Bigby Bear

FOR ALL SEASONS

By PHILIPPE COUDRAY

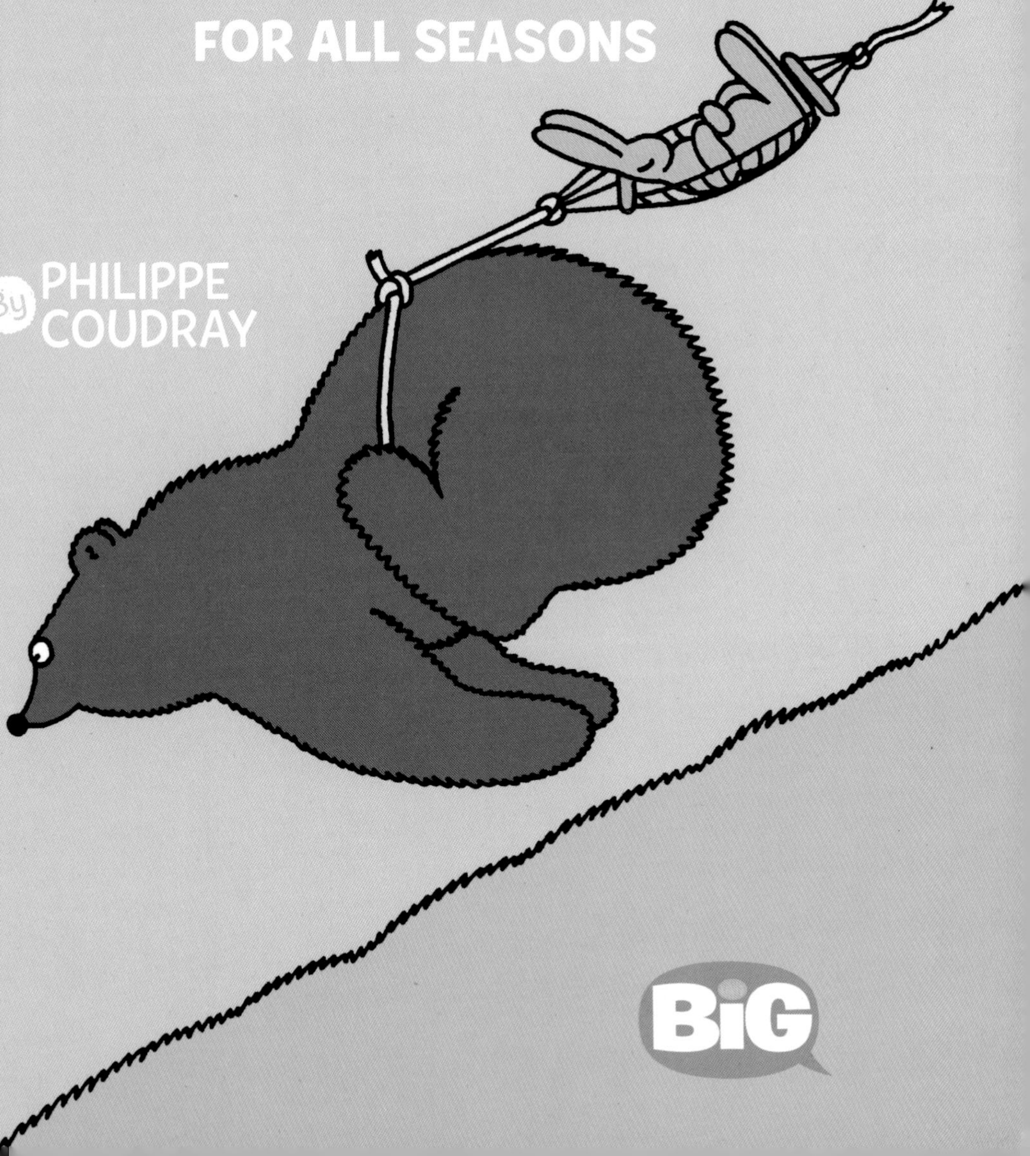

BiG

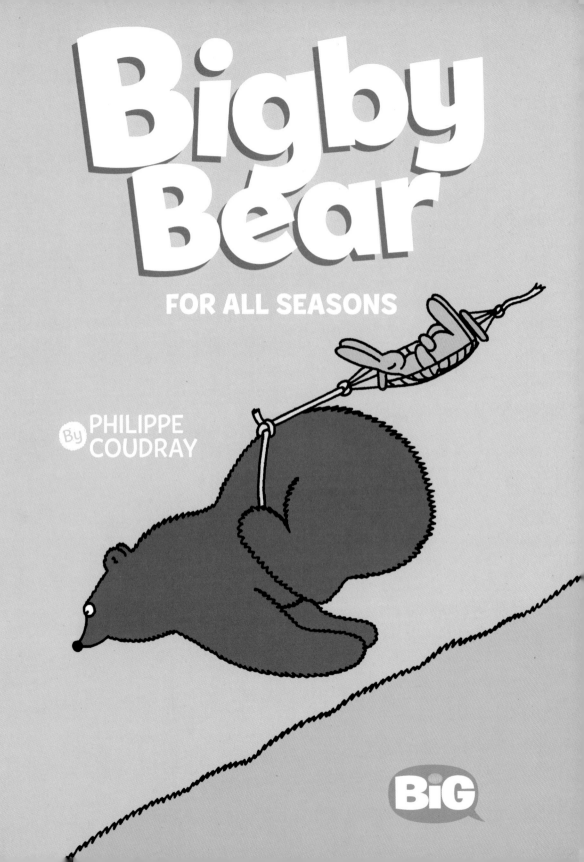

Philippe Coudray
Story & Art

•

Miceal Beausang-O'Griafa
Translator

•

Fabrice Sapolsky
& **Alex Donoghue**
US Edition Editors

Amanda Lucido
Assistant Editor

Vincent Henry
Original Edition Editor

Jerry Frissen
Senior Art Director

Fabrice Giger
Publisher

Rights and Licensing - licensing@humanoids.com
Press and Social Media - pr@humanoids.com

BIGBY BEAR: FOR ALL SEASONS. This title is a publication of Humanoids, Inc. 8033 Sunset Blvd. #628, Los Angeles, CA 90046.
Copyright © 2019 Humanoids, Inc., Los Angeles (USA). All rights reserved. Humanoids and its logos are ® and © 2019 Humanoids, Inc.
Library of Congress Control Number: 2019937624
F&P Level: Q 4

BiG is an imprint of Humanoids, Inc.

First published in France under the title *L'Ours Barnabé* Copyright © 2012–2018 La Boîte à Bulles and Philippe Coudray. All rights reserved.
All characters, the distinctive likenesses thereof and all related indicia are trademarks of La Boîte à Bulles Sarl and/or of Philippe Coudray.

FALL

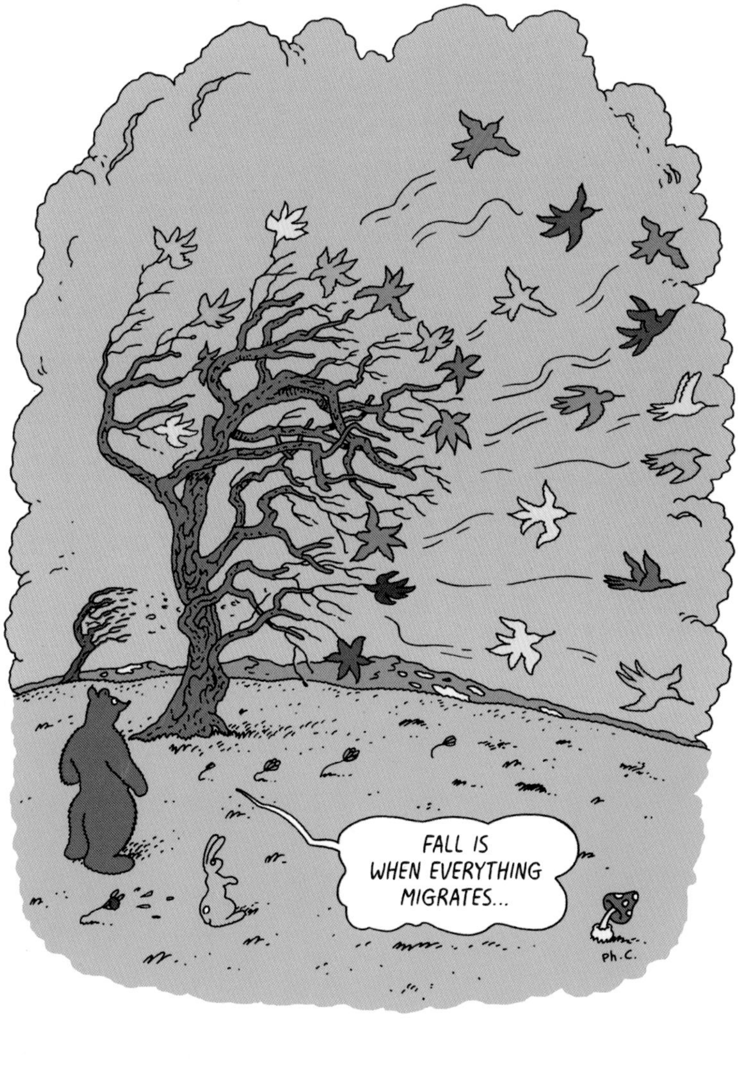
FALL IS
WHEN EVERYTHING
MIGRATES...
Ph.C.

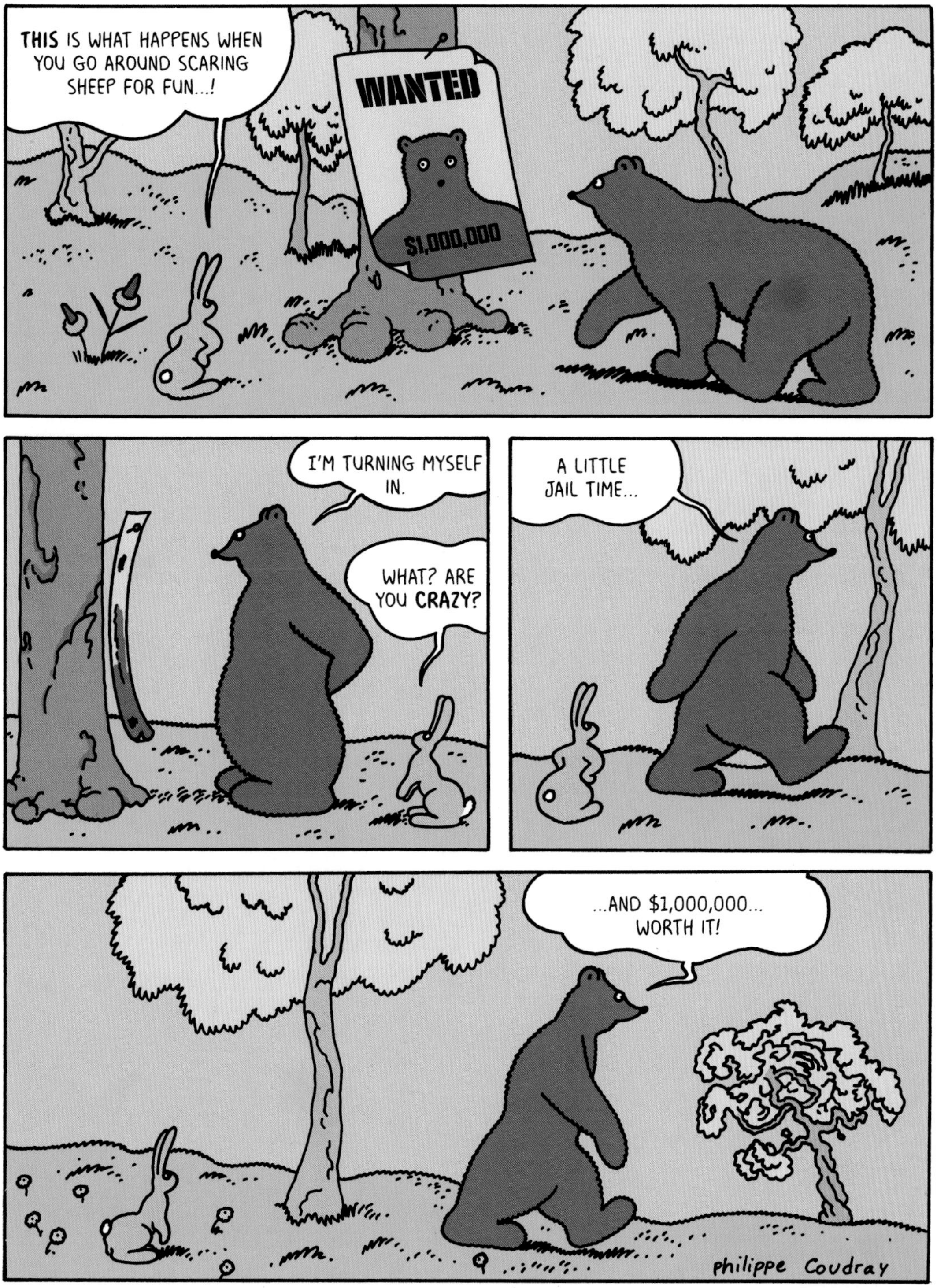
THIS IS WHAT HAPPENS WHEN YOU GO AROUND SCARING SHEEP FOR FUN...!
WANTED
$1,000,000
I'M TURNING MYSELF IN.
WHAT? ARE YOU CRAZY?
A LITTLE JAIL TIME...
...AND $1,000,000... WORTH IT!
philippe Coudray

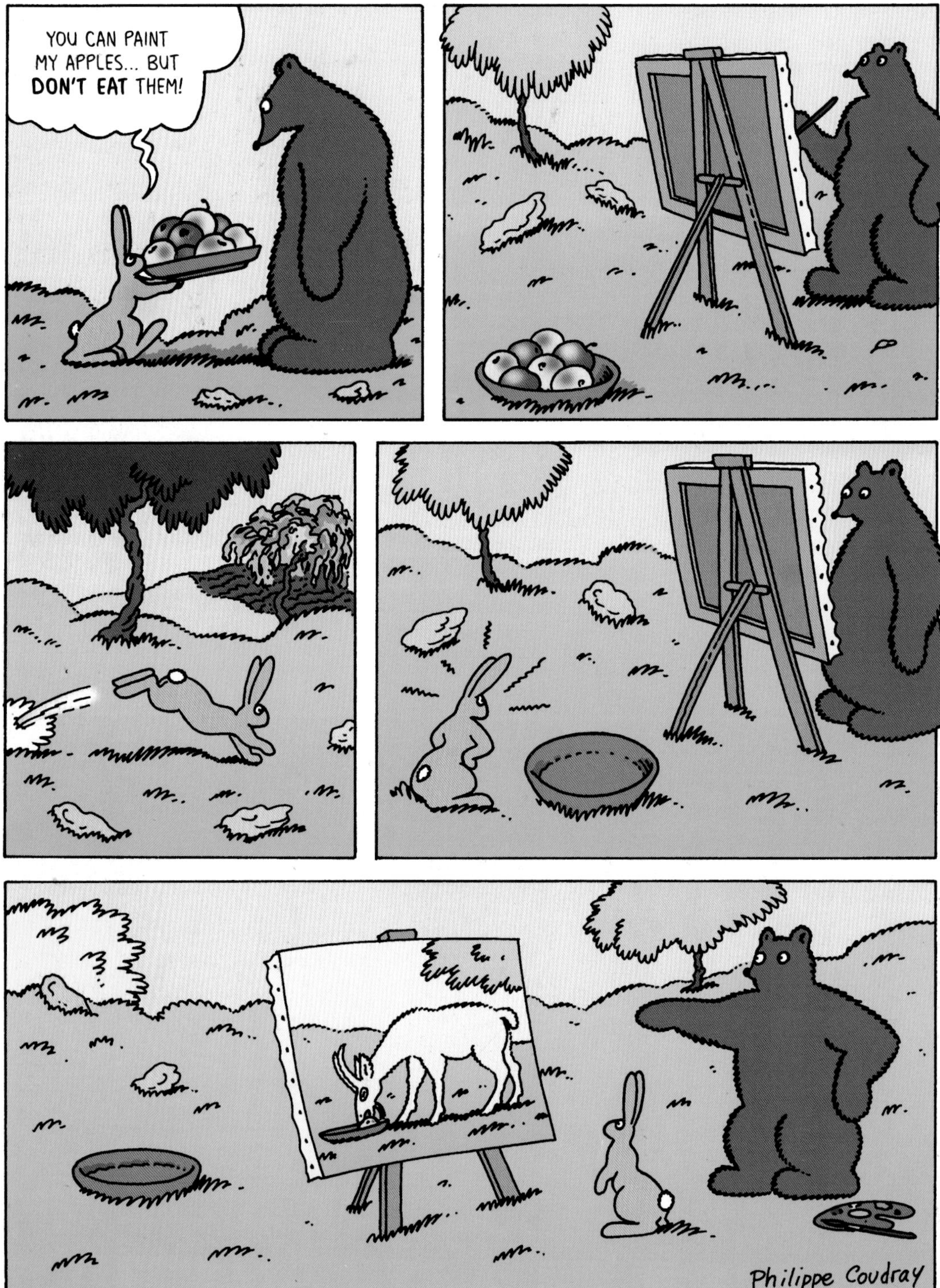
YOU CAN PAINT MY APPLES... BUT **DON'T EAT** THEM!
Philippe Coudray

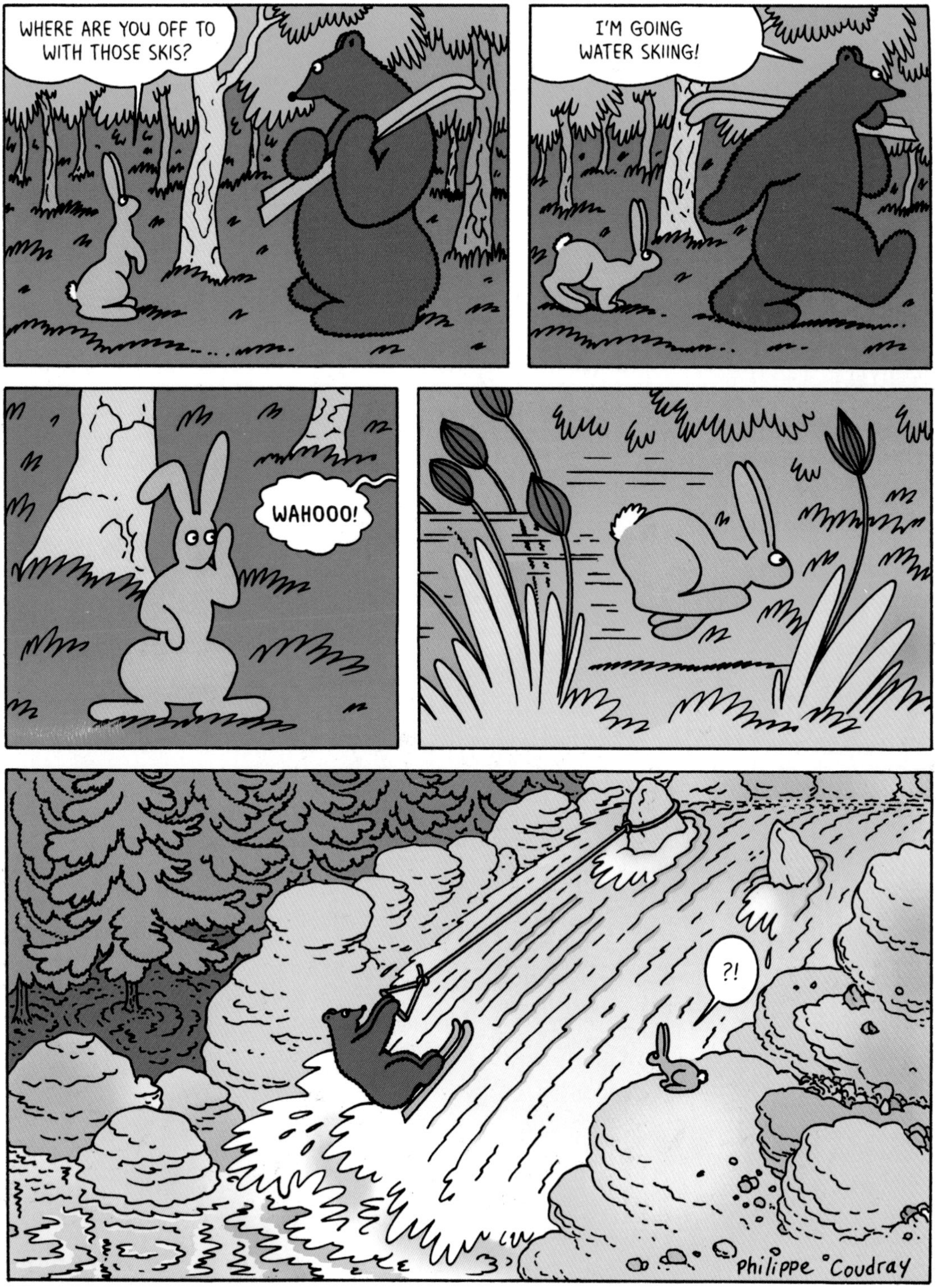
WHERE ARE YOU OFF TO WITH THOSE SKIS?
I'M GOING WATER SKIING!
WAHOOO!
?!
Philippe Coudray

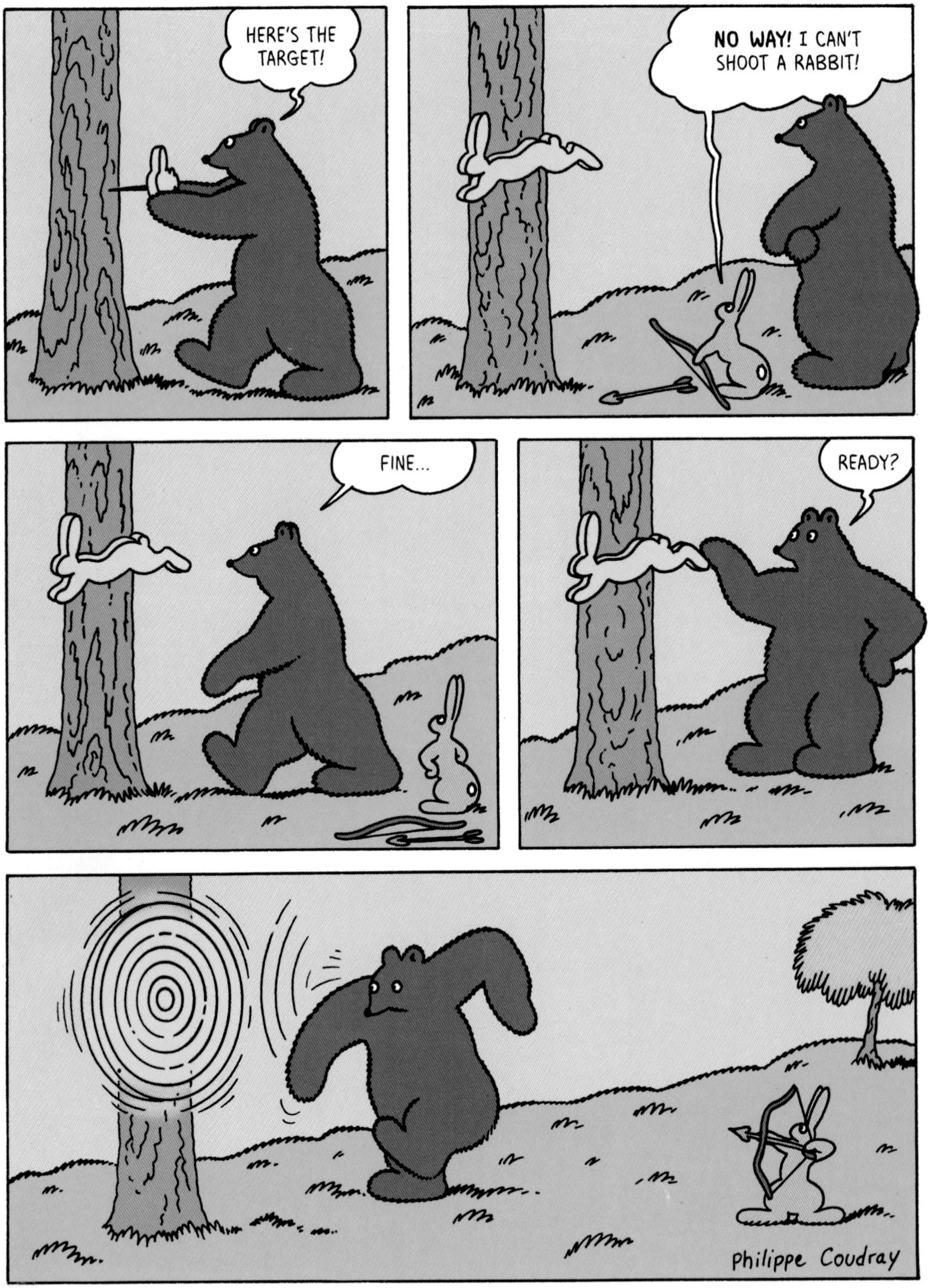
HERE'S THE TARGET!
NO WAY! I CAN'T SHOOT A RABBIT!
FINE...
READY?
Philippe Coudray

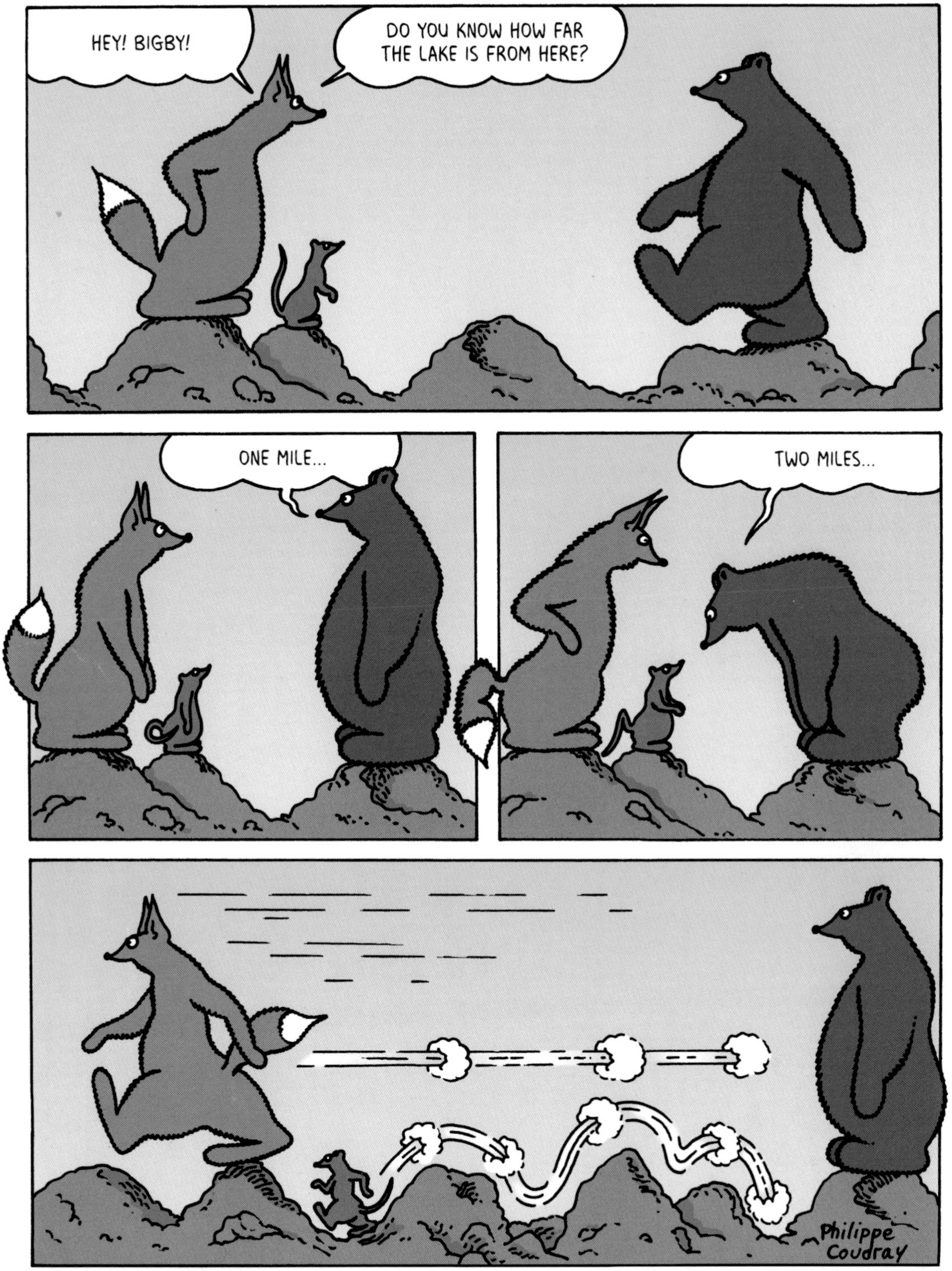
HEY! BIGBY!
DO YOU KNOW HOW FAR THE LAKE IS FROM HERE?
ONE MILE...
TWO MILES...
Philippe Coudray

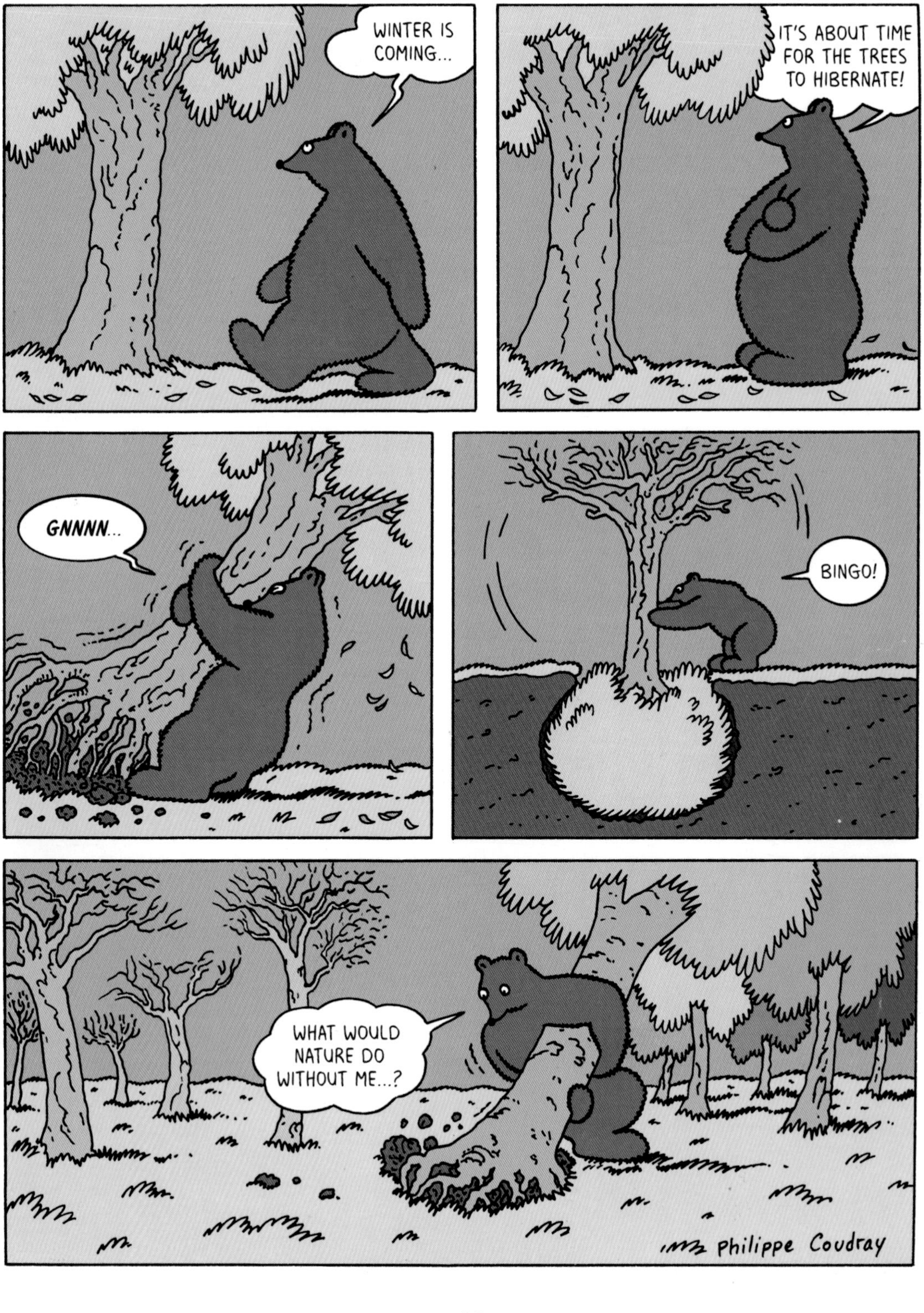
WINTER IS COMING...
IT'S ABOUT TIME FOR THE TREES TO HIBERNATE!
GNNNN...
BINGO!
WHAT WOULD NATURE DO WITHOUT ME...?
Philippe Coudray

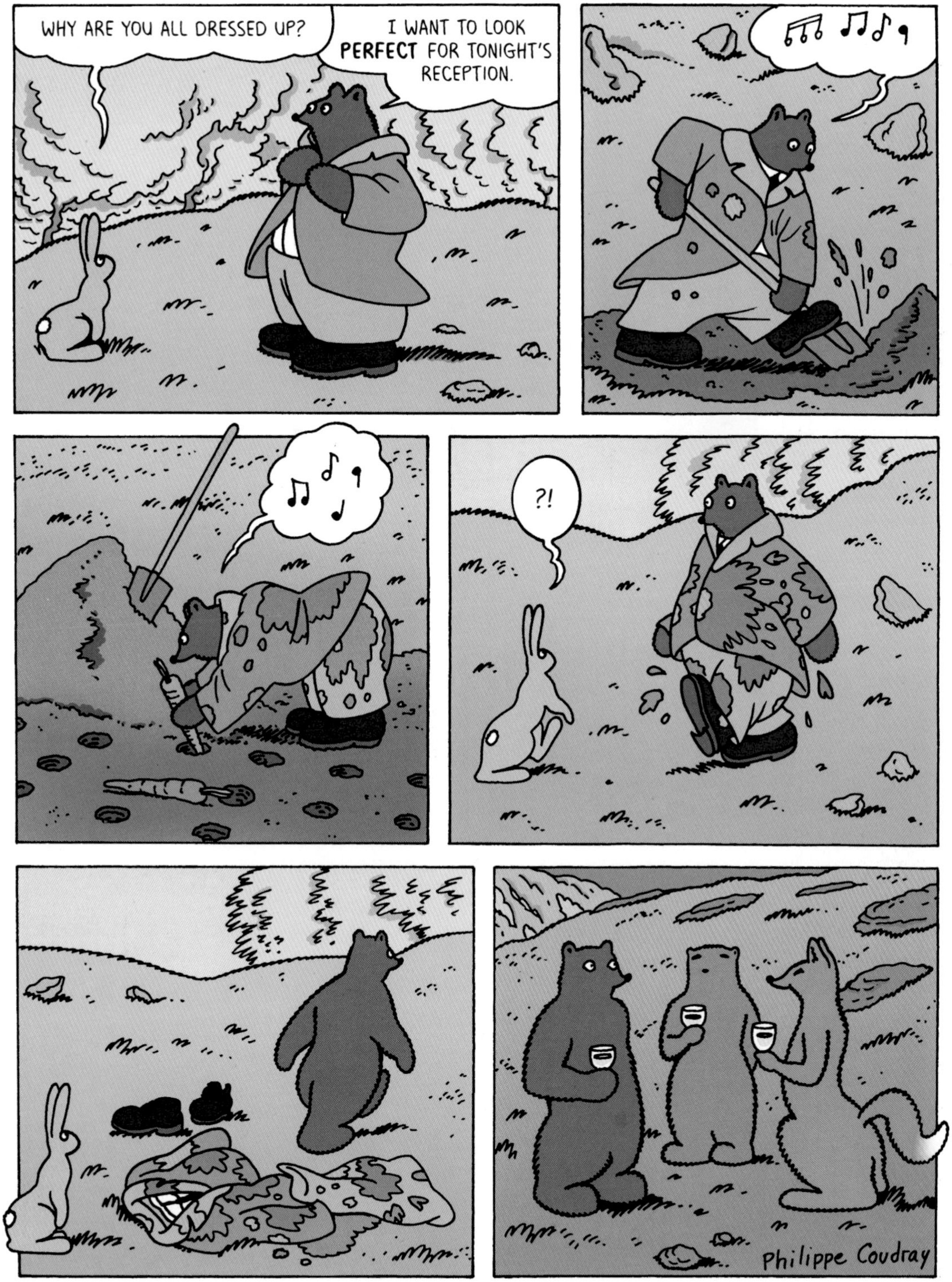
WHY ARE YOU ALL DRESSED UP?
I WANT TO LOOK **PERFECT** FOR TONIGHT'S RECEPTION.
?!
Philippe Coudray

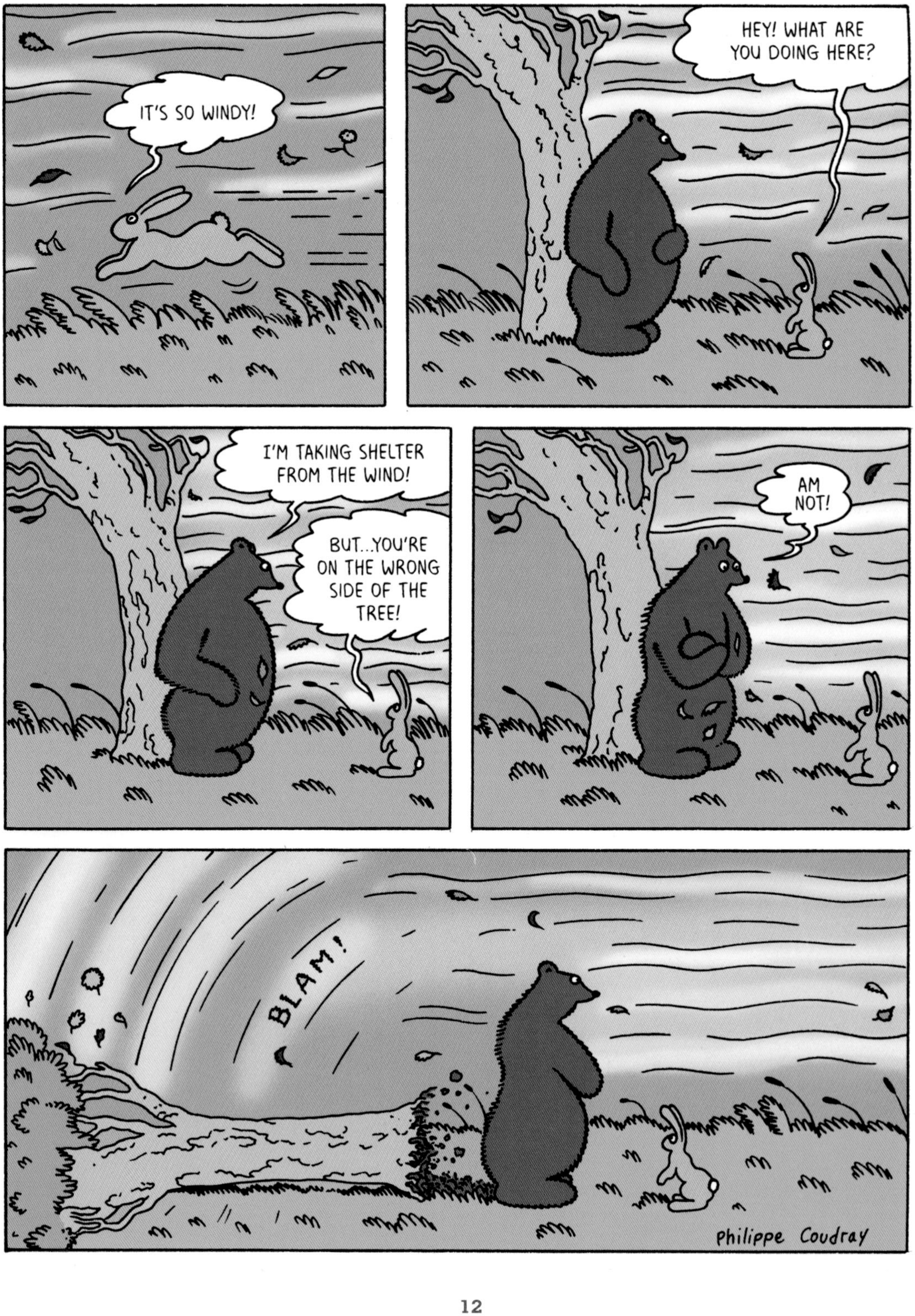
IT'S SO WINDY!
HEY! WHAT ARE YOU DOING HERE?
I'M TAKING SHELTER FROM THE WIND!
BUT...YOU'RE ON THE WRONG SIDE OF THE TREE!
AM NOT!
BLAM!
Philippe Coudray

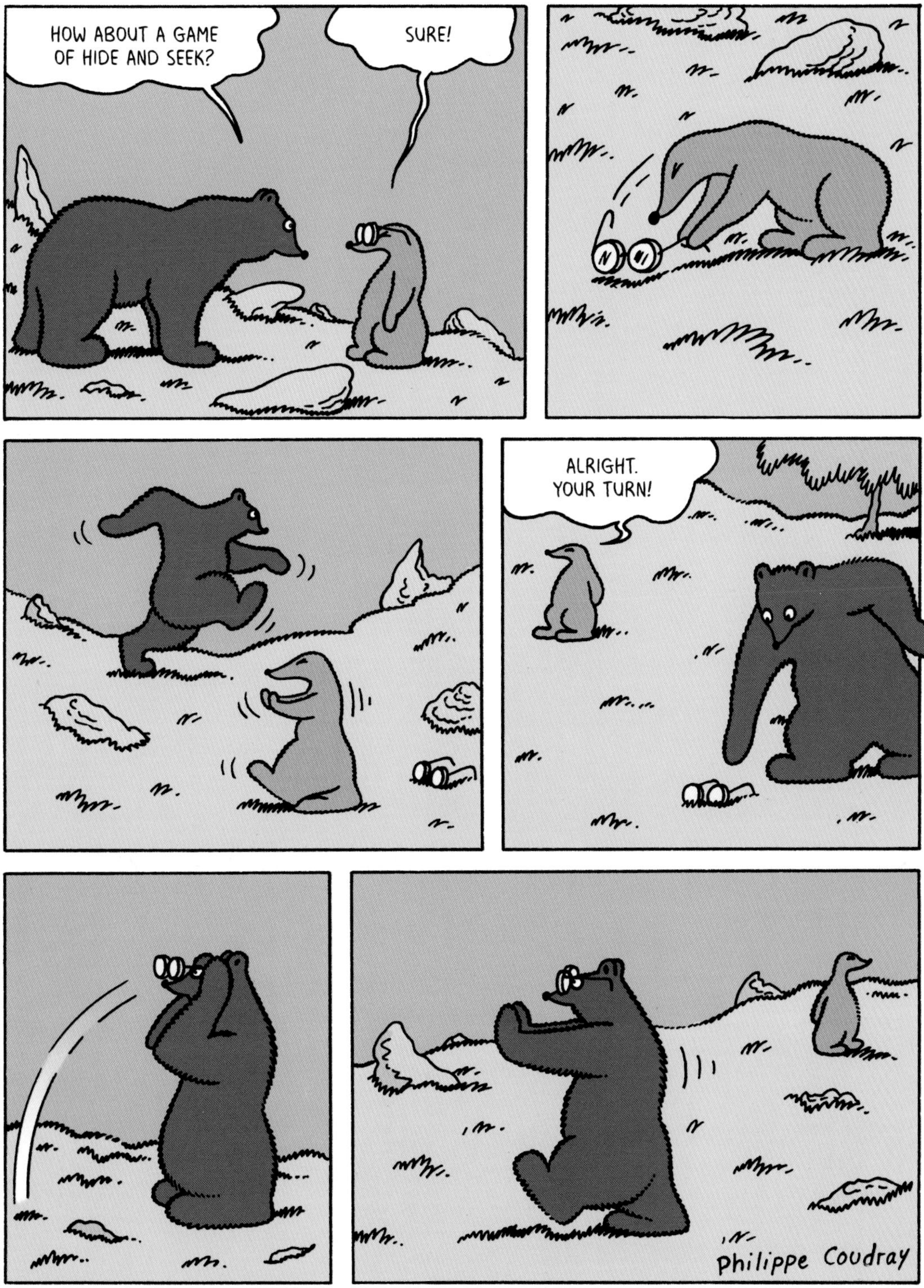
HOW ABOUT A GAME OF HIDE AND SEEK?
SURE!
ALRIGHT. YOUR TURN!
Philippe Coudray

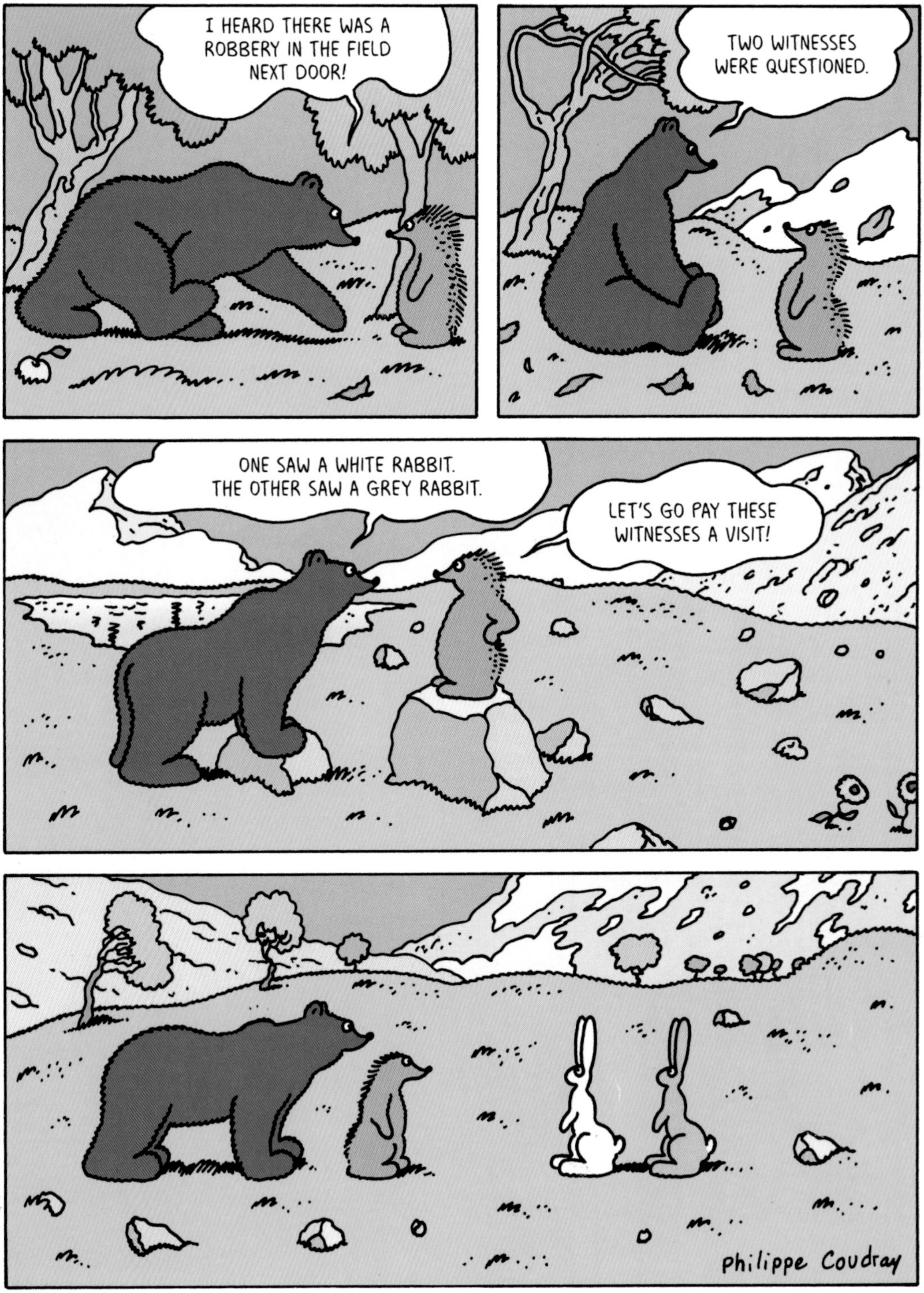
I HEARD THERE WAS A ROBBERY IN THE FIELD NEXT DOOR!
TWO WITNESSES WERE QUESTIONED.
ONE SAW A WHITE RABBIT. THE OTHER SAW A GREY RABBIT.
LET'S GO PAY THESE WITNESSES A VISIT!
Philippe Coudray

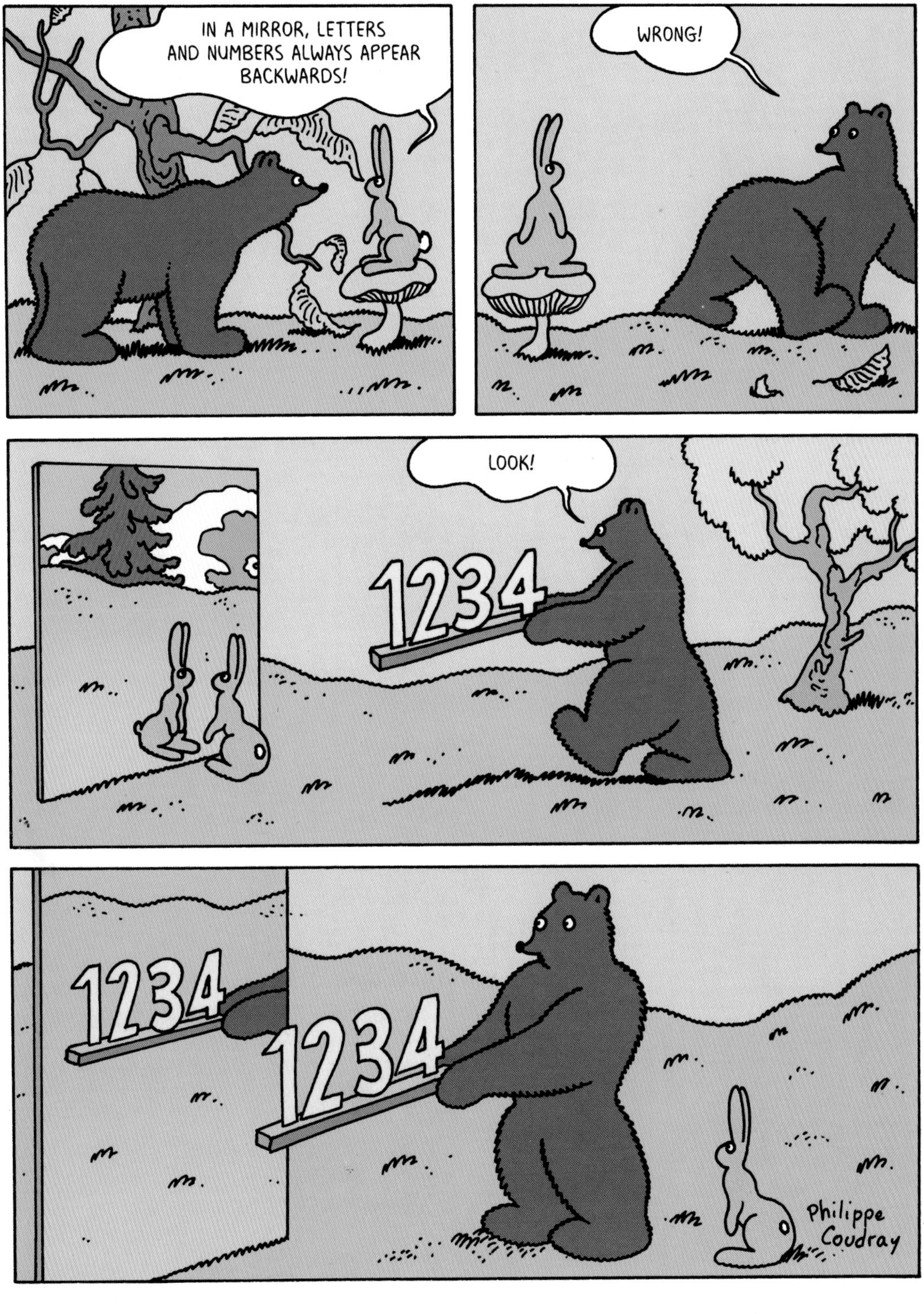
IN A MIRROR, LETTERS AND NUMBERS ALWAYS APPEAR BACKWARDS!
WRONG!
LOOK!
1234
1234
1234
Philippe Coudray

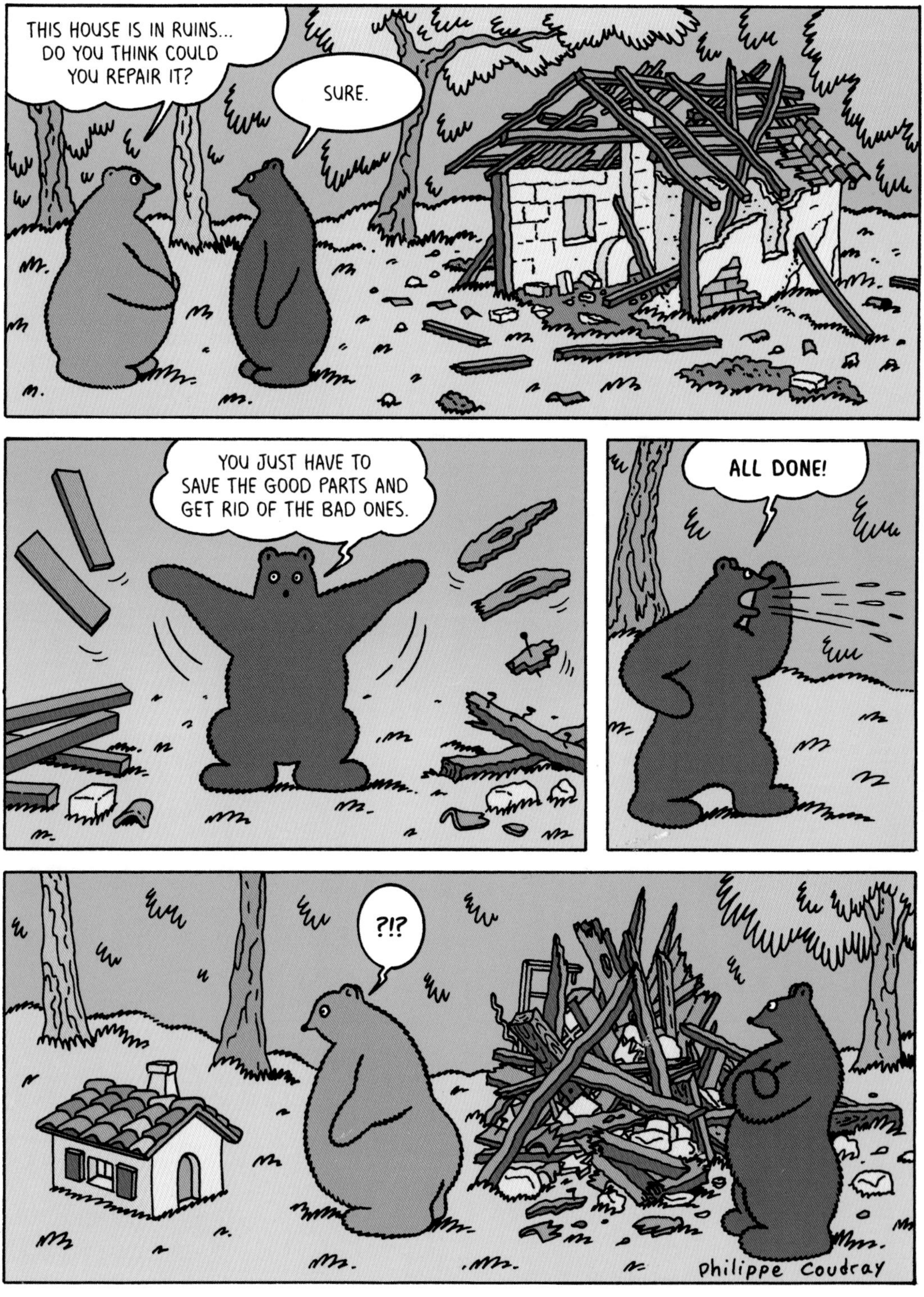
THIS HOUSE IS IN RUINS... DO YOU THINK COULD YOU REPAIR IT?
SURE.
YOU JUST HAVE TO SAVE THE GOOD PARTS AND GET RID OF THE BAD ONES.
ALL DONE!
?!?
Philippe Coudray

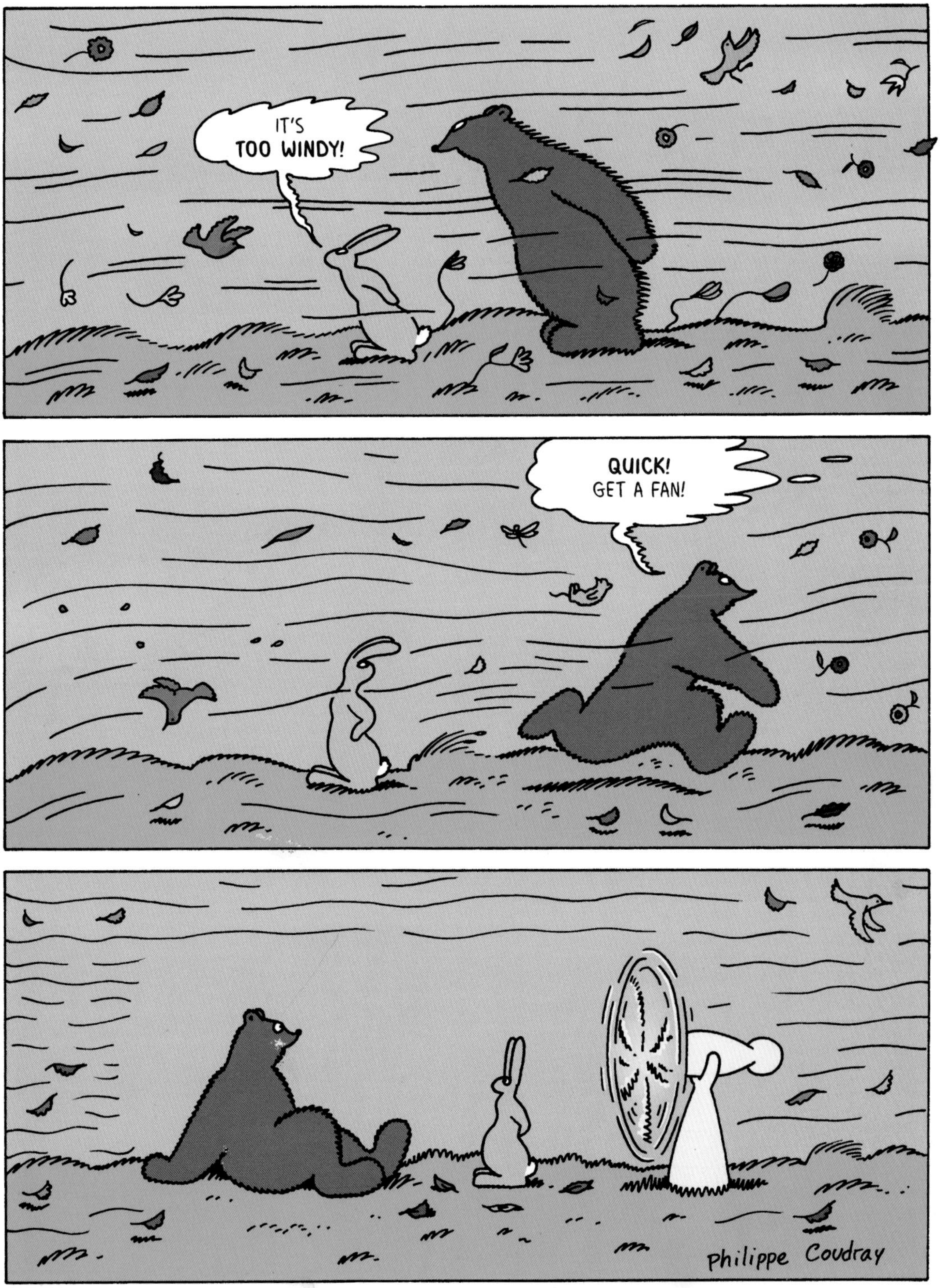
IT'S TOO WINDY!
QUICK! GET A FAN!
Philippe Coudray

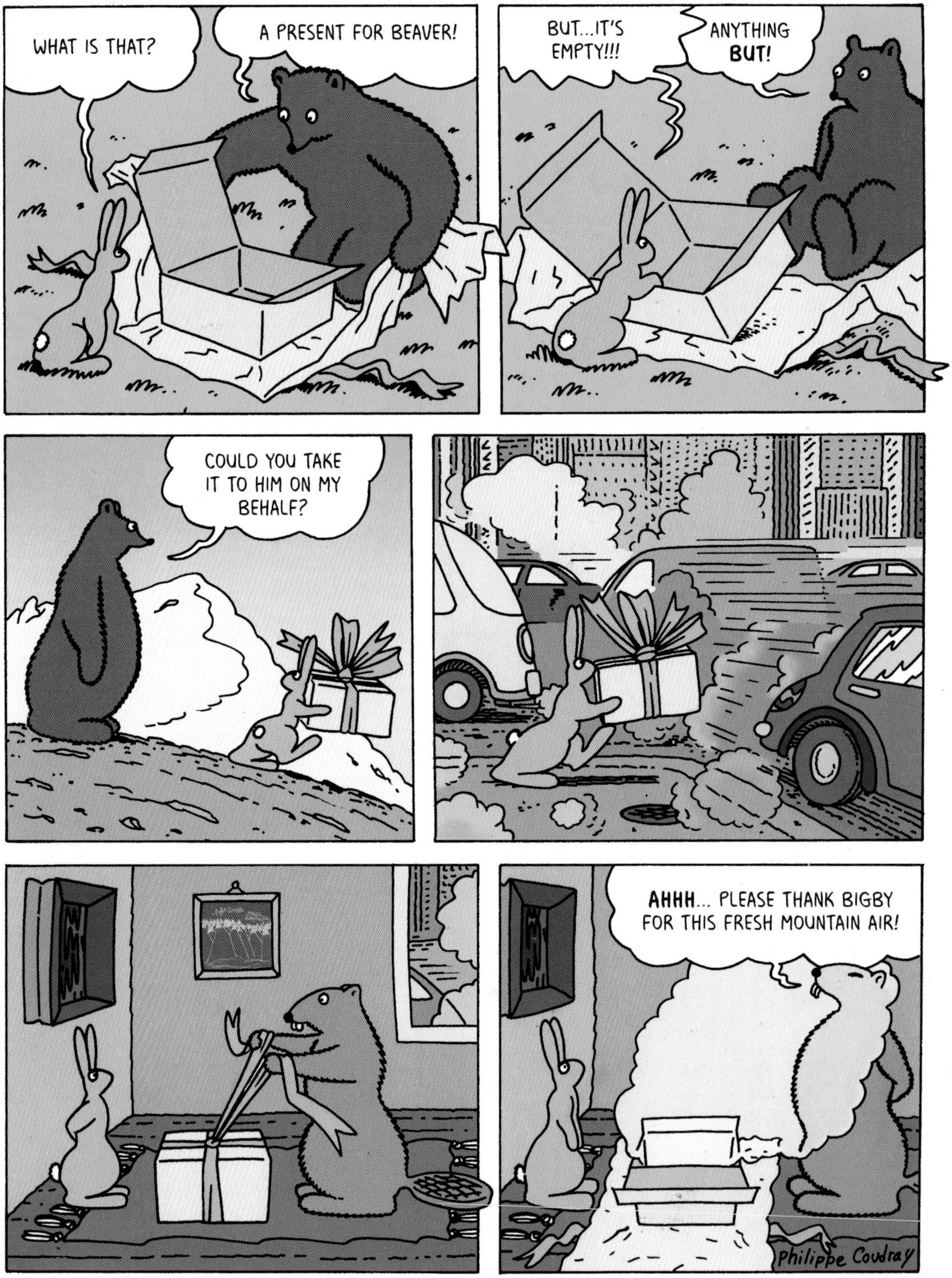
WHAT IS THAT?
A PRESENT FOR BEAVER!
BUT...IT'S EMPTY!!!
ANYTHING **BUT**!
COULD YOU TAKE IT TO HIM ON MY BEHALF?
AHHH... PLEASE THANK BIGBY FOR THIS FRESH MOUNTAIN AIR!
Philippe Coudray

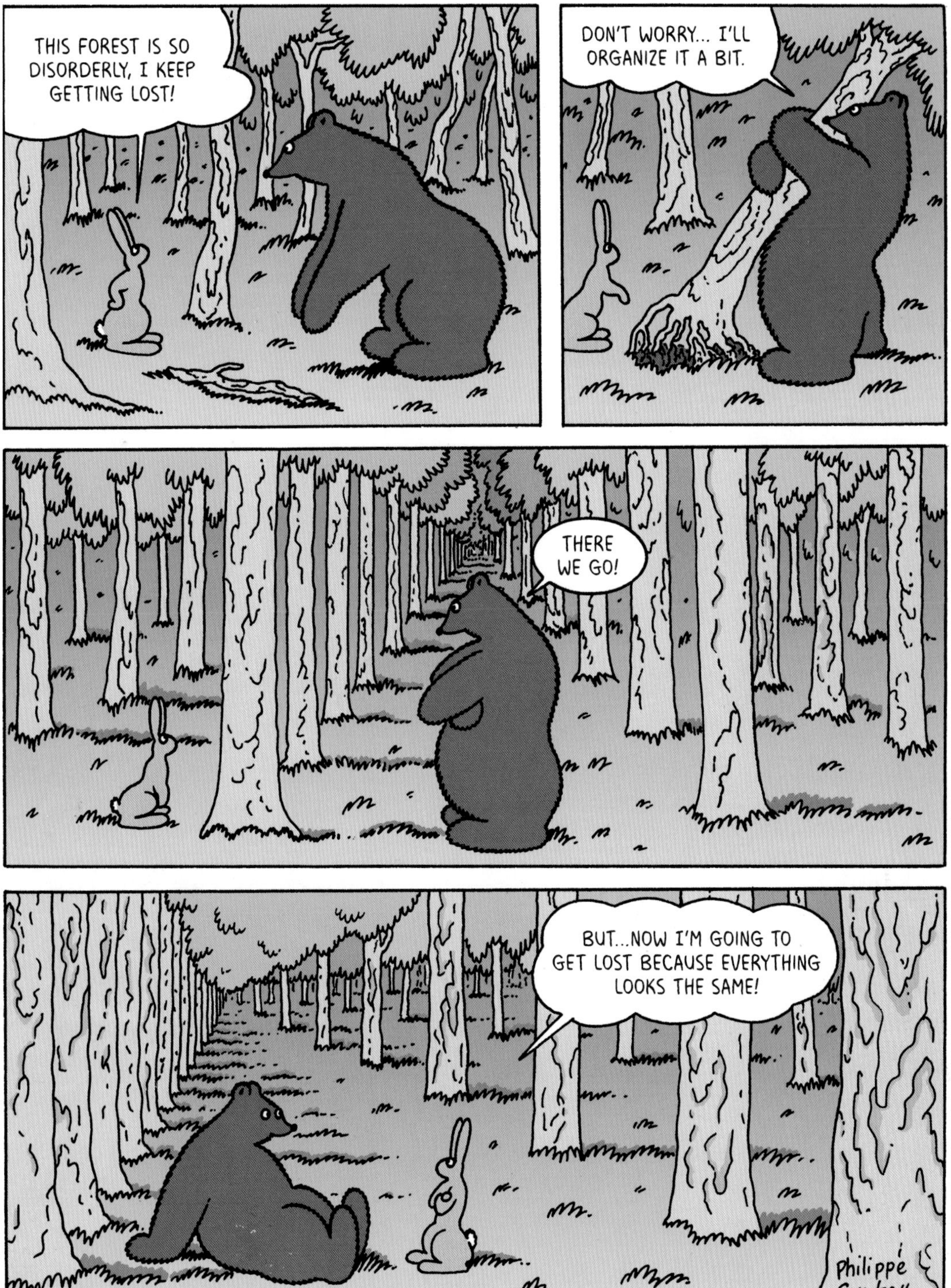
THIS FOREST IS SO DISORDERLY, I KEEP GETTING LOST!
DON'T WORRY... I'LL ORGANIZE IT A BIT.
THERE WE GO!
BUT...NOW I'M GOING TO GET LOST BECAUSE EVERYTHING LOOKS THE SAME!
Philippe Coudray

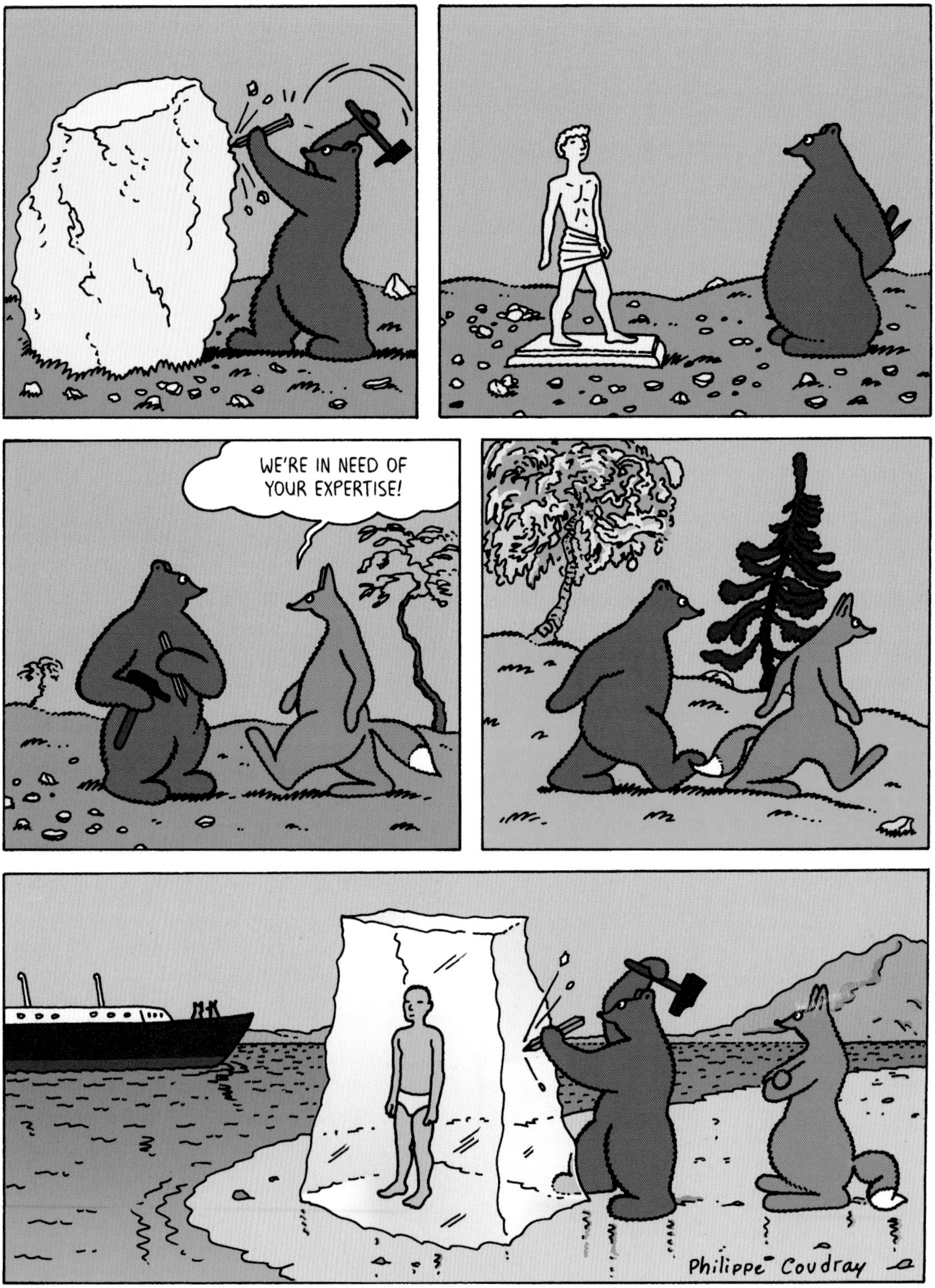
WE'RE IN NEED OF YOUR EXPERTISE!
Philippe Coudray

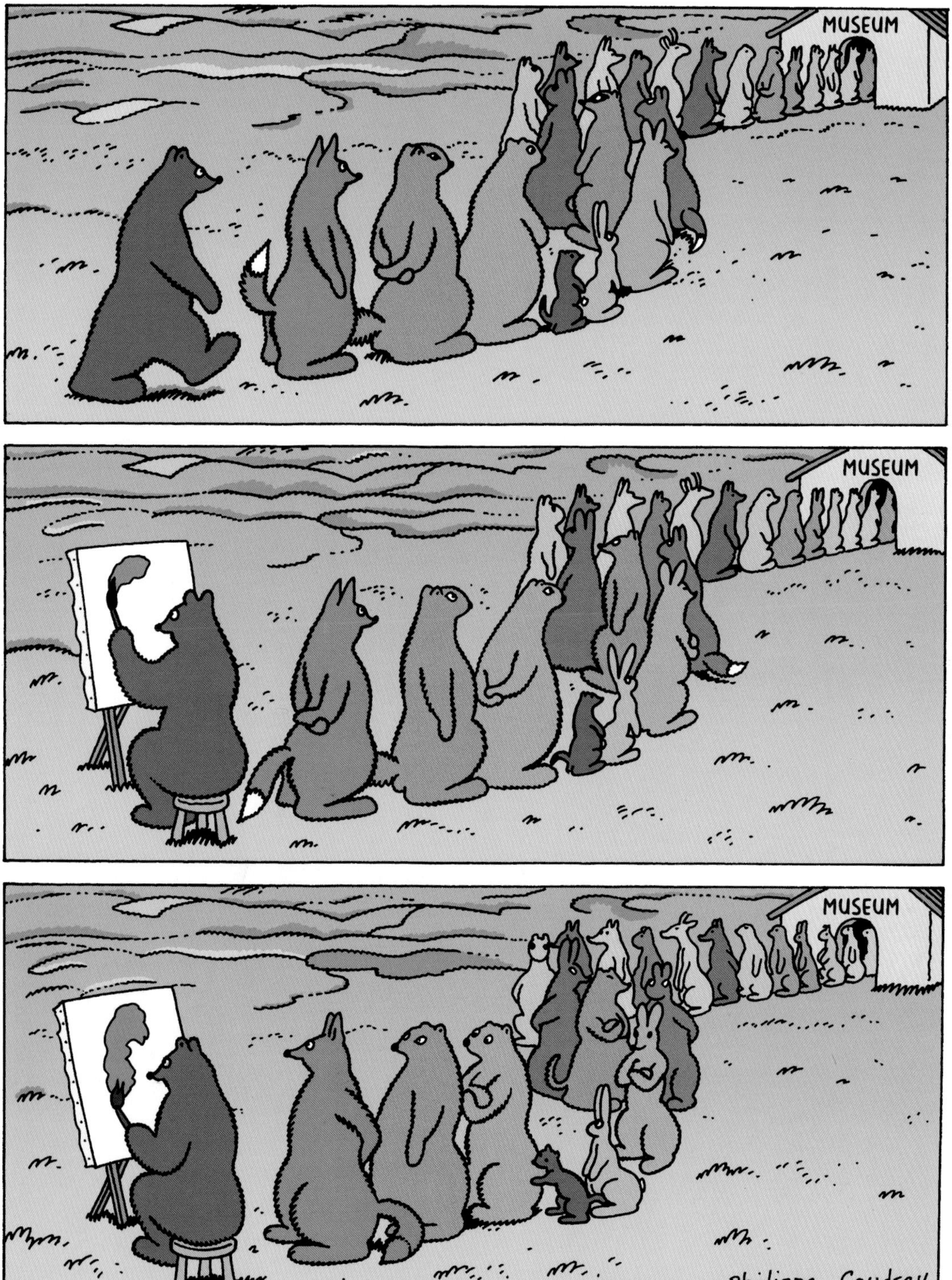
MUSEUM
MUSEUM
MUSEUM
Philippe Coudray

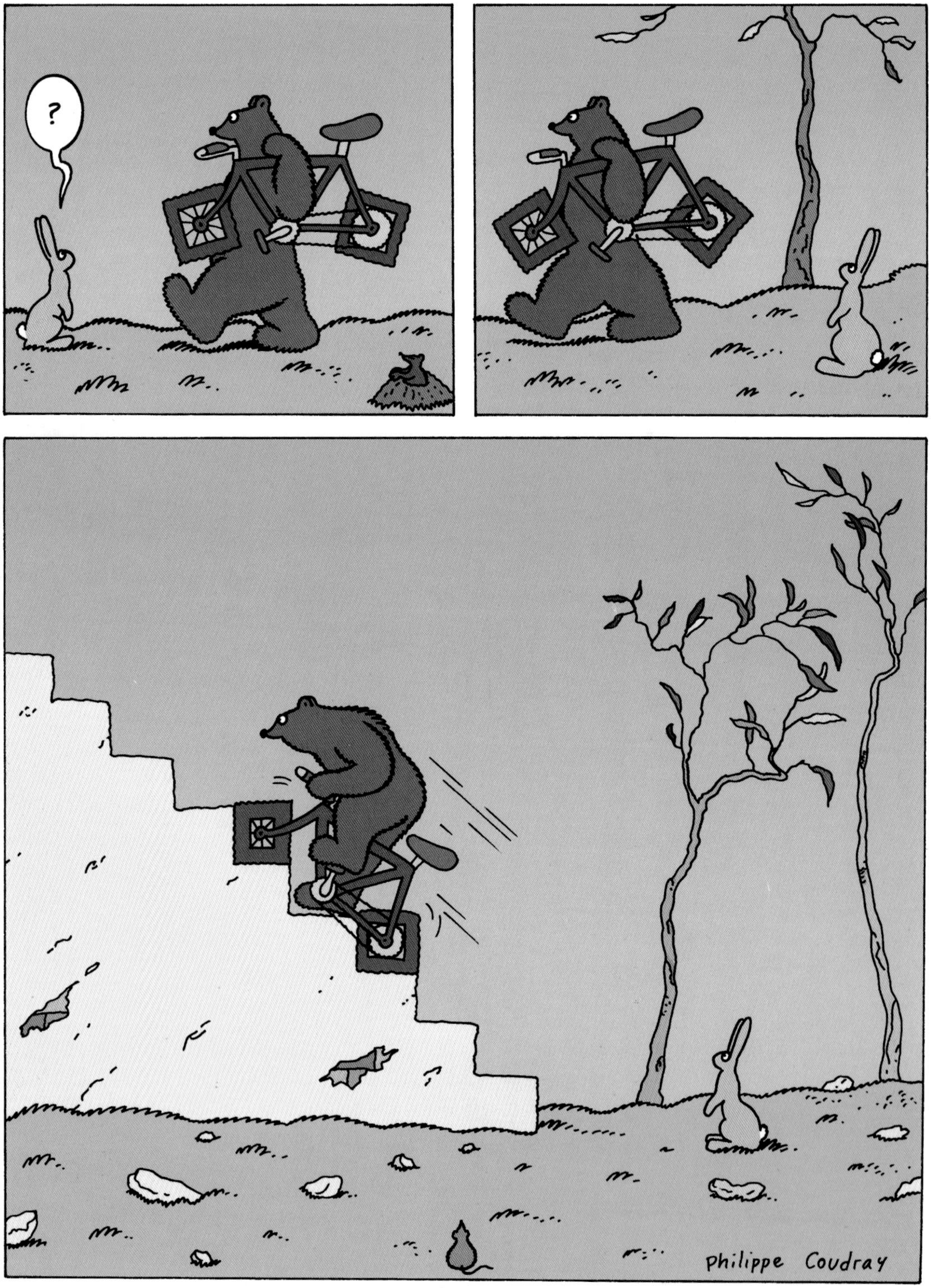
?
philippe Coudray

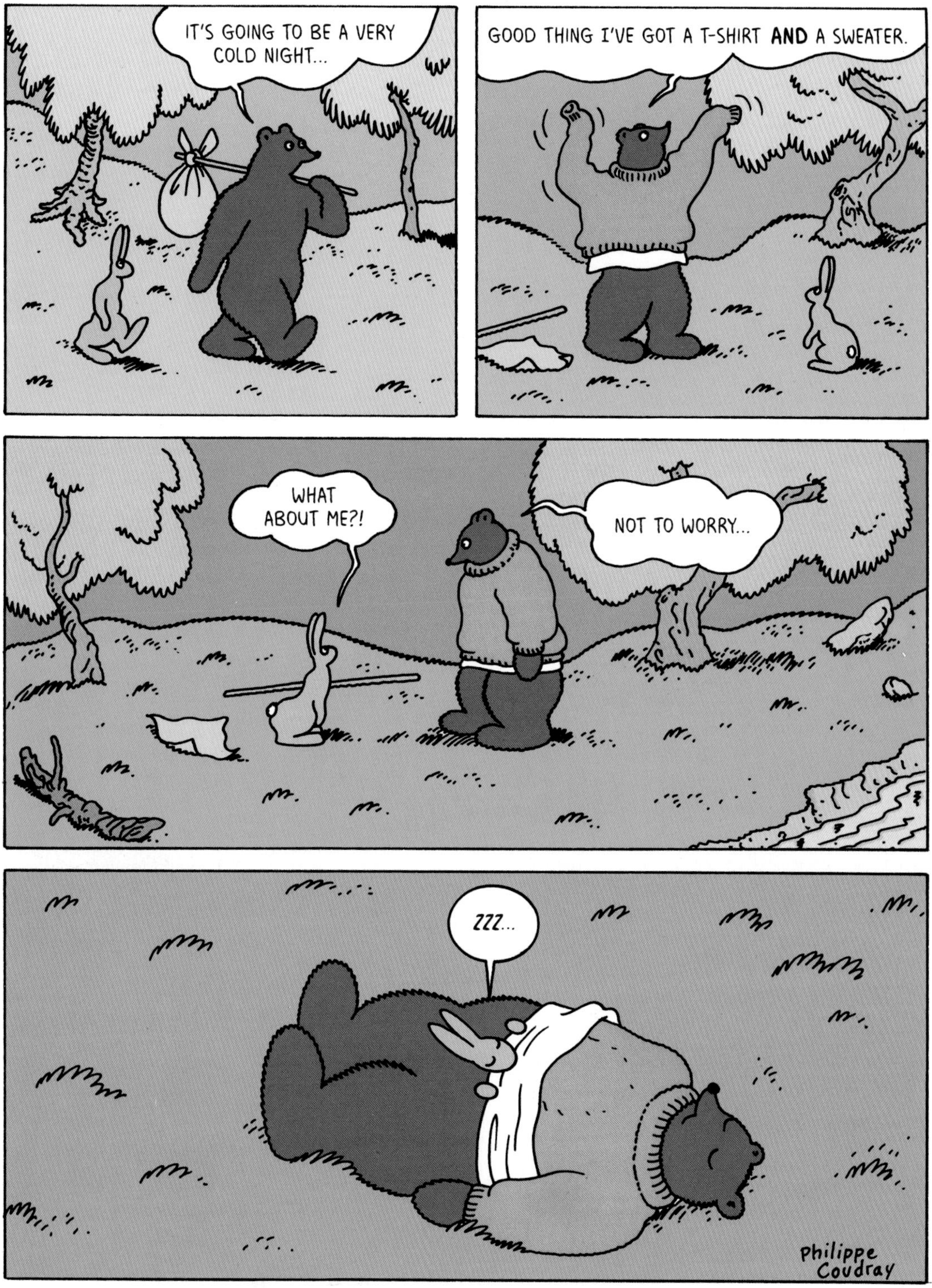
IT'S GOING TO BE A VERY COLD NIGHT...
GOOD THING I'VE GOT A T-SHIRT AND A SWEATER.
WHAT ABOUT ME?!
NOT TO WORRY...
ZZZ...
Philippe Coudray

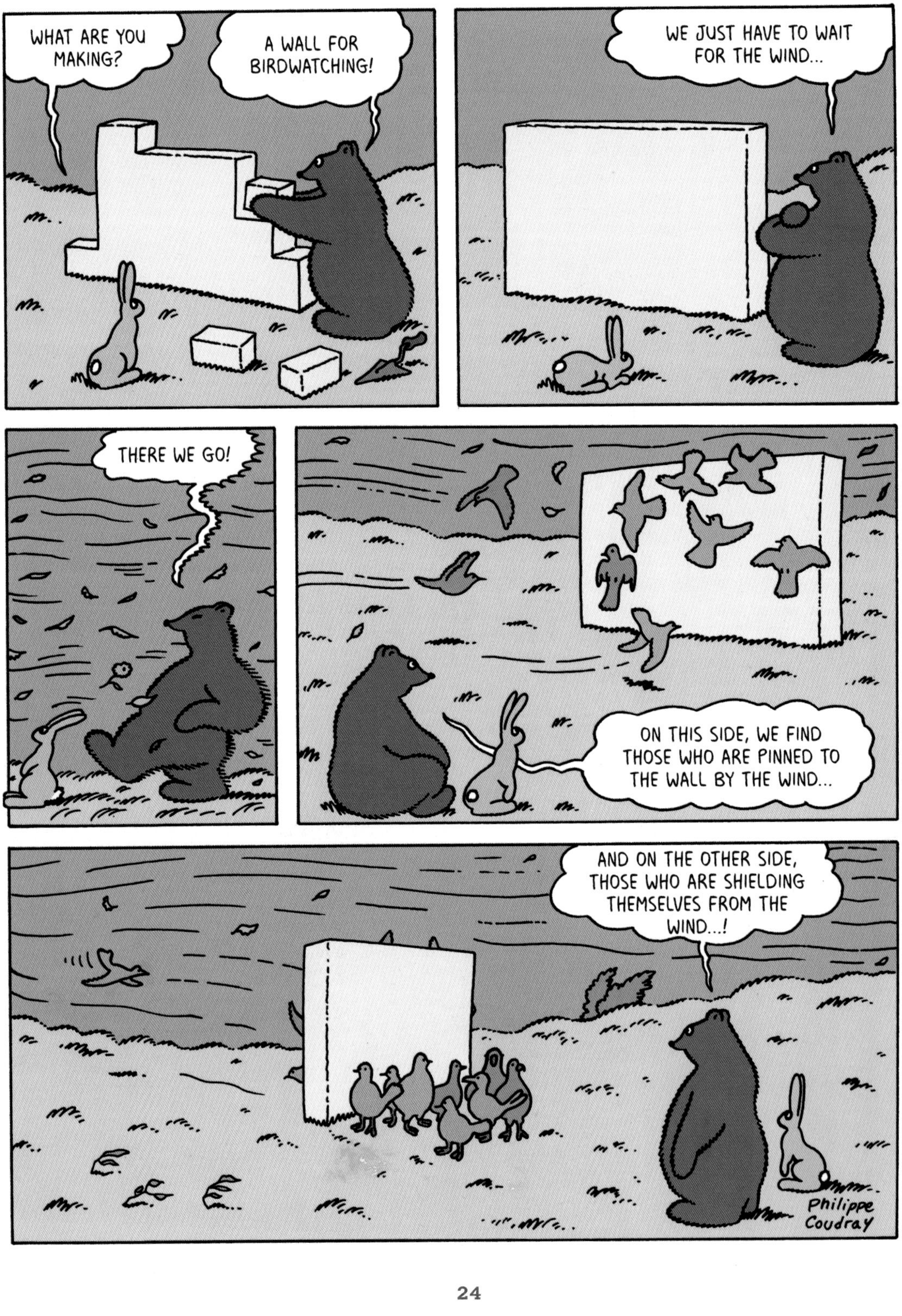
WHAT ARE YOU MAKING?
A WALL FOR BIRDWATCHING!
WE JUST HAVE TO WAIT FOR THE WIND...
THERE WE GO!
ON THIS SIDE, WE FIND THOSE WHO ARE PINNED TO THE WALL BY THE WIND...
AND ON THE OTHER SIDE, THOSE WHO ARE SHIELDING THEMSELVES FROM THE WIND...!
Philippe Coudray

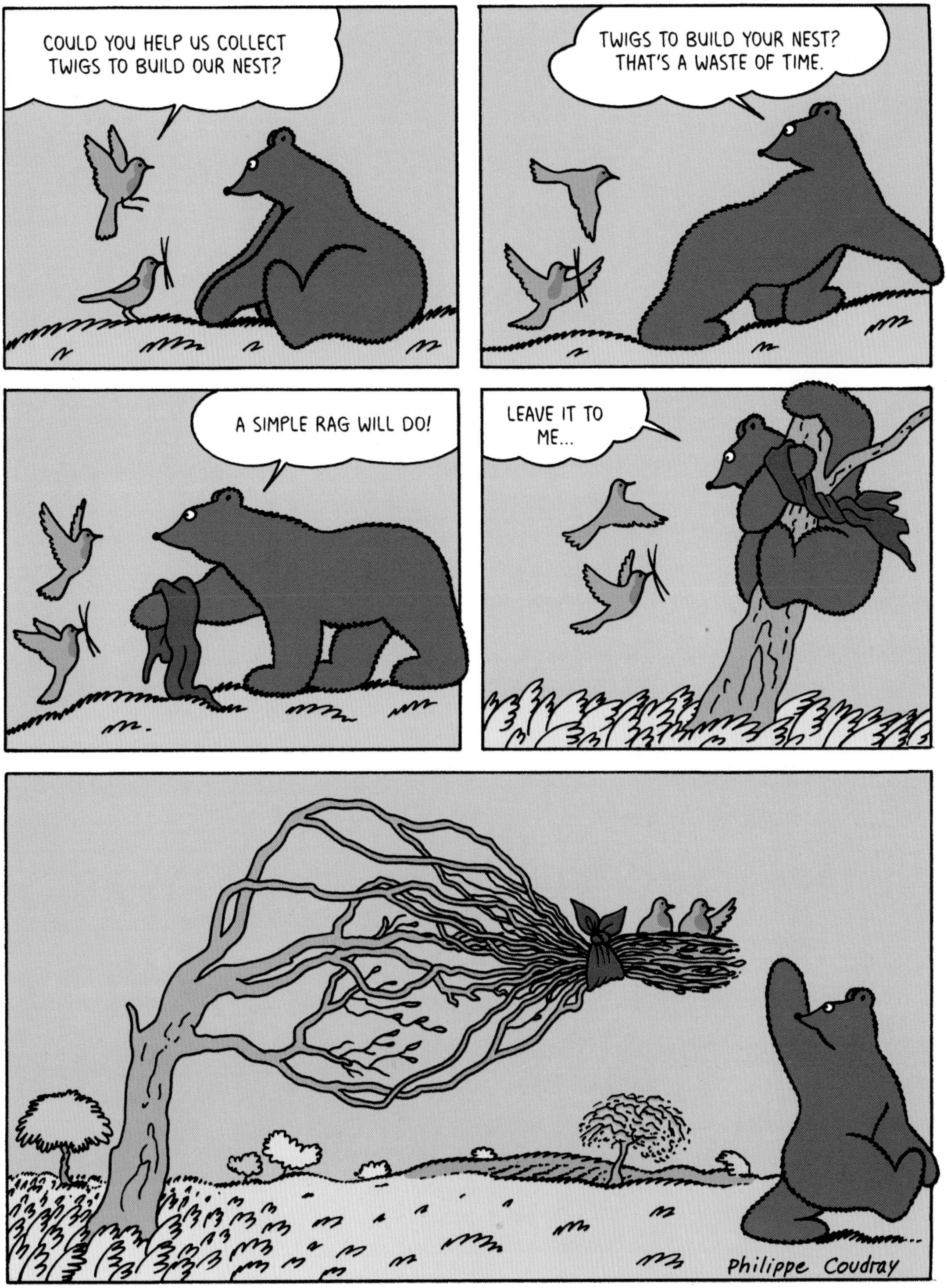
COULD YOU HELP US COLLECT TWIGS TO BUILD OUR NEST?
TWIGS TO BUILD YOUR NEST? THAT'S A WASTE OF TIME.
A SIMPLE RAG WILL DO!
LEAVE IT TO ME...
Philippe Coudray

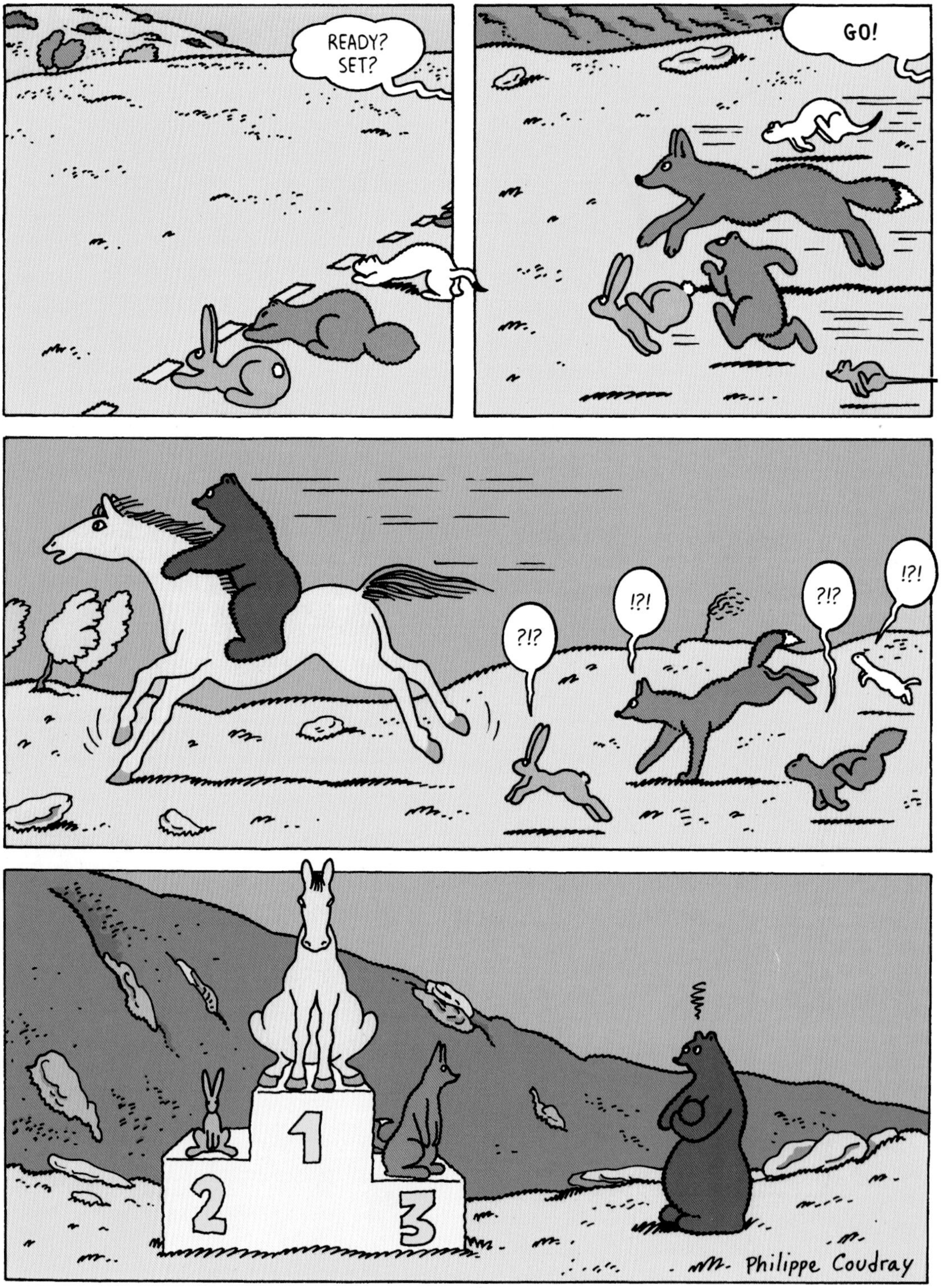
READY? SET?
GO!
?!?
!?!
?!?
!?!
Philippe Coudray

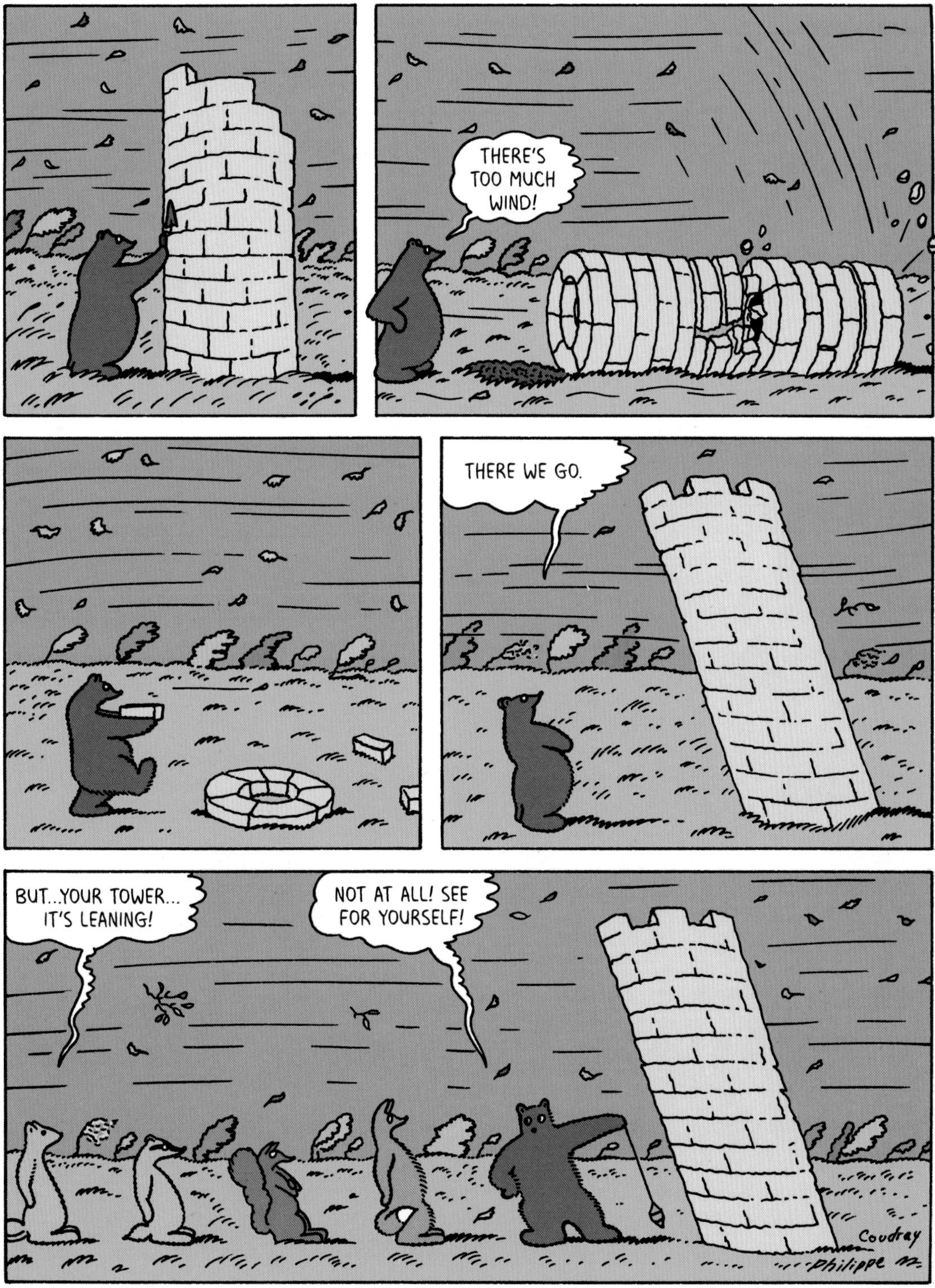
THERE'S TOO MUCH WIND!
THERE WE GO.
BUT... YOUR TOWER... IT'S LEANING!
NOT AT ALL! SEE FOR YOURSELF!
Coudray
Philippe

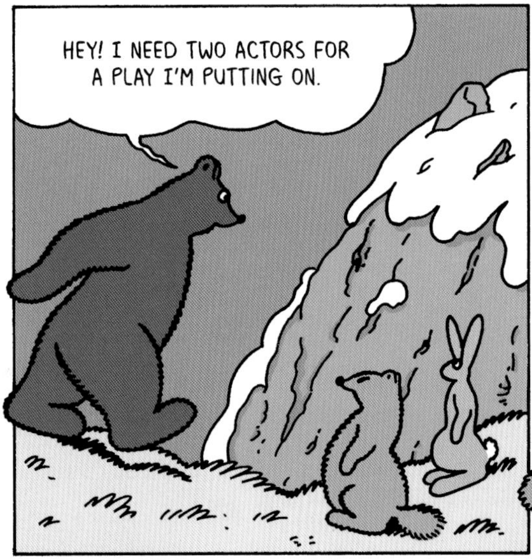
HEY! I NEED TWO ACTORS FOR A PLAY I'M PUTTING ON.

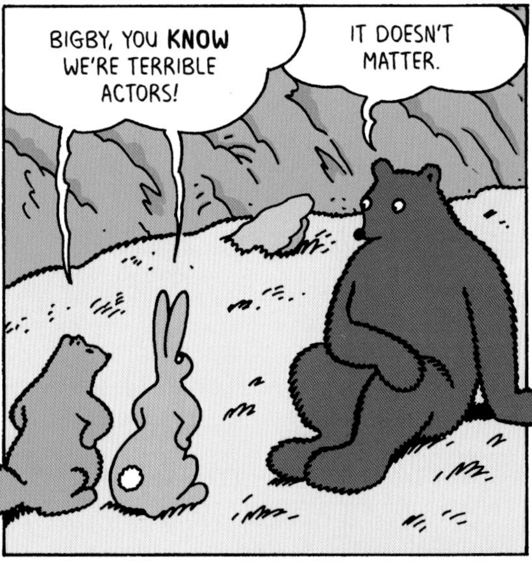
BIGBY, YOU **KNOW** WE'RE TERRIBLE ACTORS!
IT DOESN'T MATTER.

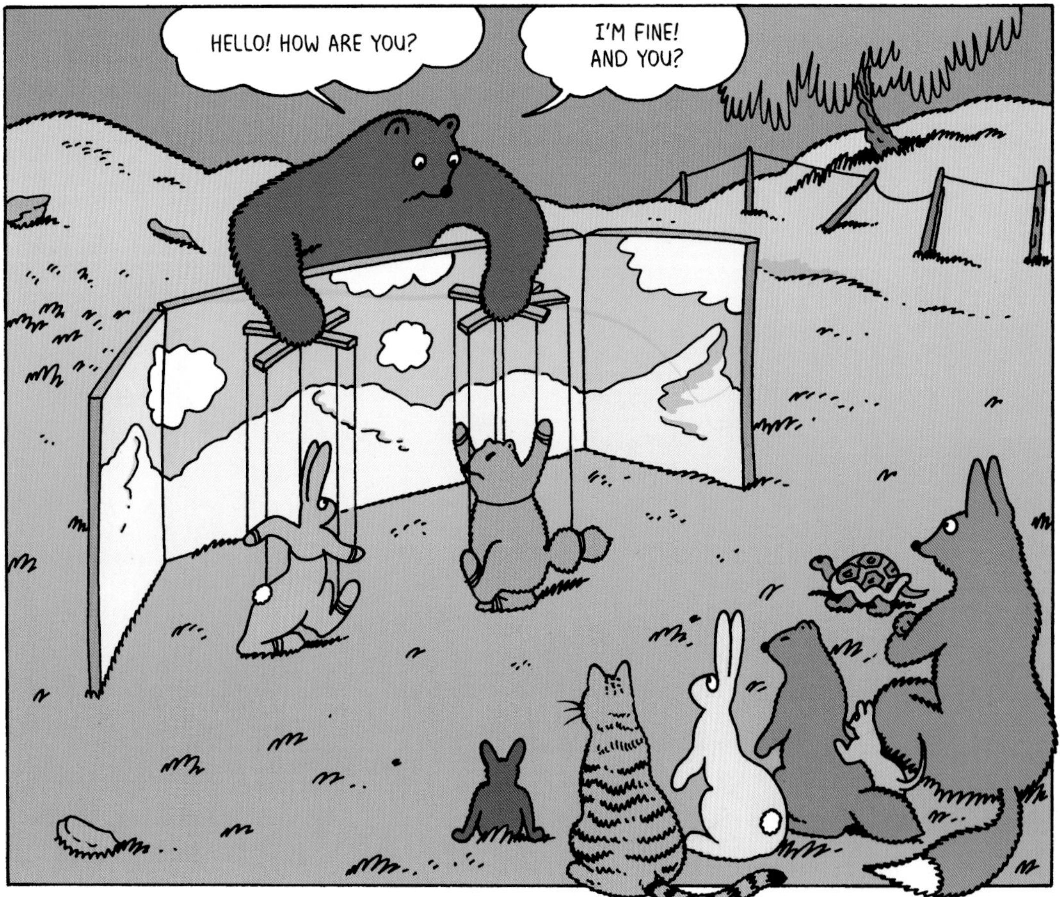
HELLO! HOW ARE YOU?
I'M FINE! AND YOU?

WINTER

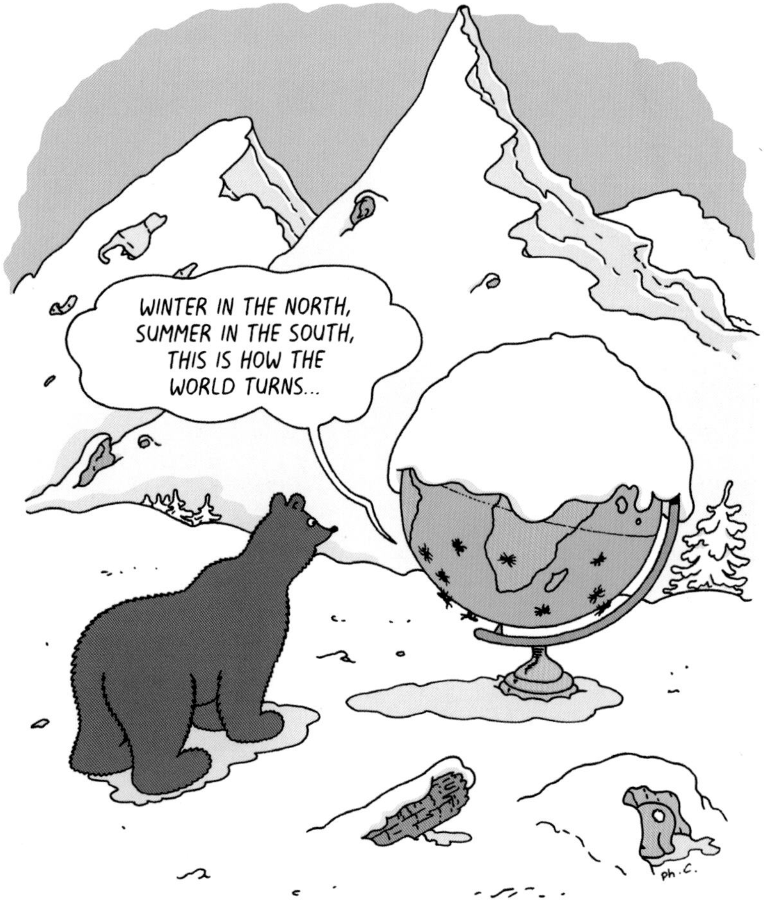

WINTER IN THE NORTH, SUMMER IN THE SOUTH, THIS IS HOW THE WORLD TURNS...
ph.C.

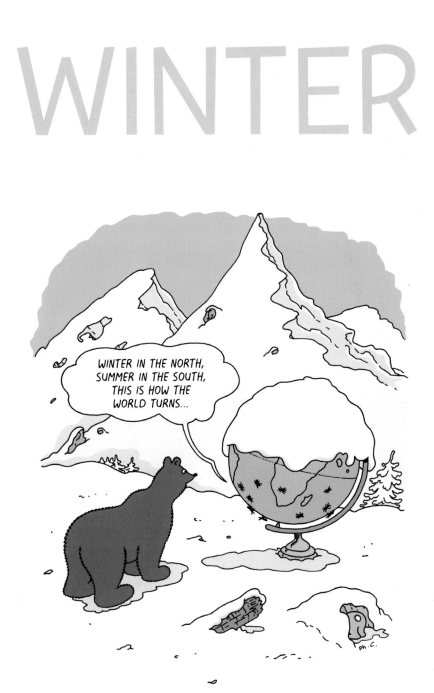

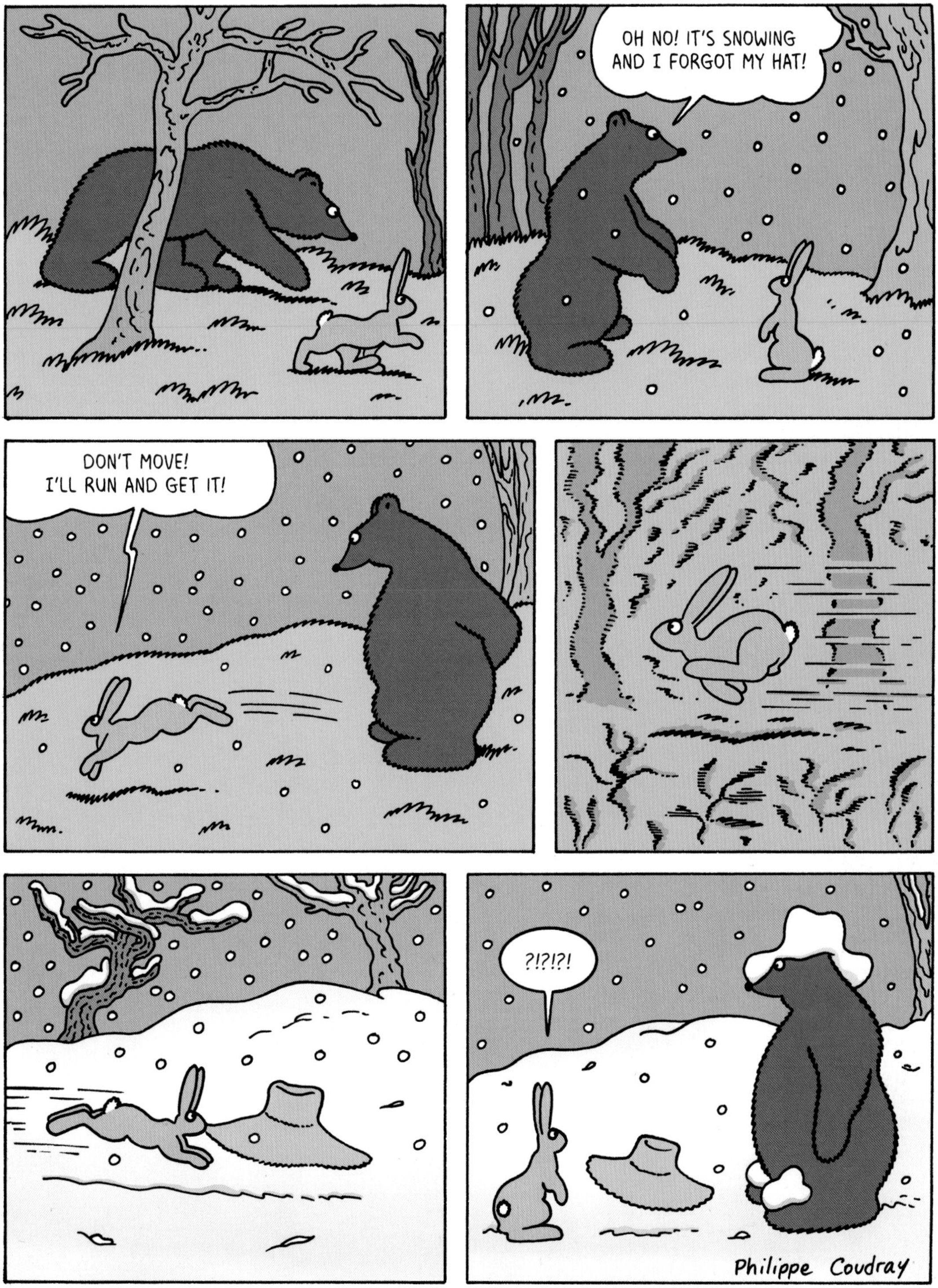
OH NO! IT'S SNOWING AND I FORGOT MY HAT!
DON'T MOVE! I'LL RUN AND GET IT!
?!?!?!
Philippe Coudray

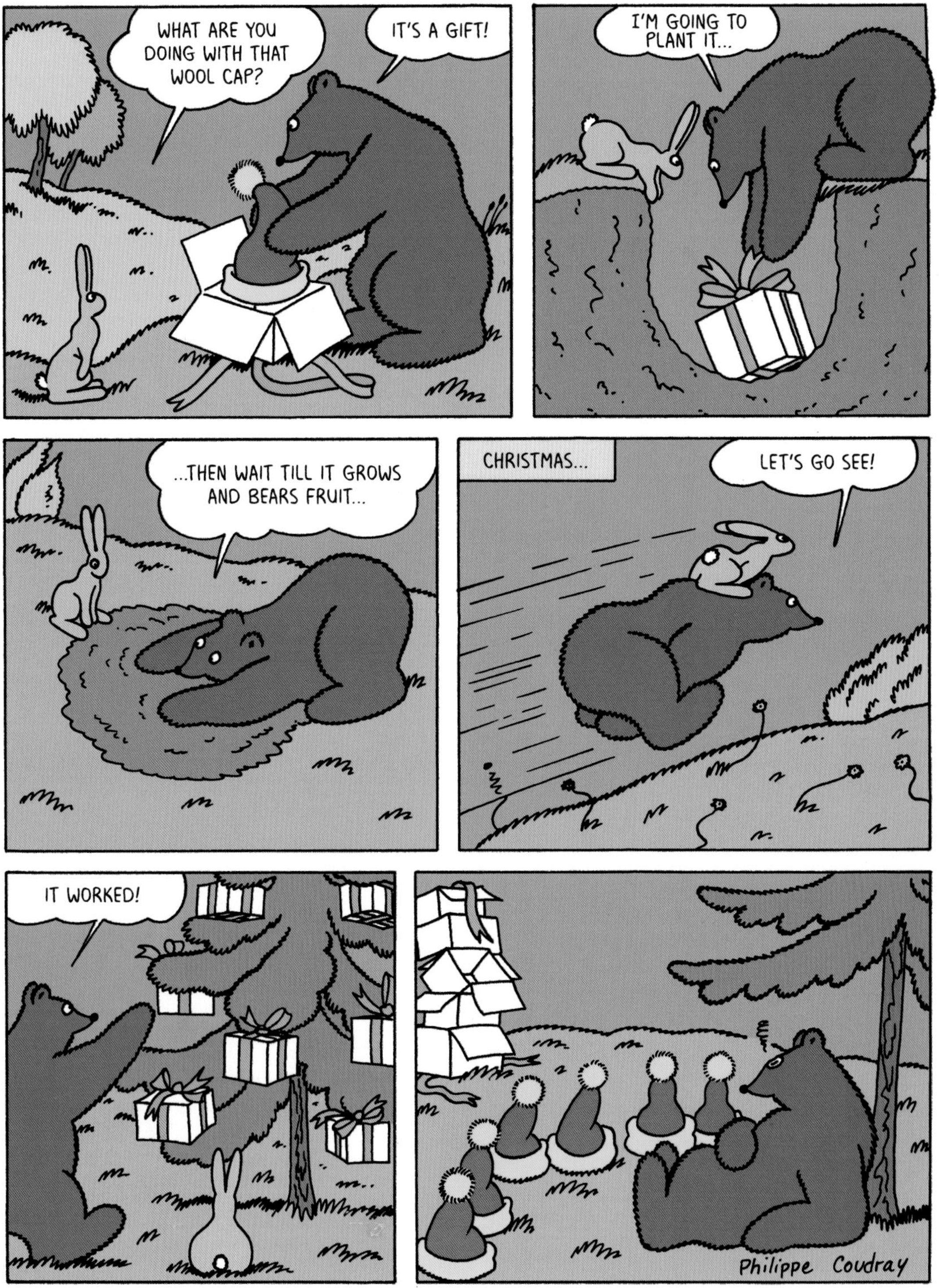
WHAT ARE YOU DOING WITH THAT WOOL CAP?
IT'S A GIFT!
I'M GOING TO PLANT IT...
...THEN WAIT TILL IT GROWS AND BEARS FRUIT...
CHRISTMAS...
LET'S GO SEE!
IT WORKED!
Philippe Coudray

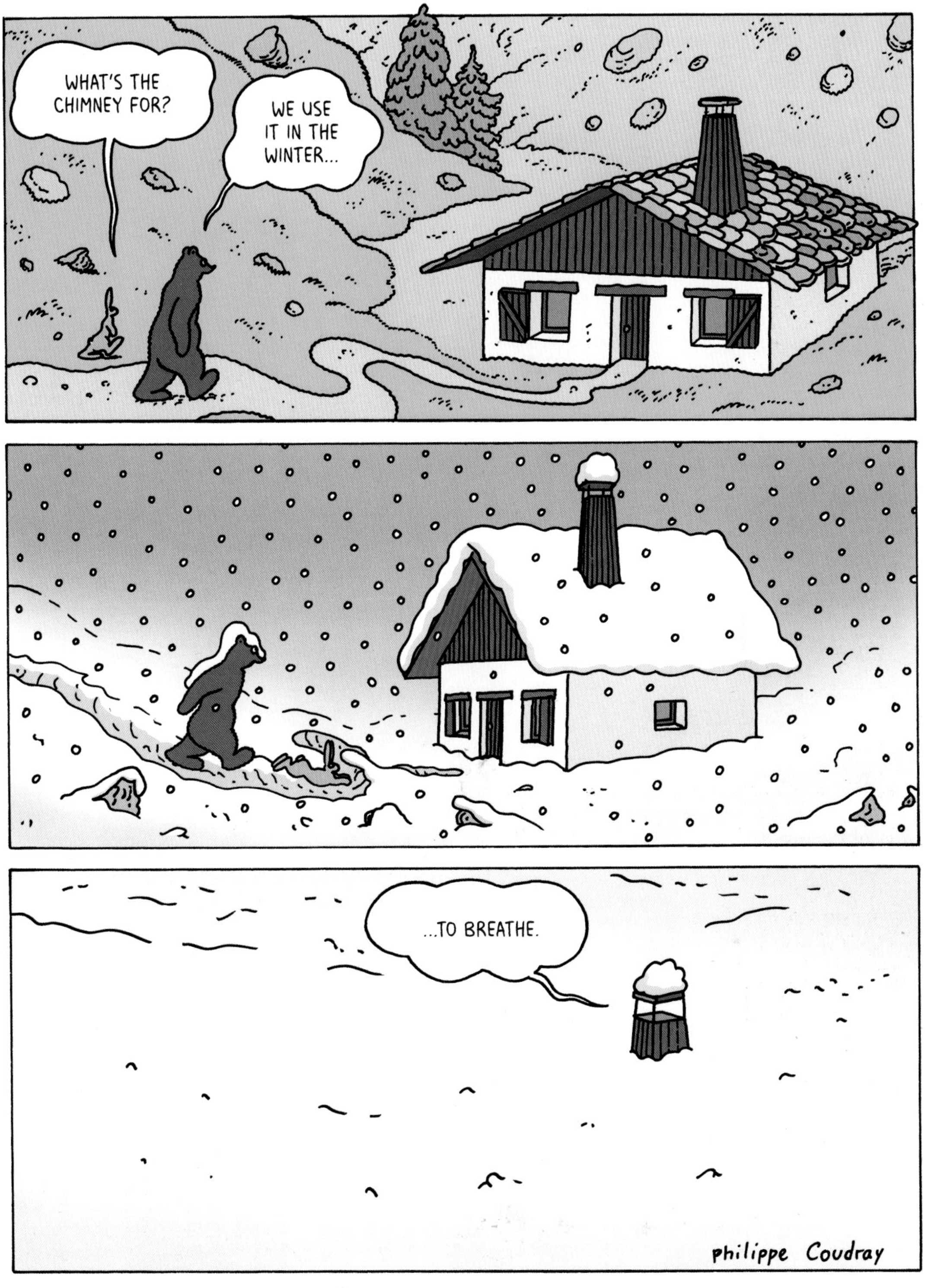
WHAT'S THE CHIMNEY FOR?
WE USE IT IN THE WINTER...
...TO BREATHE.
philippe Coudray

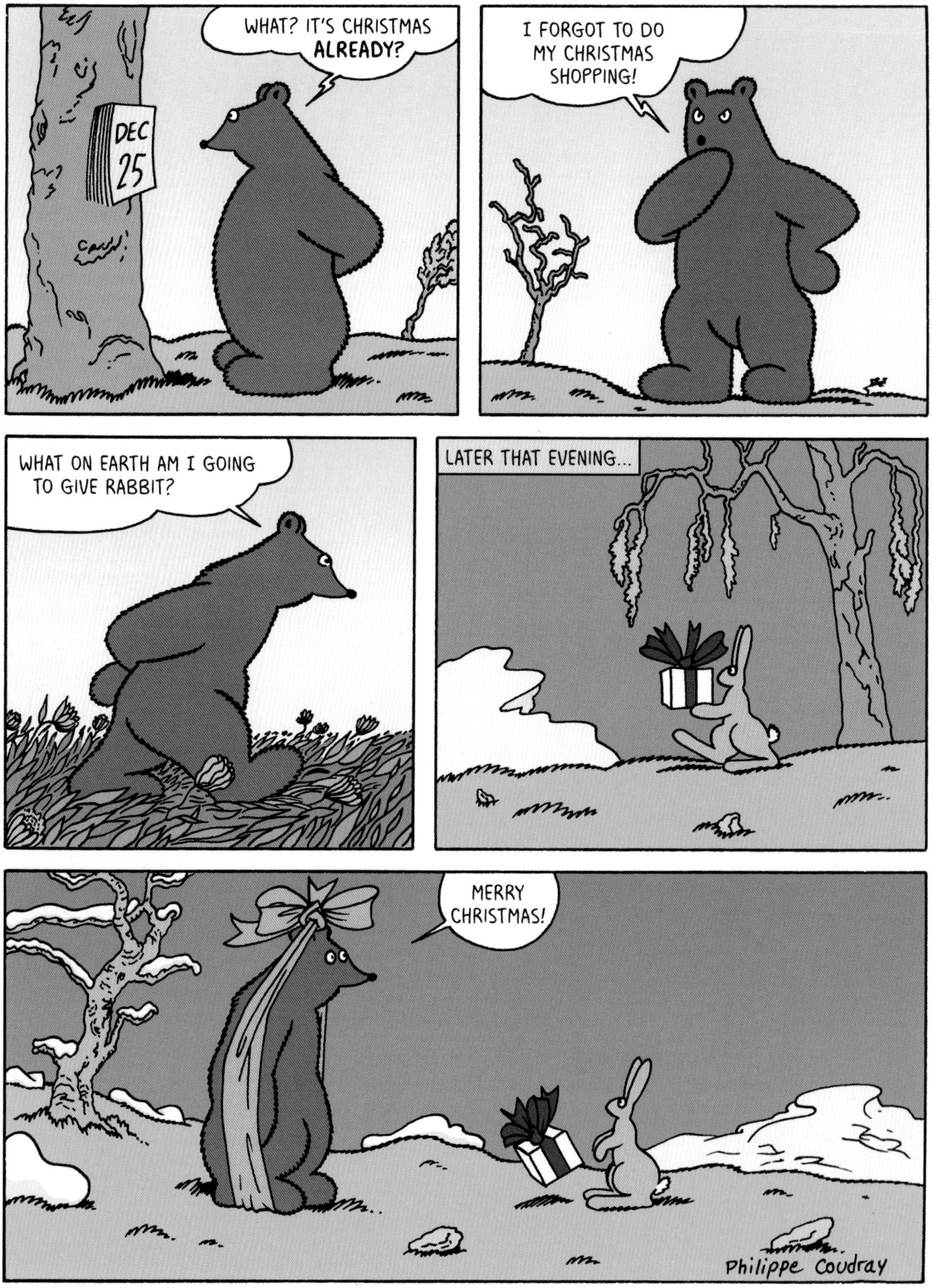
WHAT? IT'S CHRISTMAS **ALREADY?**
DEC 25
I FORGOT TO DO MY CHRISTMAS SHOPPING!
WHAT ON EARTH AM I GOING TO GIVE RABBIT?
LATER THAT EVENING...
MERRY CHRISTMAS!
Philippe Coudray

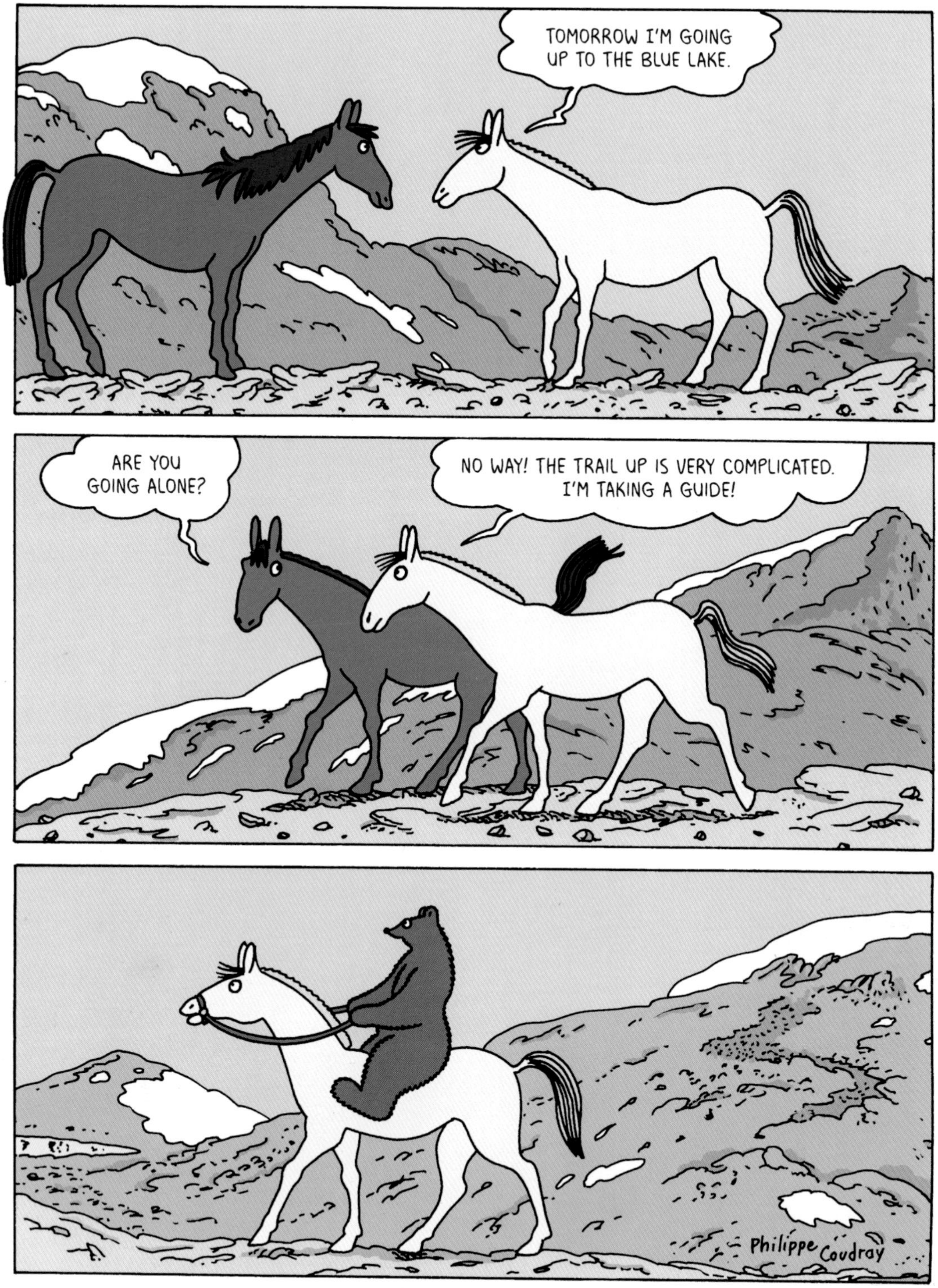

TOMORROW I'M GOING UP TO THE BLUE LAKE.
ARE YOU GOING ALONE?
NO WAY! THE TRAIL UP IS VERY COMPLICATED. I'M TAKING A GUIDE!
Philippe Coudray

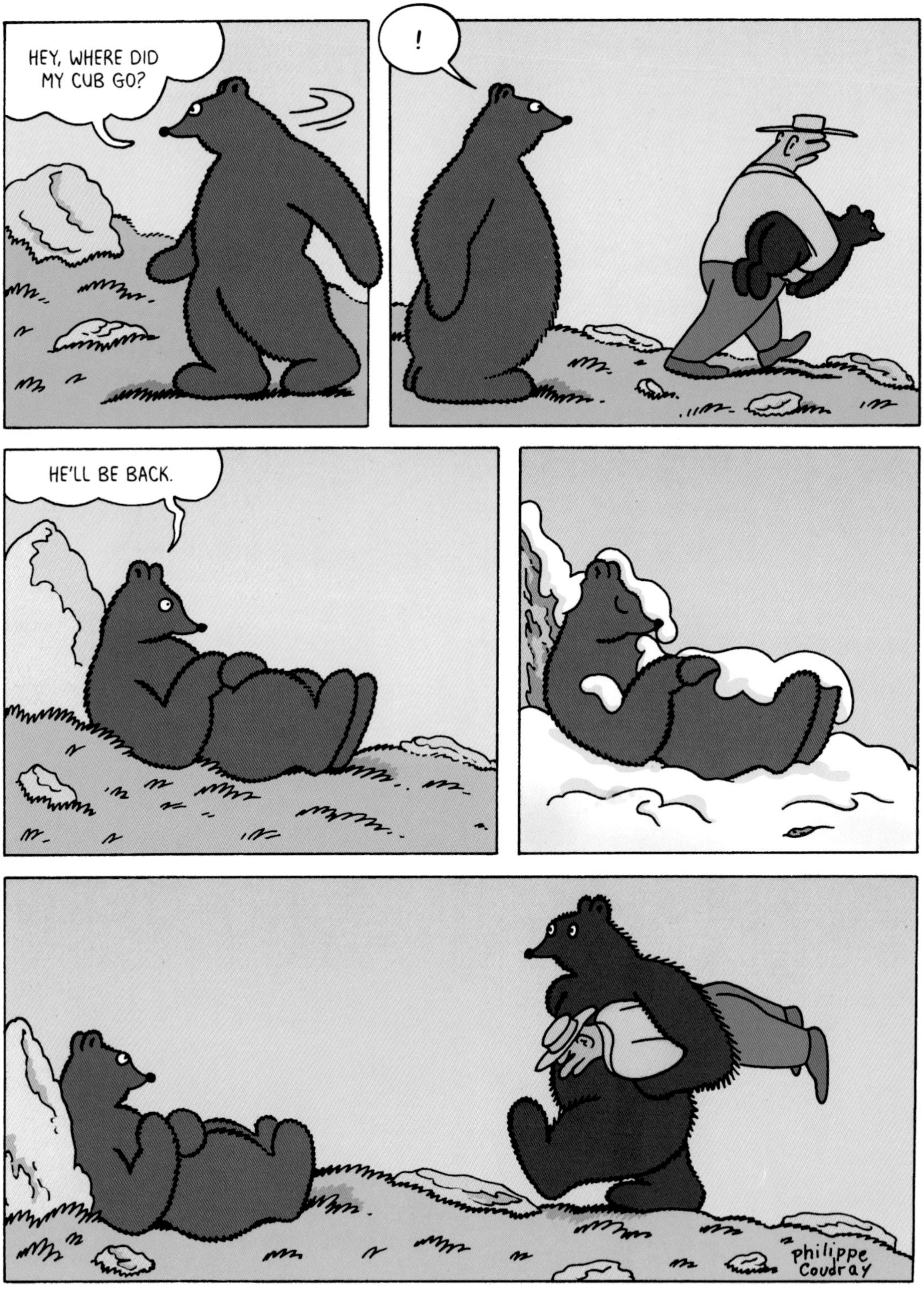
HEY, WHERE DID MY CUB GO?
!
HE'LL BE BACK.
Philippe Coudray

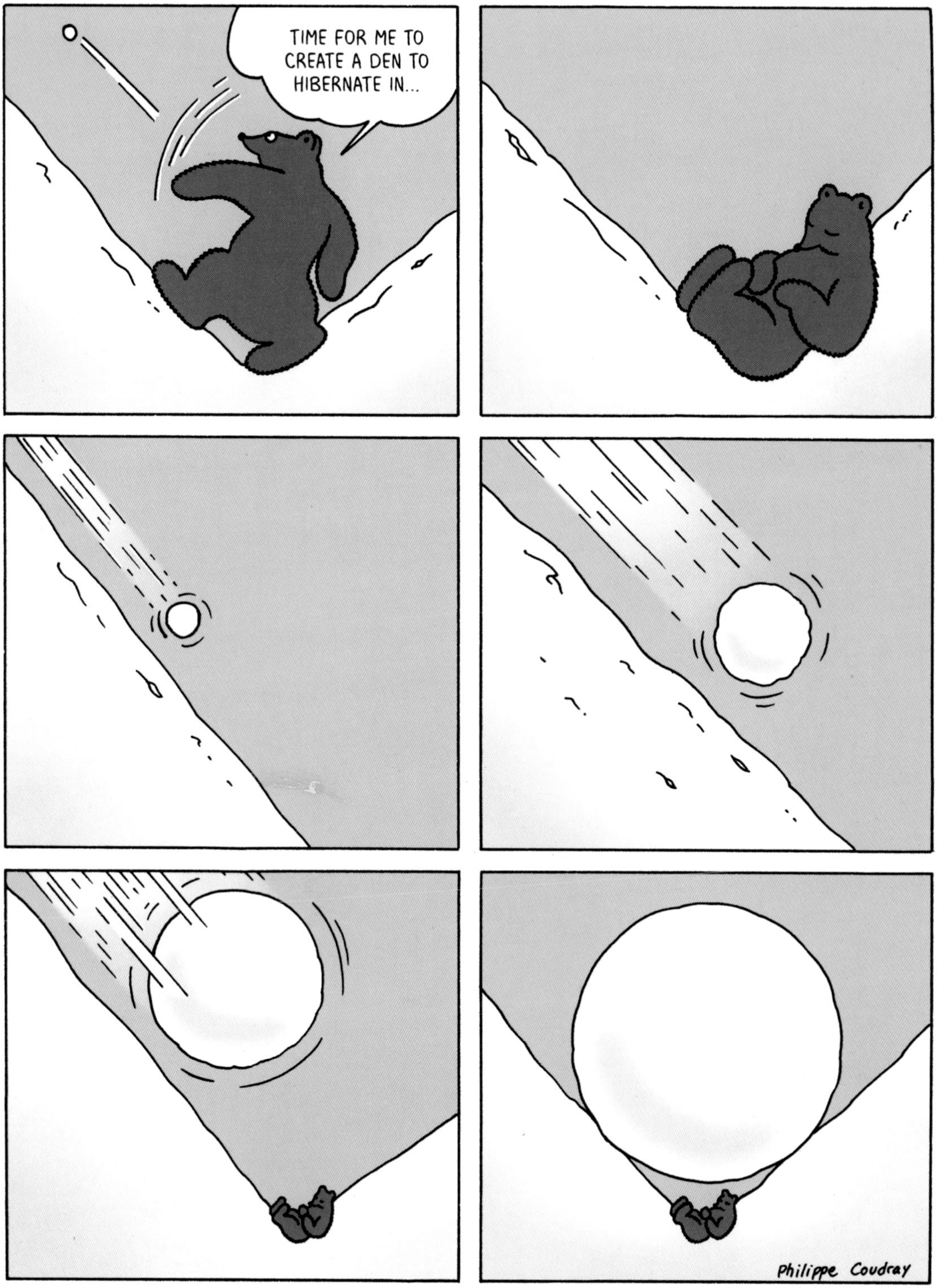
TIME FOR ME TO CREATE A DEN TO HIBERNATE IN...
Philippe Coudray

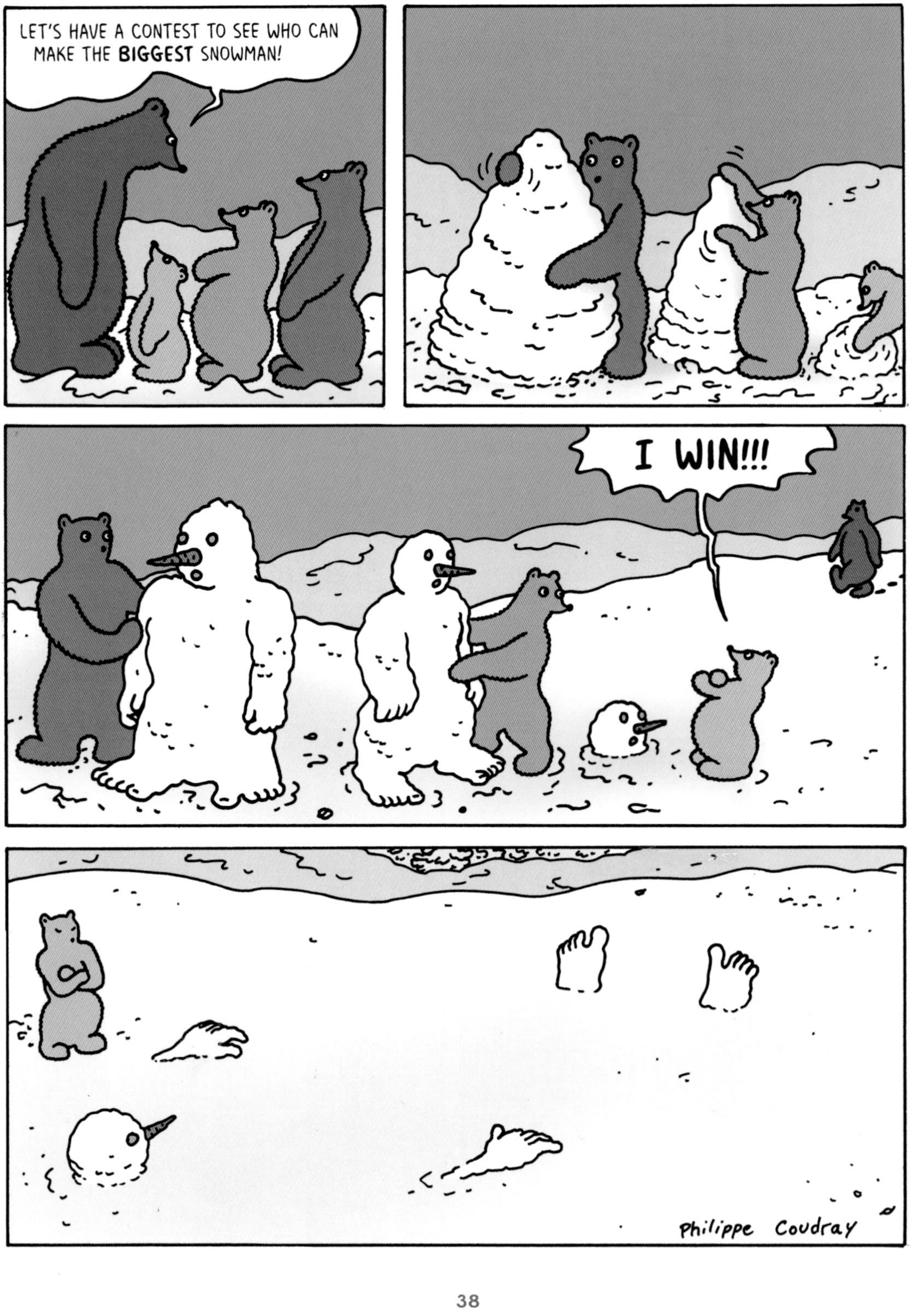
LET'S HAVE A CONTEST TO SEE WHO CAN MAKE THE **BIGGEST** SNOWMAN!
I WIN!!!
Philippe Coudray

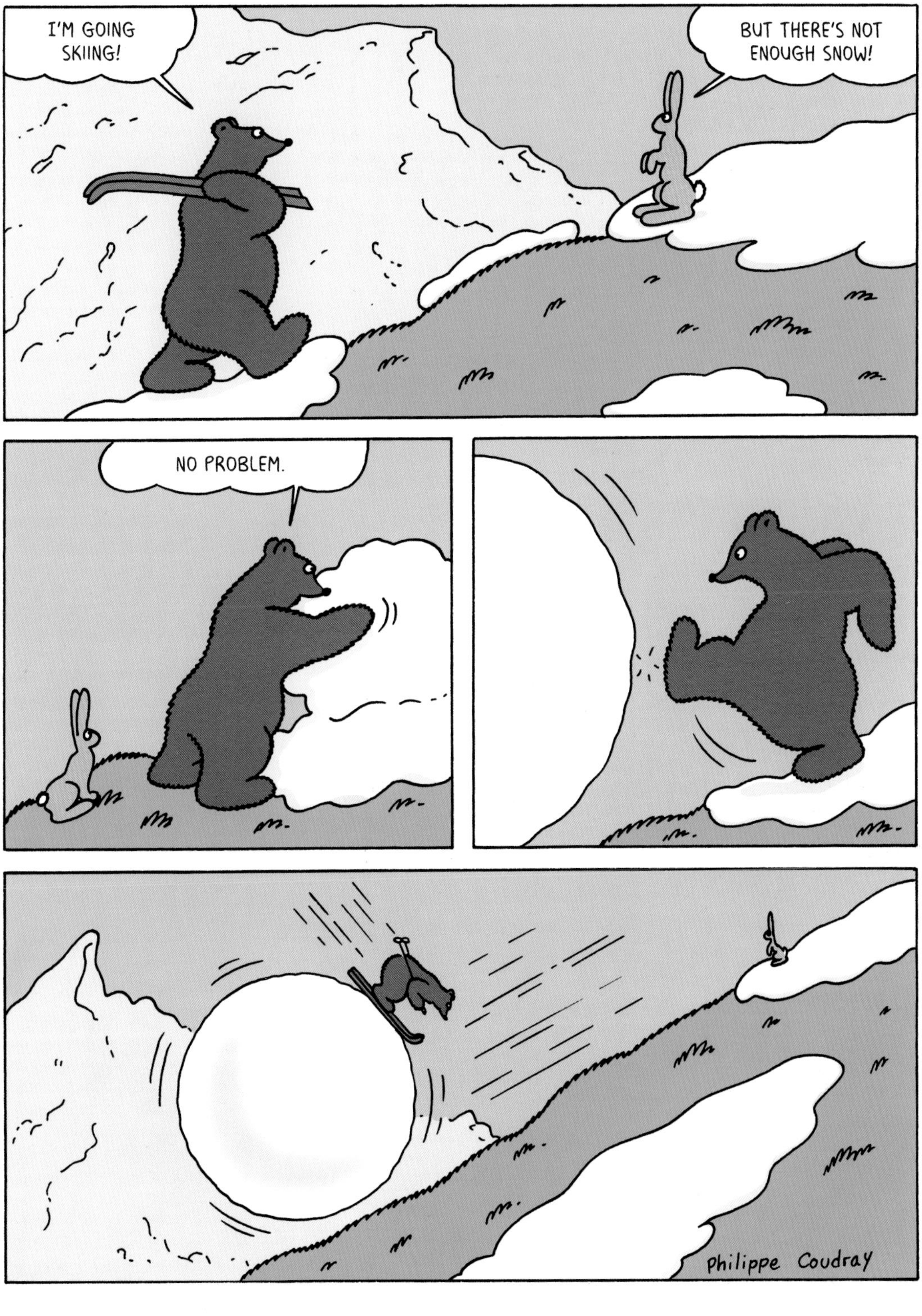
I'M GOING SKIING!
BUT THERE'S NOT ENOUGH SNOW!
NO PROBLEM.
Philippe Coudray

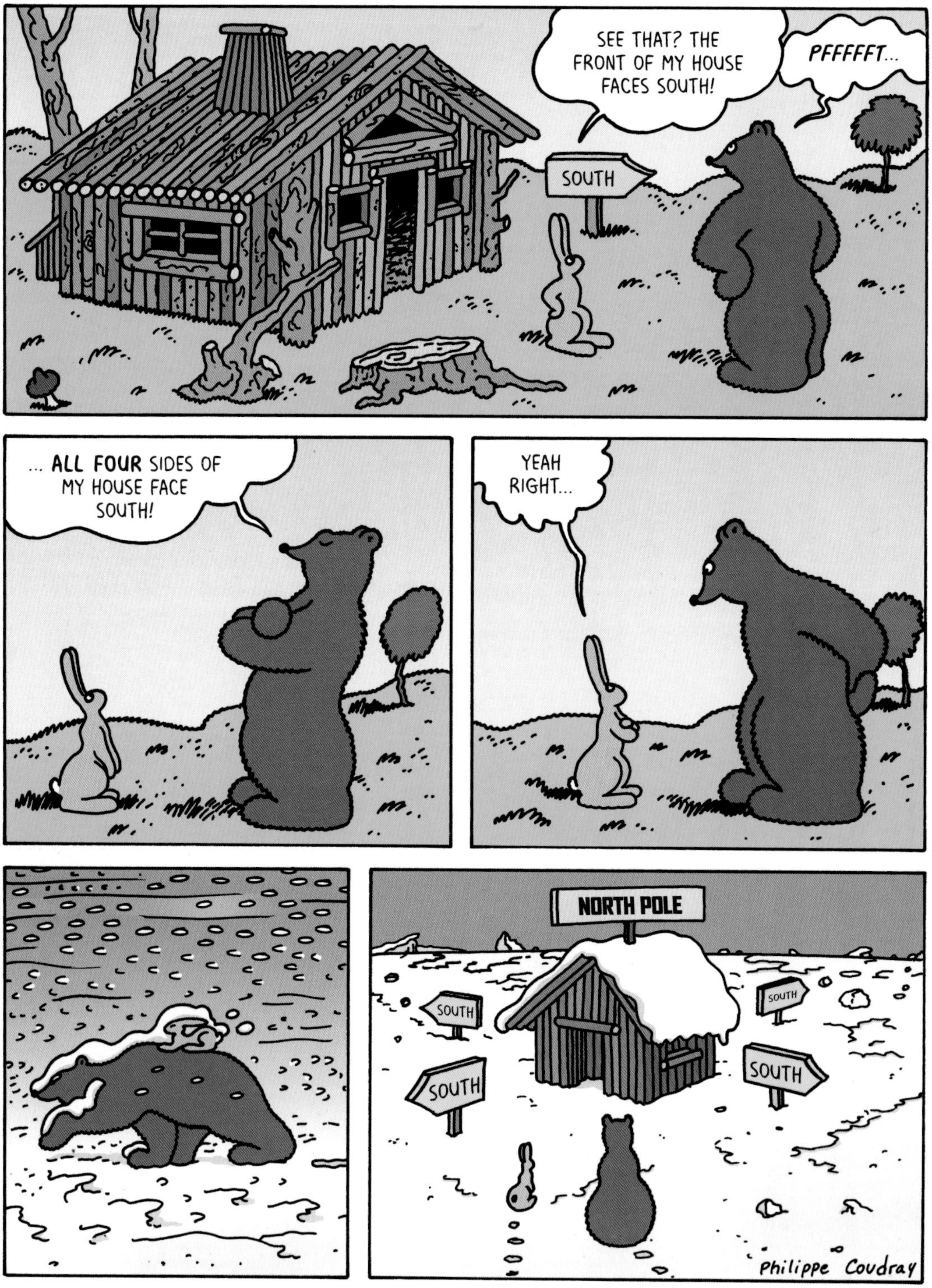

SEE THAT? THE FRONT OF MY HOUSE FACES SOUTH!
PFFFFFT...
SOUTH
... **ALL FOUR** SIDES OF MY HOUSE FACE SOUTH!
YEAH RIGHT...
NORTH POLE
SOUTH
SOUTH
SOUTH
SOUTH
Philippe Coudray

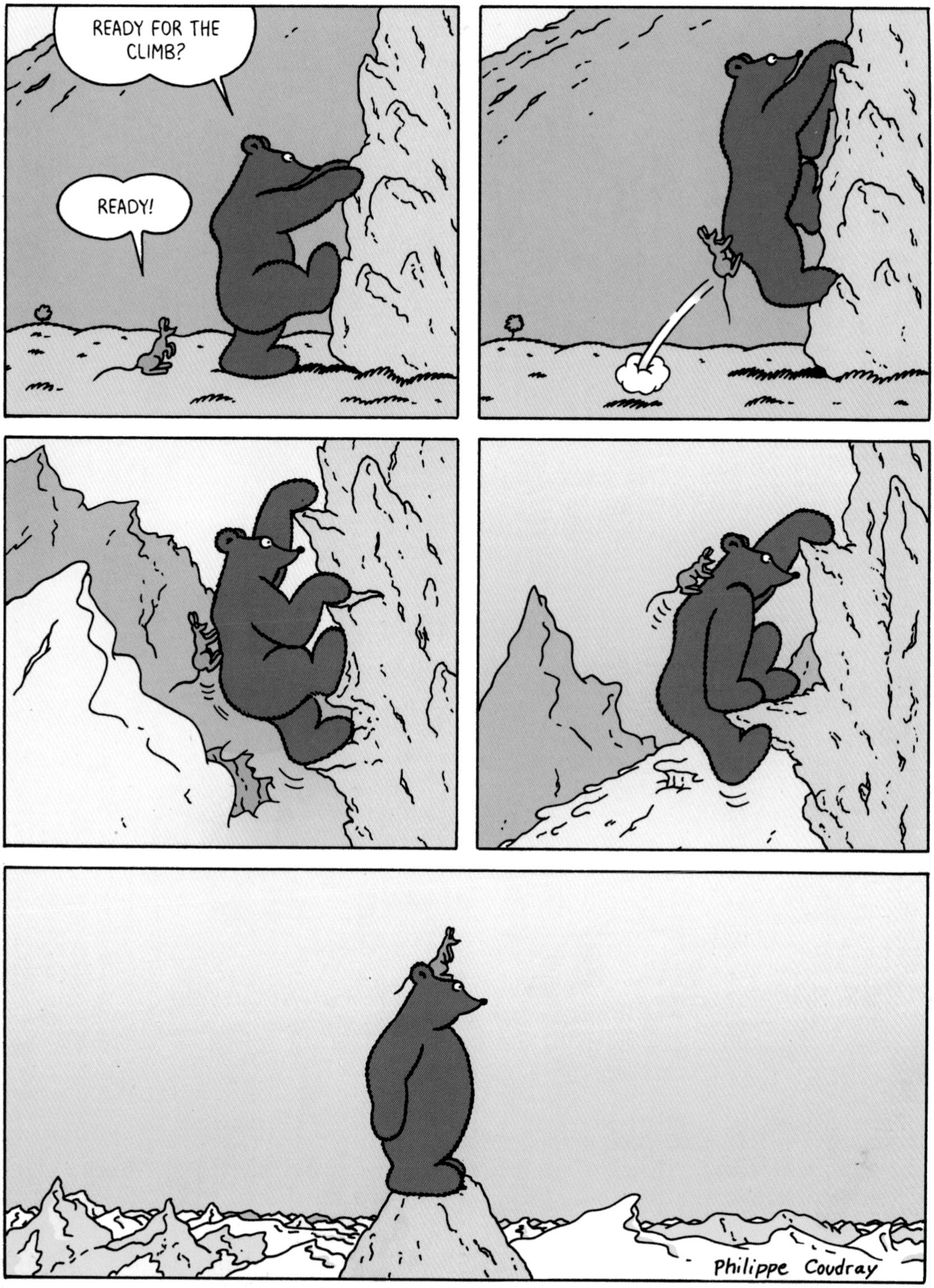
READY FOR THE CLIMB?
READY!
Philippe Coudray

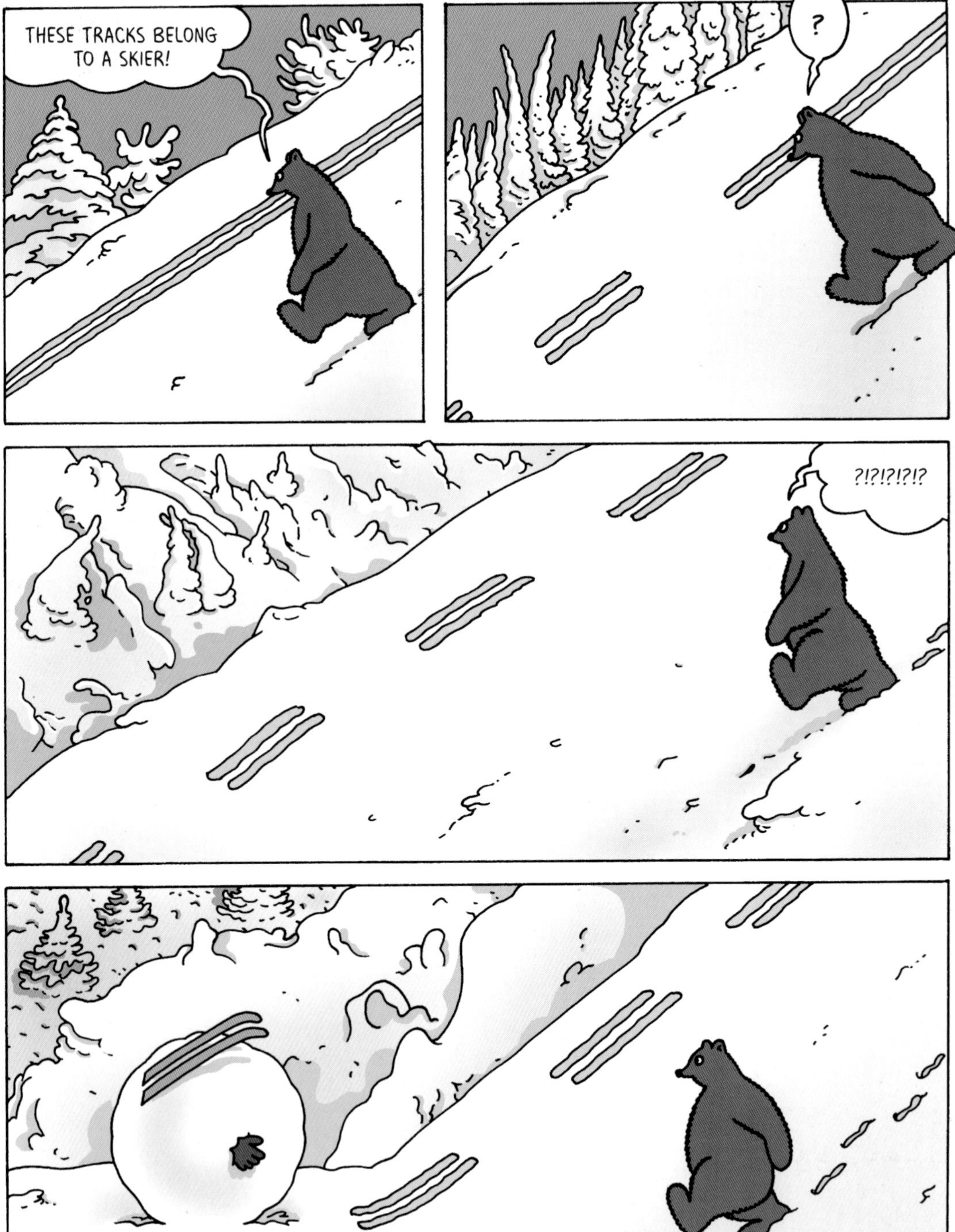
THESE TRACKS BELONG TO A SKIER!
?
?!?!?!?!?
Philippe Coudray

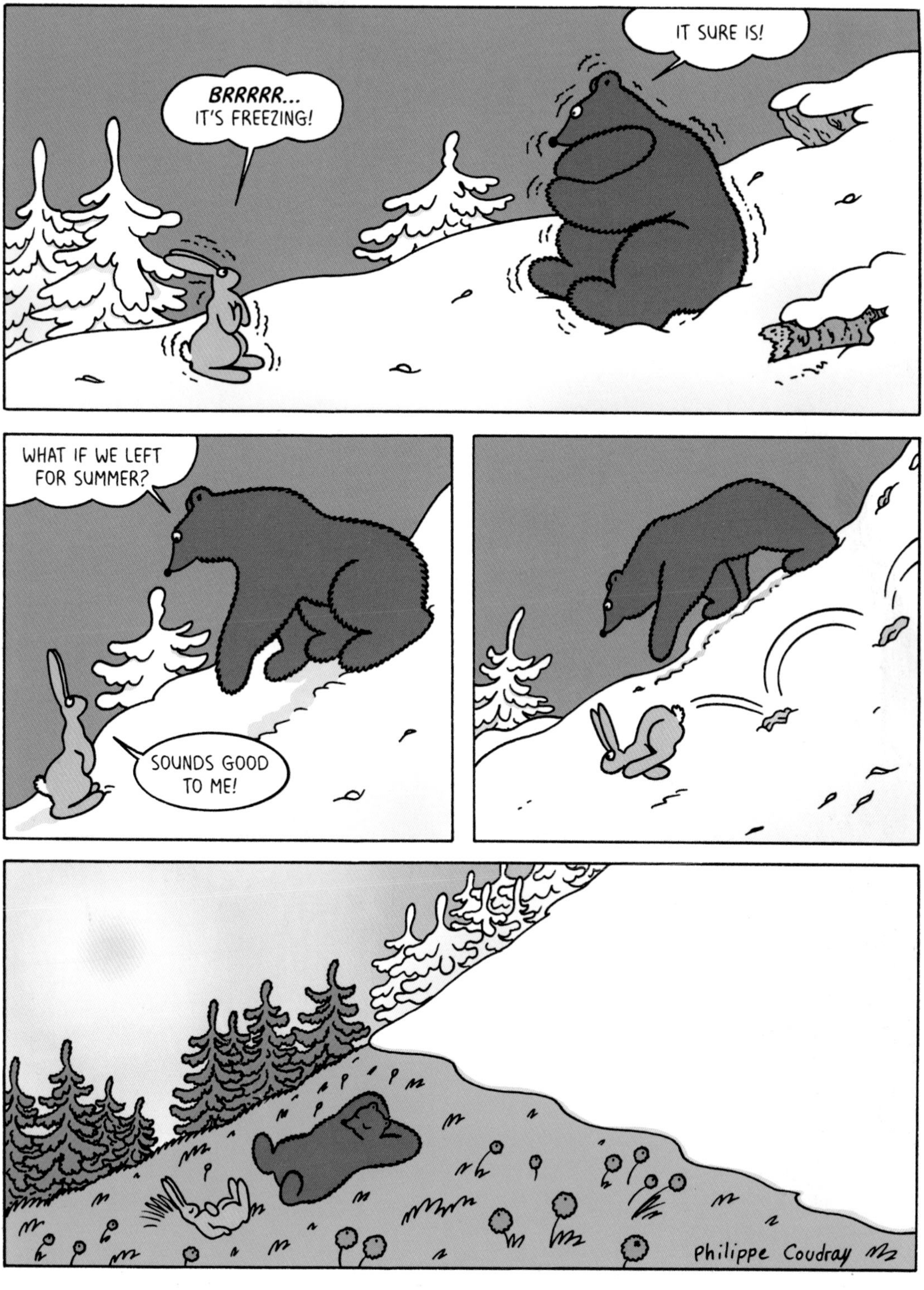
BRRRRR...
IT'S FREEZING!
IT SURE IS!
WHAT IF WE LEFT FOR SUMMER?
SOUNDS GOOD TO ME!
Philippe Coudray

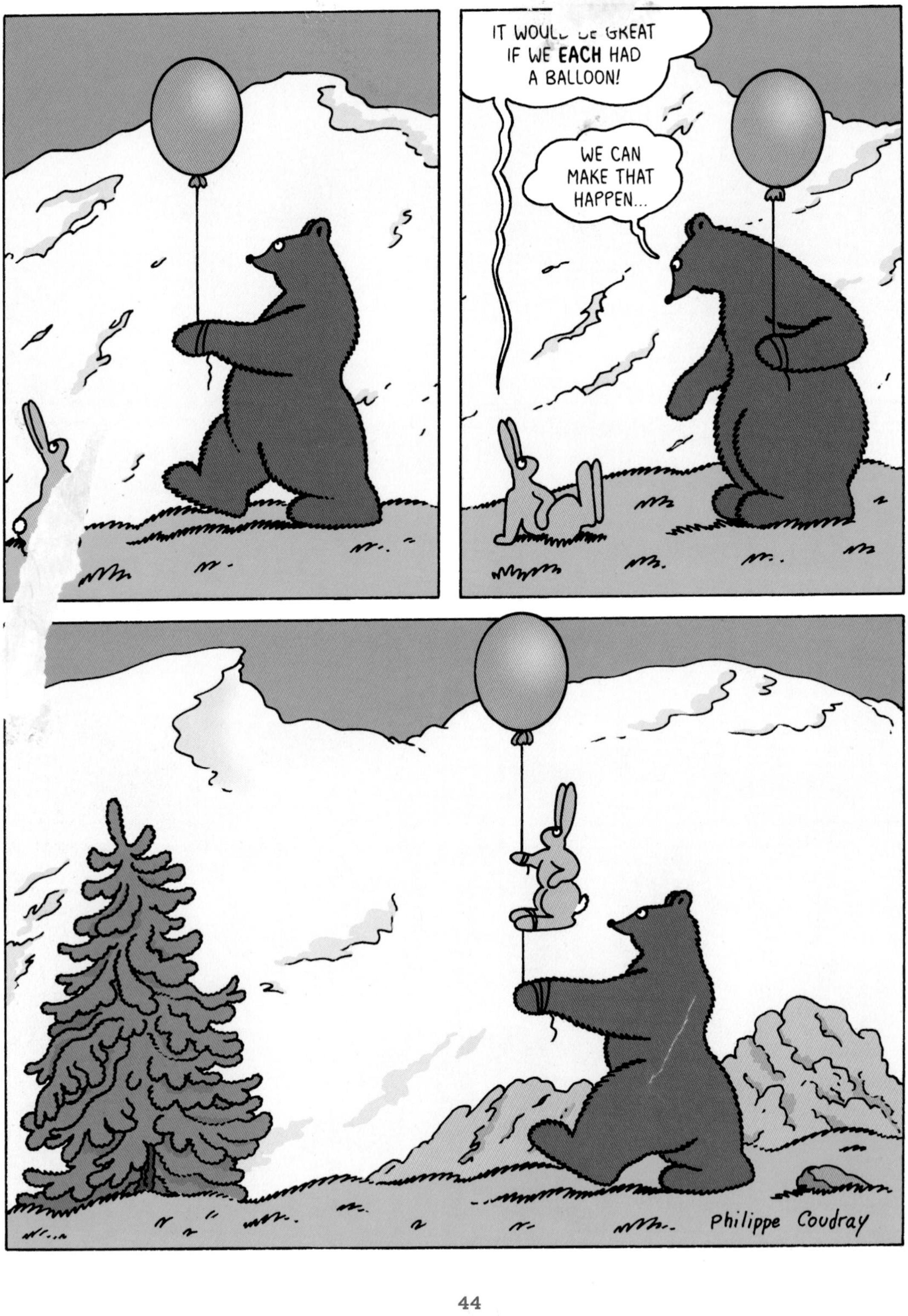
IT WOULD BE GREAT IF WE **EACH** HAD A BALLOON!
WE CAN MAKE THAT HAPPEN...
Philippe Coudray

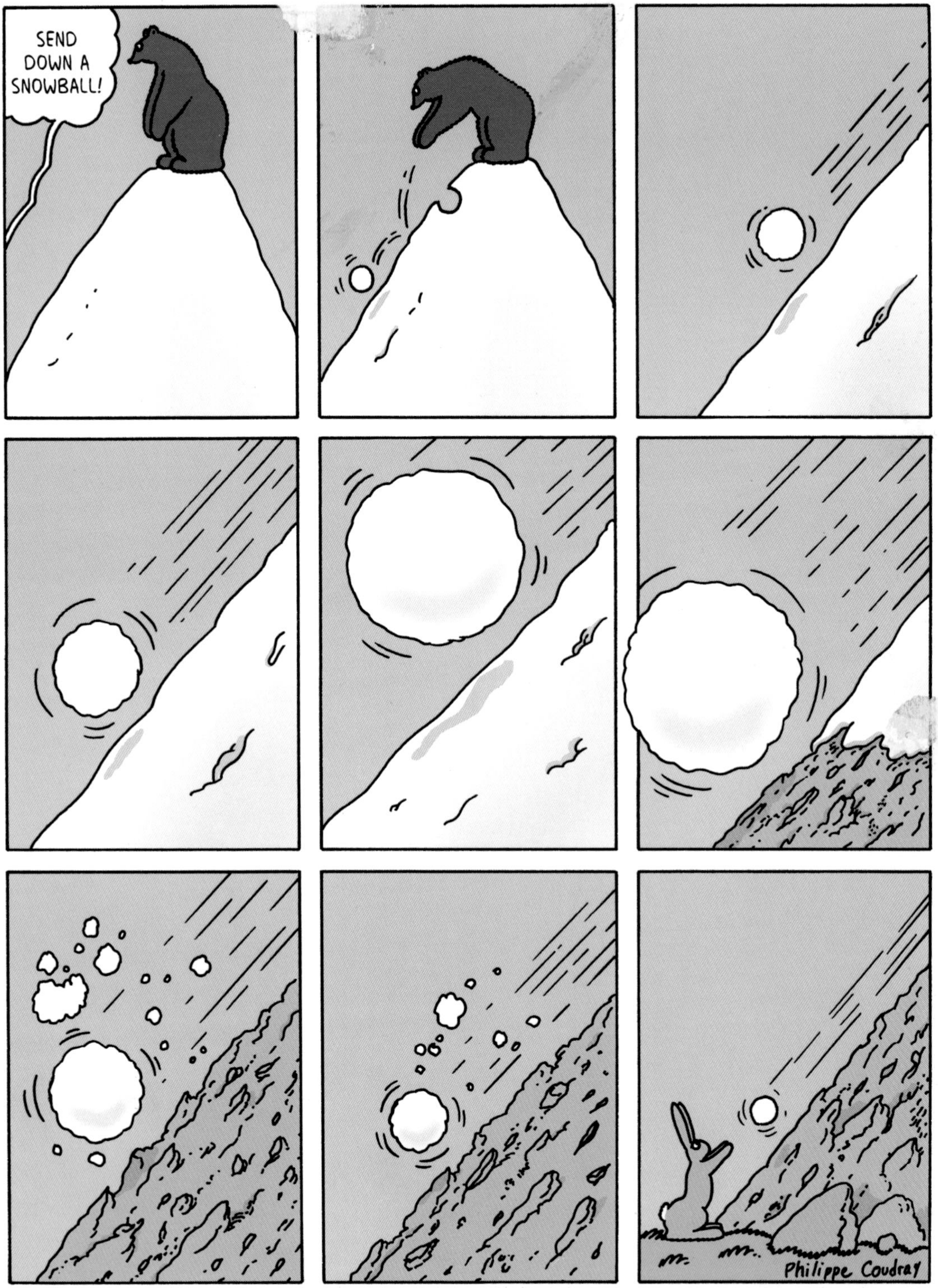
SEND DOWN A SNOWBALL!
Philippe Coudray

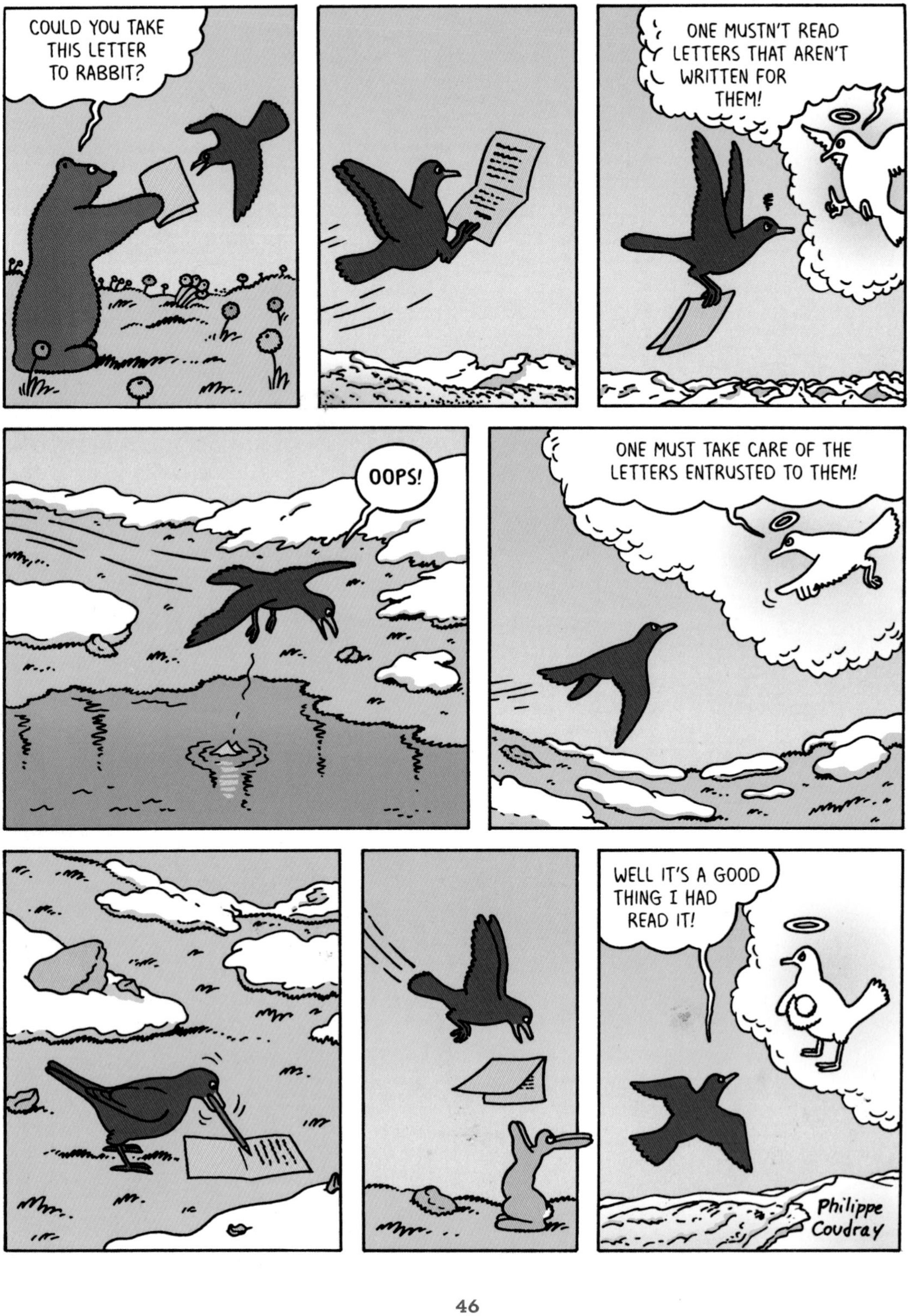
COULD YOU TAKE THIS LETTER TO RABBIT?
ONE MUSTN'T READ LETTERS THAT AREN'T WRITTEN FOR THEM!
OOPS!
ONE MUST TAKE CARE OF THE LETTERS ENTRUSTED TO THEM!
WELL IT'S A GOOD THING I HAD READ IT!
Philippe Coudray

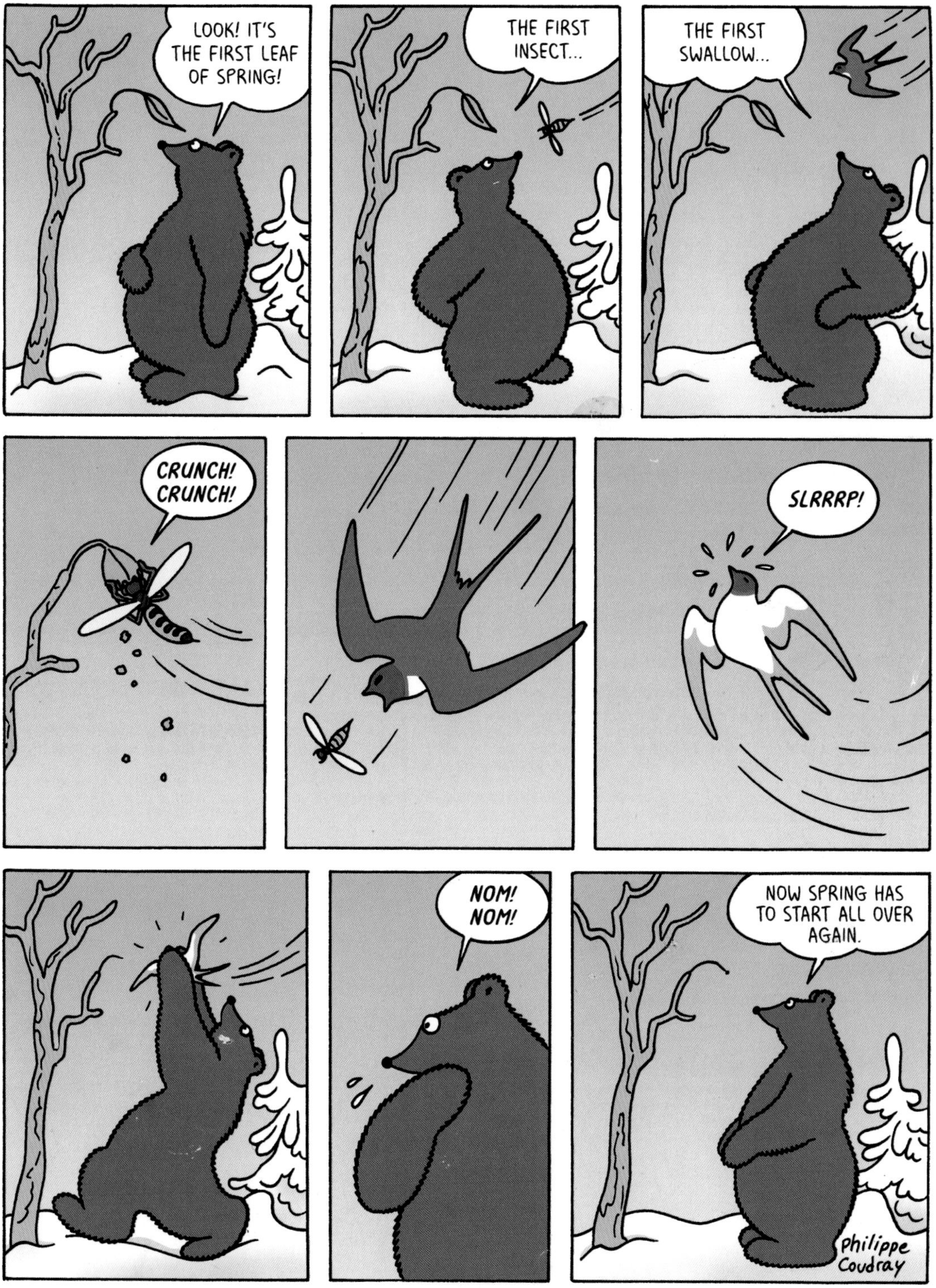

LOOK! IT'S THE FIRST LEAF OF SPRING!
THE FIRST INSECT...
THE FIRST SWALLOW...
CRUNCH! CRUNCH!
SLRRRP!
NOM! NOM!
NOW SPRING HAS TO START ALL OVER AGAIN.
Philippe Coudray

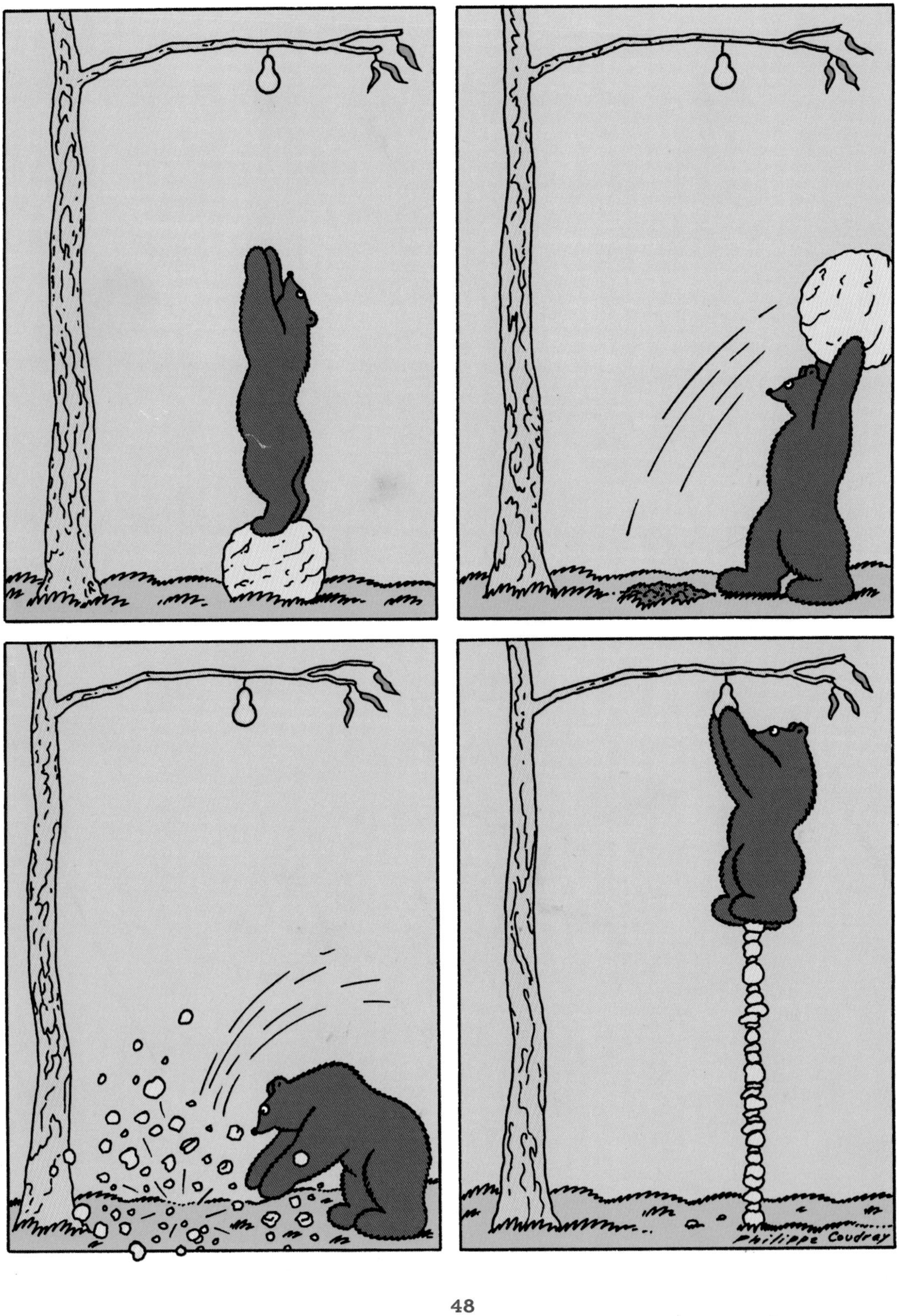
Philippe Coudray

SPRING

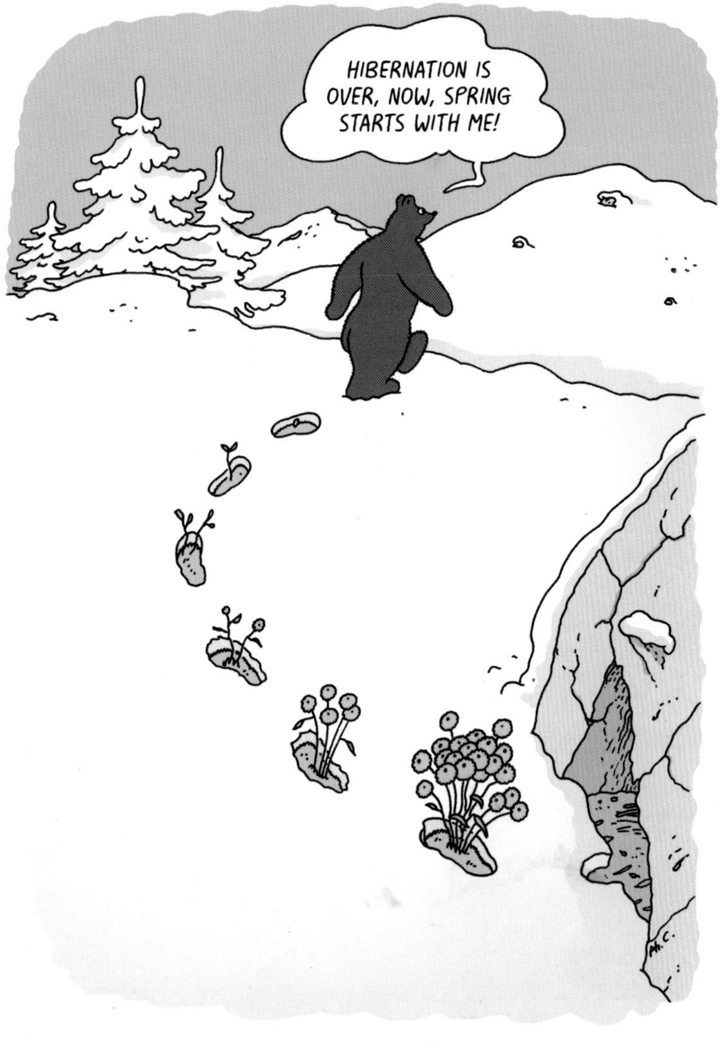
HIBERNATION IS OVER, NOW, SPRING STARTS WITH ME!
ph. C.

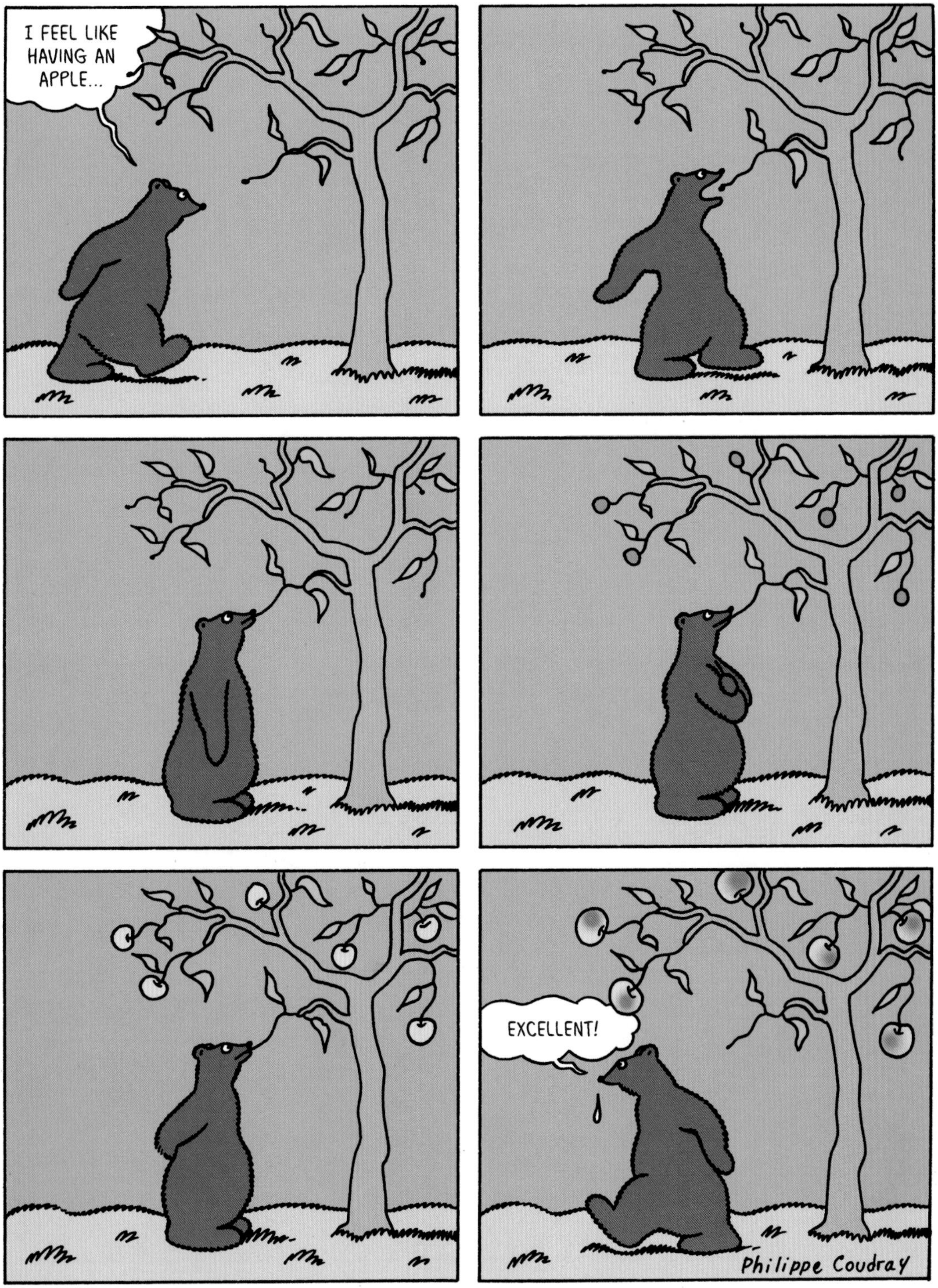
I FEEL LIKE HAVING AN APPLE...
EXCELLENT!
Philippe Coudray

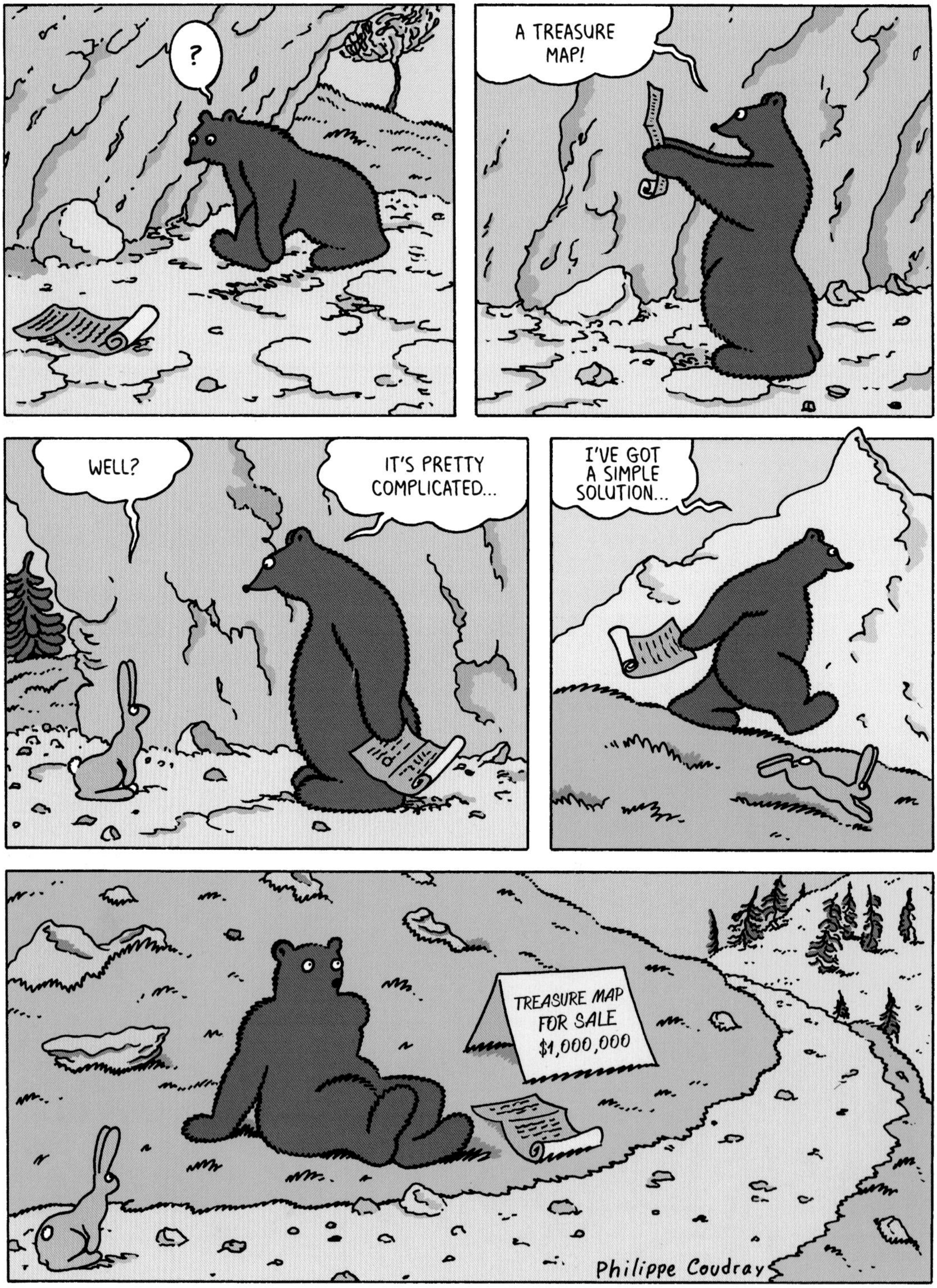
?
A TREASURE MAP!
WELL?
IT'S PRETTY COMPLICATED...
I'VE GOT A SIMPLE SOLUTION...
TREASURE MAP FOR SALE $1,000,000
Philippe Coudray

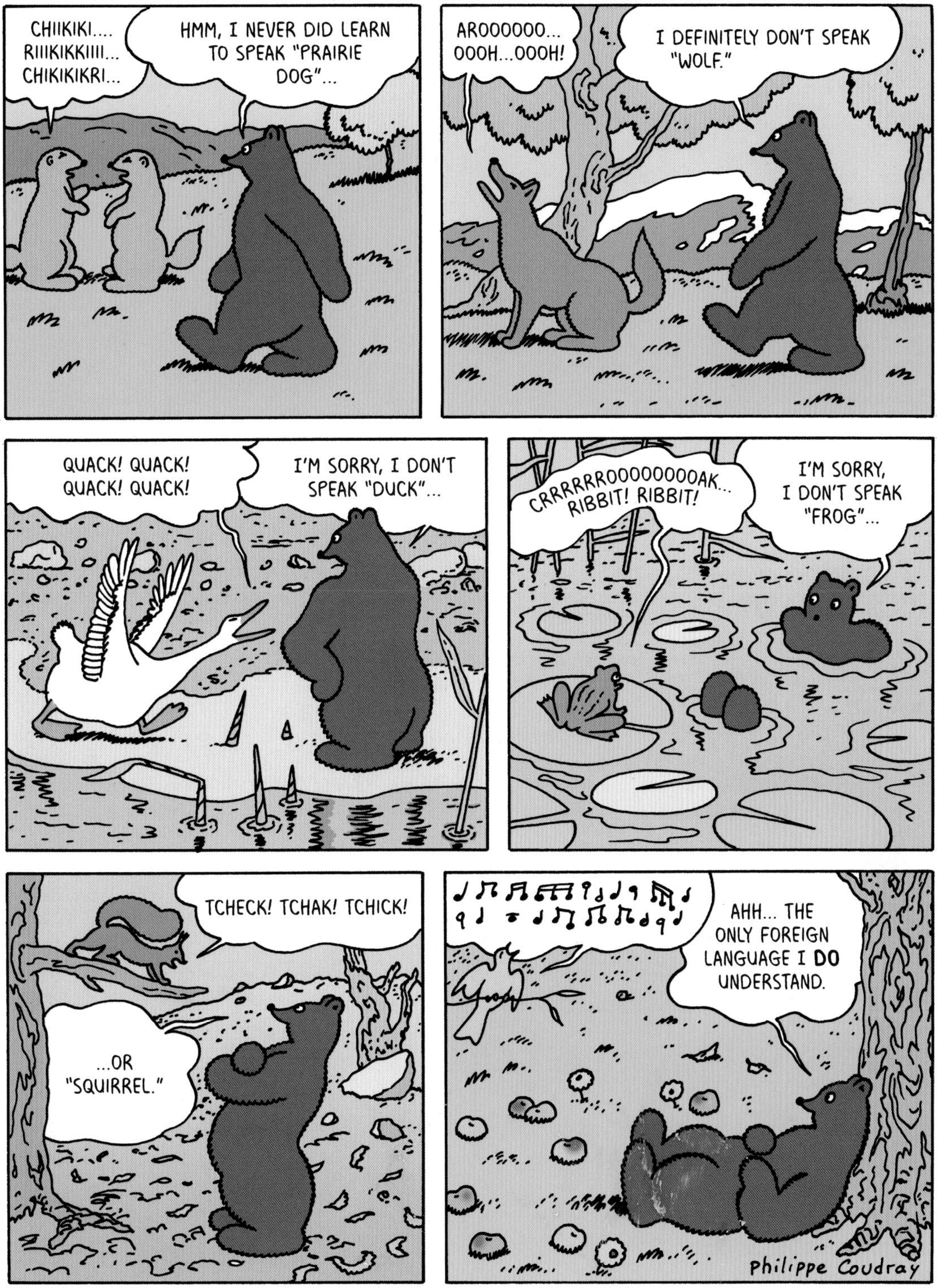
CHIIKIKI.... RIIIKIKKIIII... CHIKIKIKRI...
HMM, I NEVER DID LEARN TO SPEAK "PRAIRIE DOG"...
AROOOOOO... OOOH...OOOH!
I DEFINITELY DON'T SPEAK "WOLF."
QUACK! QUACK! QUACK! QUACK!
I'M SORRY, I DON'T SPEAK "DUCK"...
CRRRRRROOOOOOOOOAK... RIBBIT! RIBBIT!
I'M SORRY, I DON'T SPEAK "FROG"...
TCHECK! TCHAK! TCHICK!
...OR "SQUIRREL."
AHH... THE ONLY FOREIGN LANGUAGE I **DO** UNDERSTAND.
Philippe Coudray

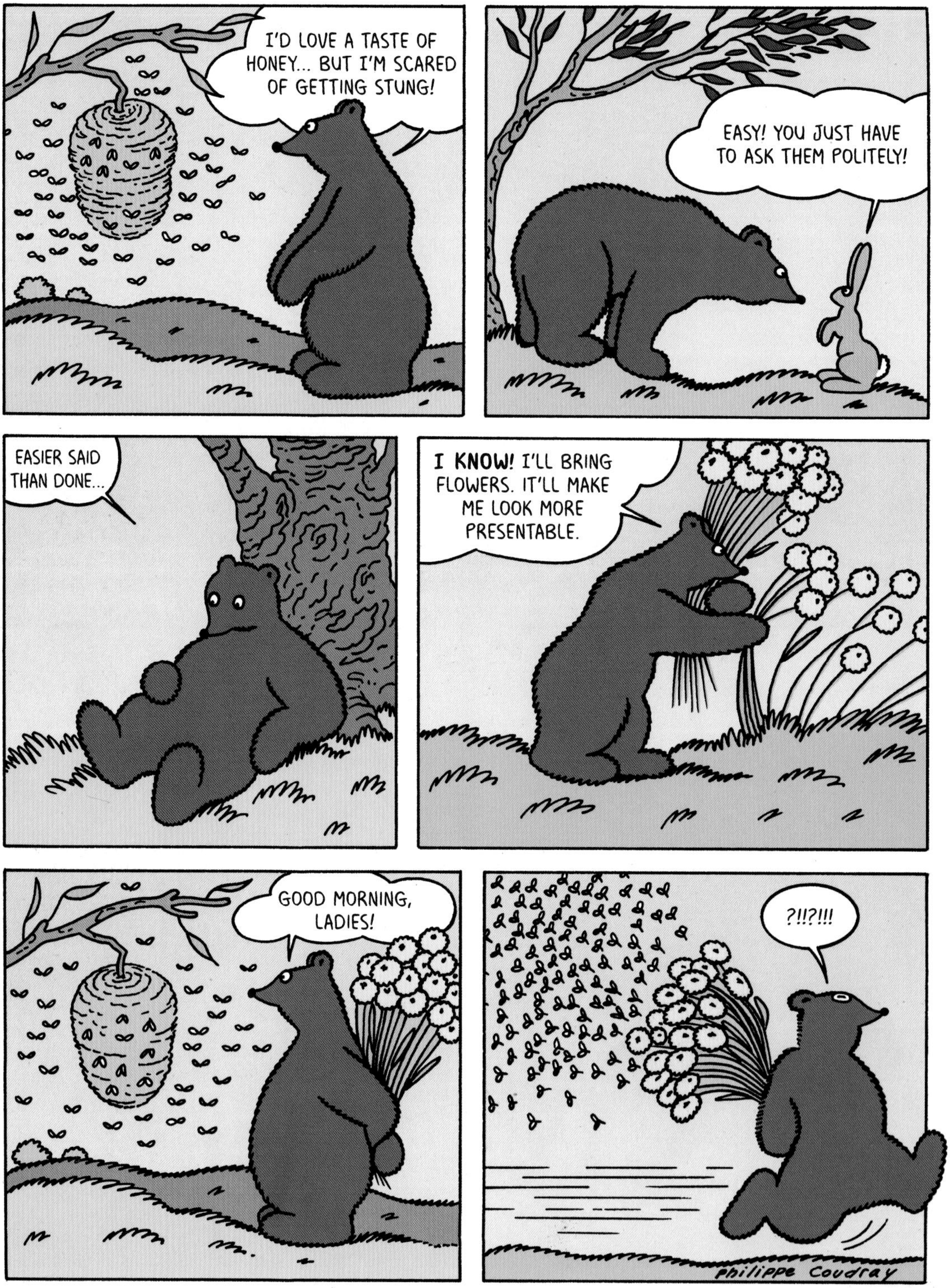

I'D LOVE A TASTE OF HONEY... BUT I'M SCARED OF GETTING STUNG!
EASY! YOU JUST HAVE TO ASK THEM POLITELY!
EASIER SAID THAN DONE...
I KNOW! I'LL BRING FLOWERS. IT'LL MAKE ME LOOK MORE PRESENTABLE.
GOOD MORNING, LADIES!
?!!?!!!
Philippe Coudray

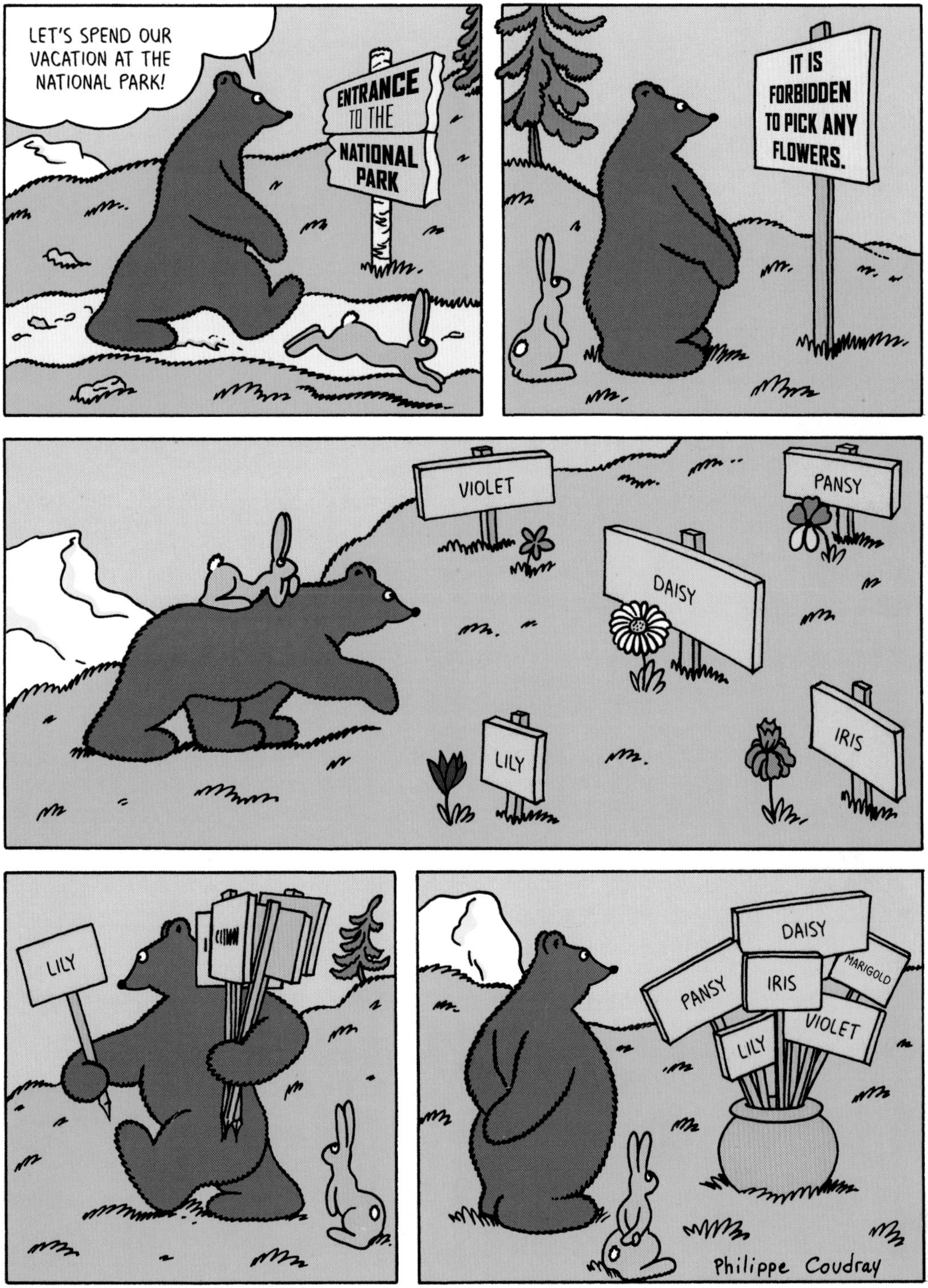
LET'S SPEND OUR VACATION AT THE NATIONAL PARK!
ENTRANCE TO THE
NATIONAL PARK
IT IS FORBIDDEN TO PICK ANY FLOWERS.
VIOLET
PANSY
DAISY
LILY
IRIS
LILY
DAISY
PANSY
IRIS
MARIGOLD
VIOLET
LILY
Philippe Coudray

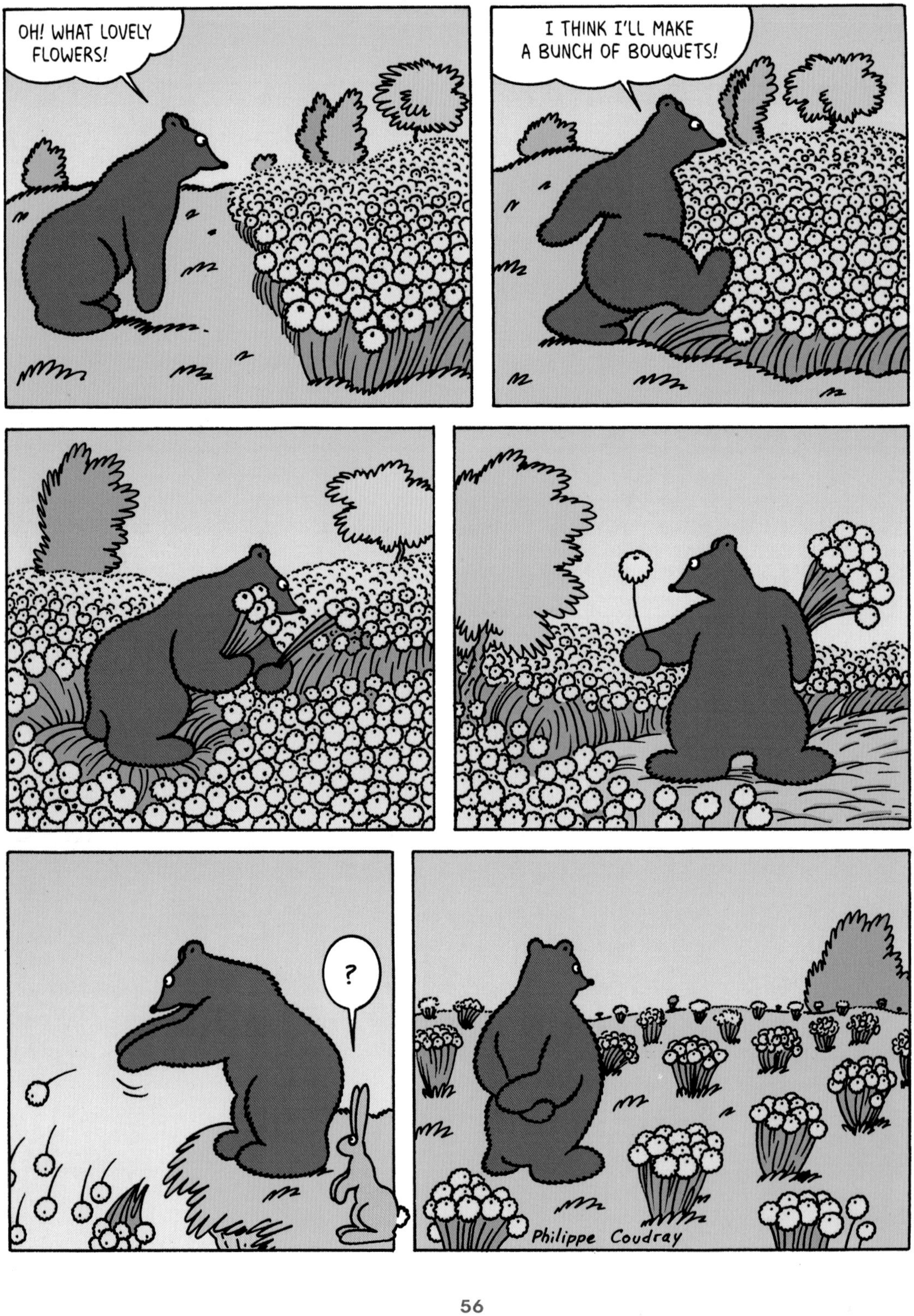
OH! WHAT LOVELY FLOWERS!
I THINK I'LL MAKE A BUNCH OF BOUQUETS!
?
Philippe Coudray

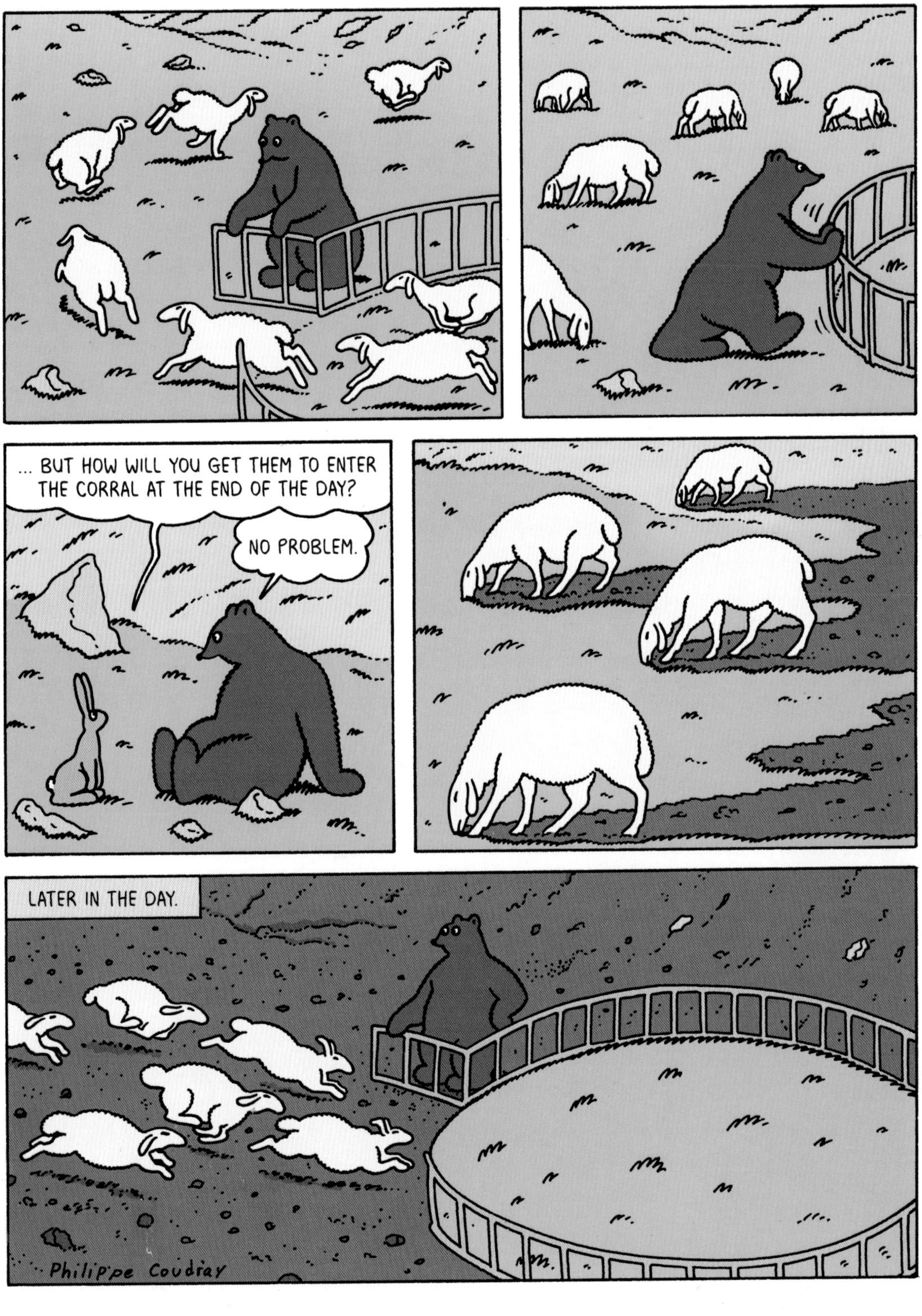
... BUT HOW WILL YOU GET THEM TO ENTER THE CORRAL AT THE END OF THE DAY?
NO PROBLEM.
LATER IN THE DAY.
Philippe Coudray

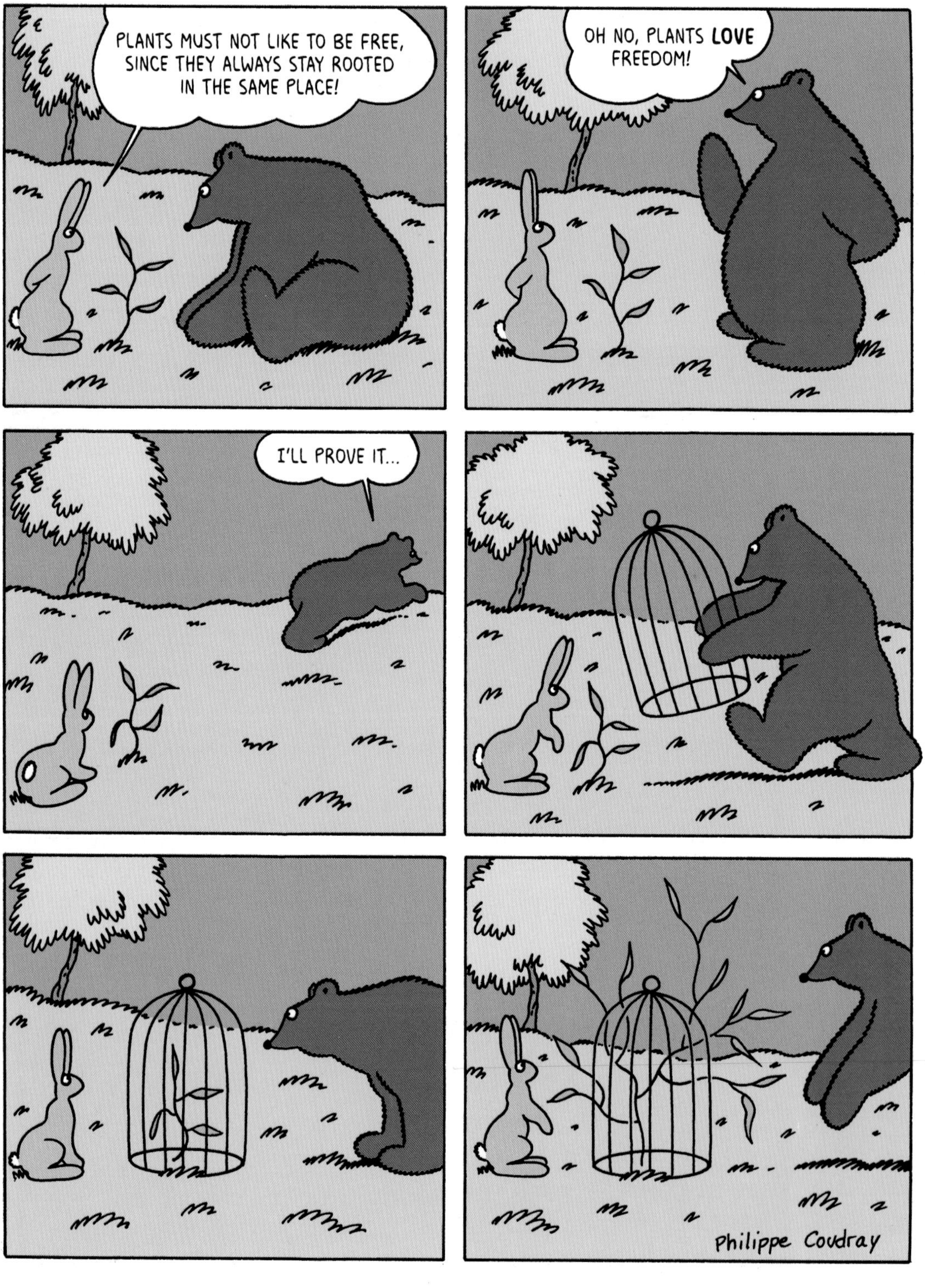
PLANTS MUST NOT LIKE TO BE FREE, SINCE THEY ALWAYS STAY ROOTED IN THE SAME PLACE!
OH NO, PLANTS **LOVE** FREEDOM!
I'LL PROVE IT...
Philippe Coudray

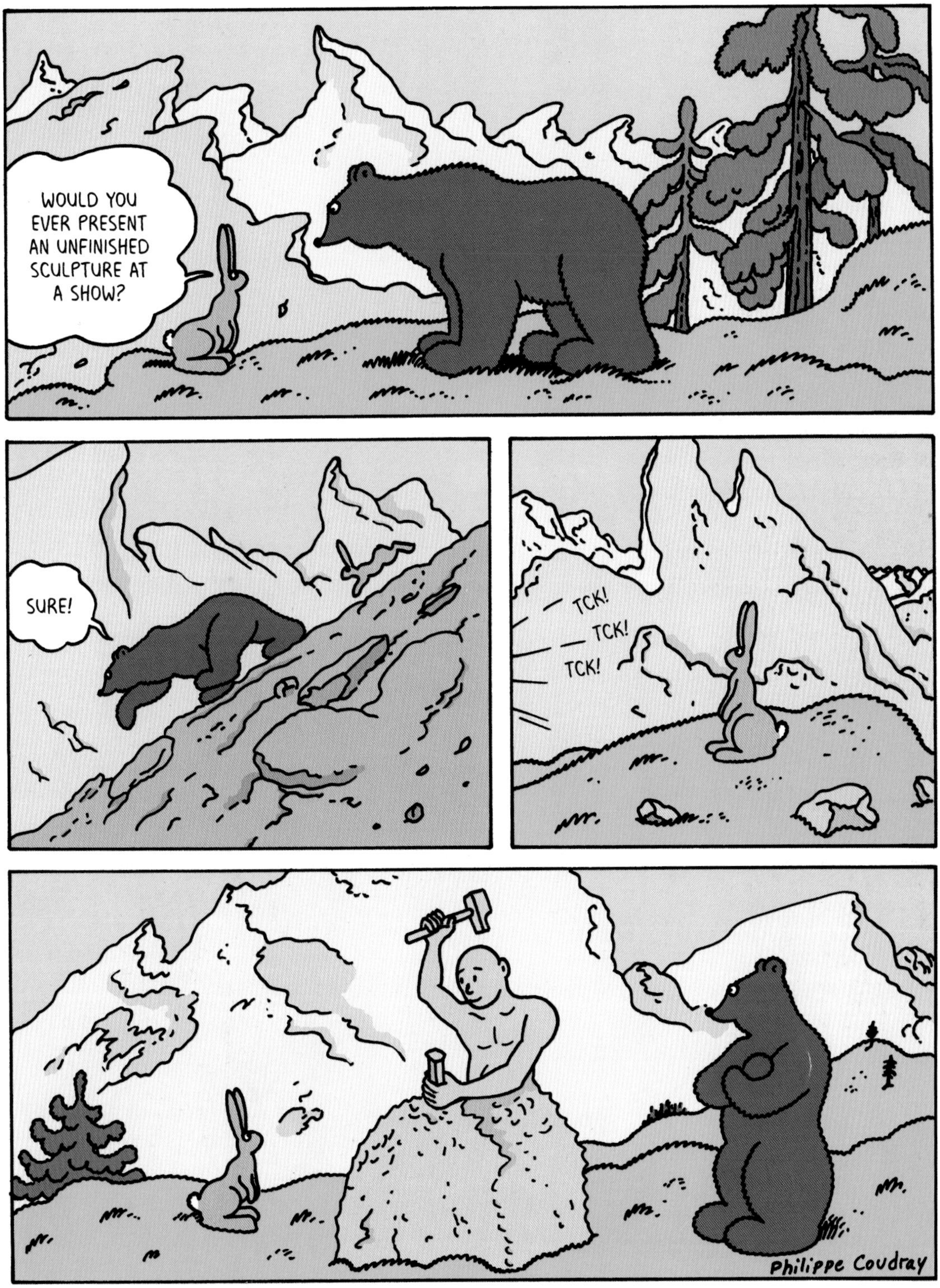
WOULD YOU EVER PRESENT AN UNFINISHED SCULPTURE AT A SHOW?
SURE!
TCK!
TCK!
TCK!
Philippe Coudray

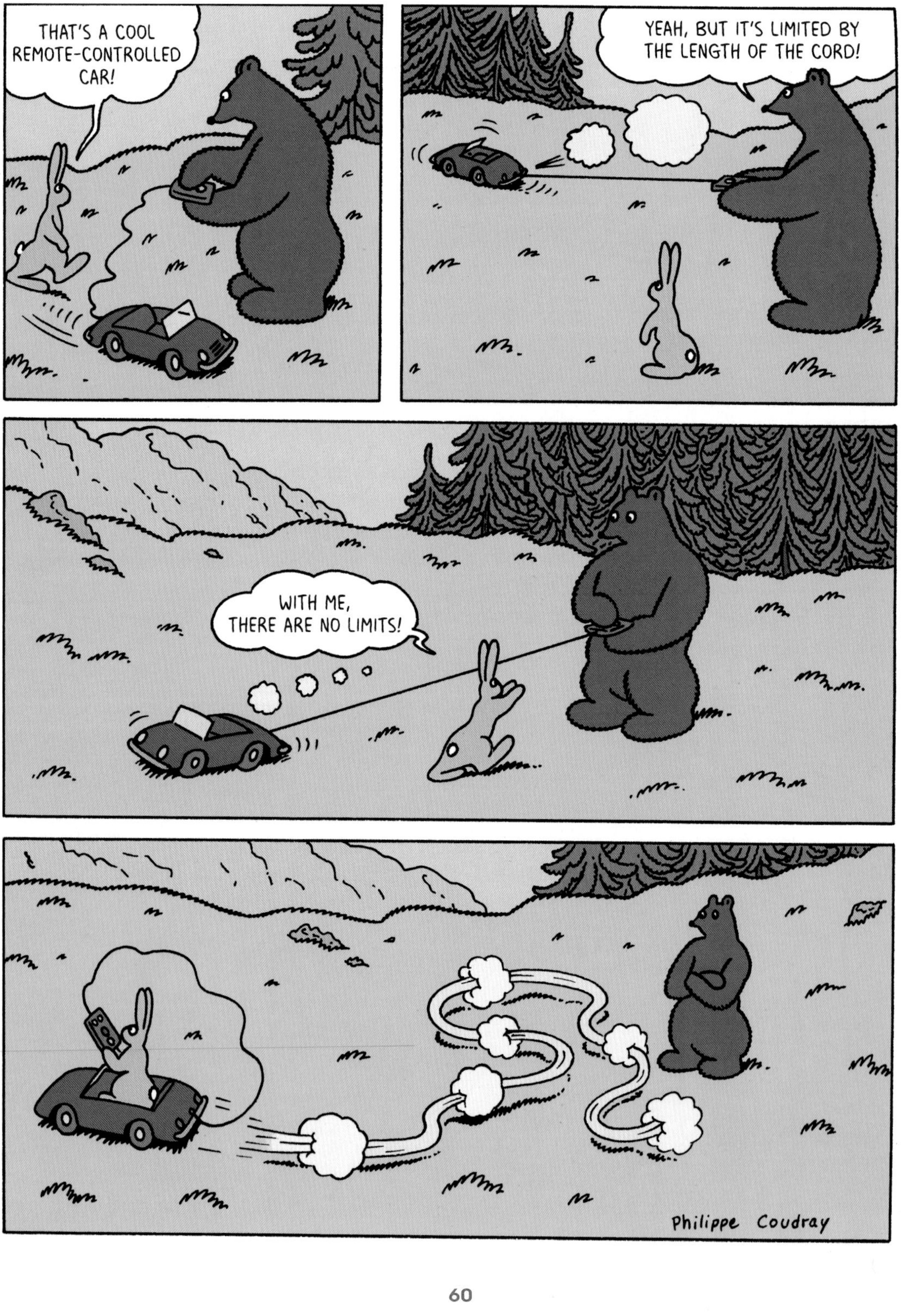

THAT'S A COOL REMOTE-CONTROLLED CAR!
YEAH, BUT IT'S LIMITED BY THE LENGTH OF THE CORD!
WITH ME, THERE ARE NO LIMITS!
Philippe Coudray

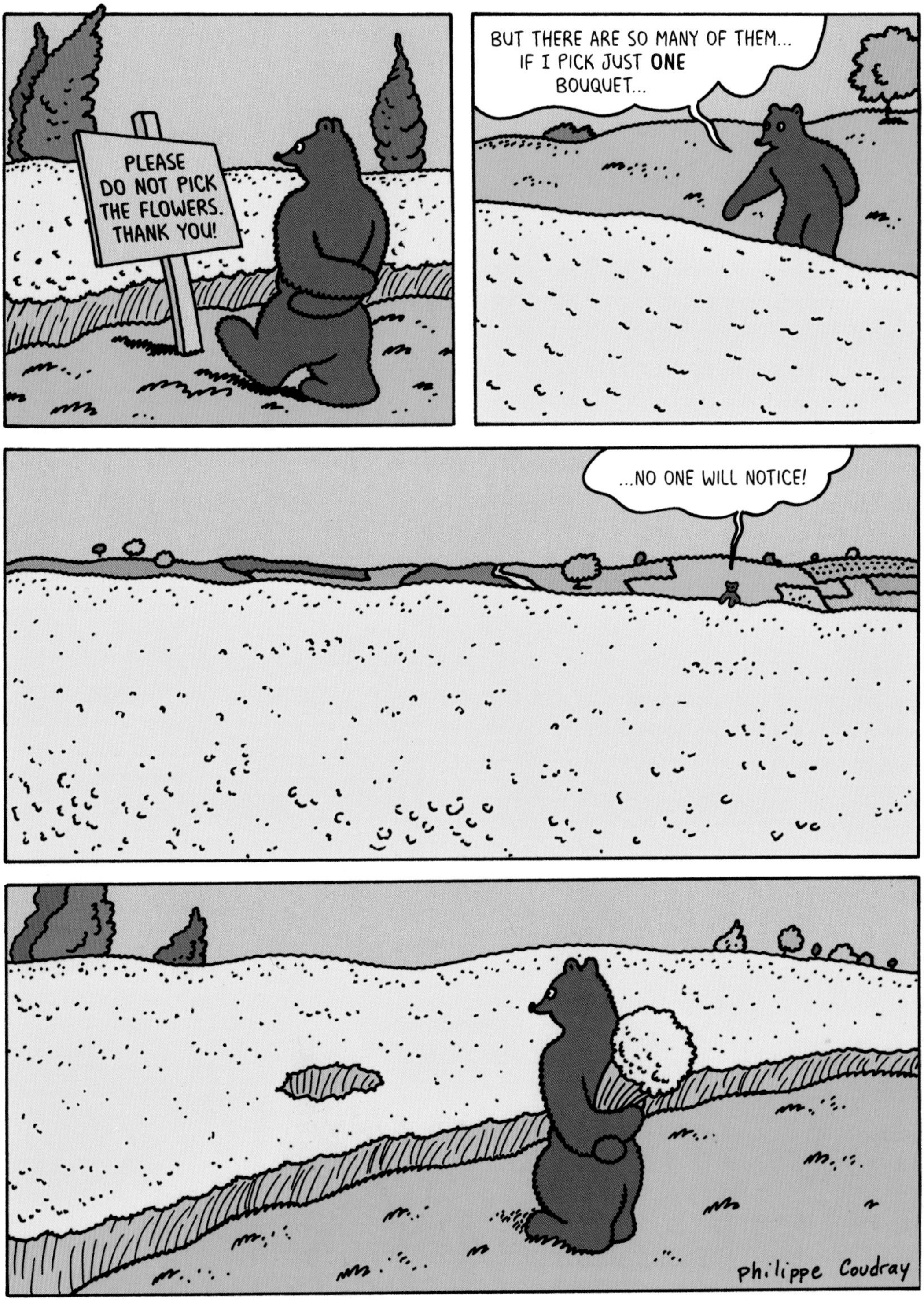
PLEASE DO NOT PICK THE FLOWERS. THANK YOU!
BUT THERE ARE SO MANY OF THEM... IF I PICK JUST **ONE** BOUQUET...
...NO ONE WILL NOTICE!
Philippe Coudray

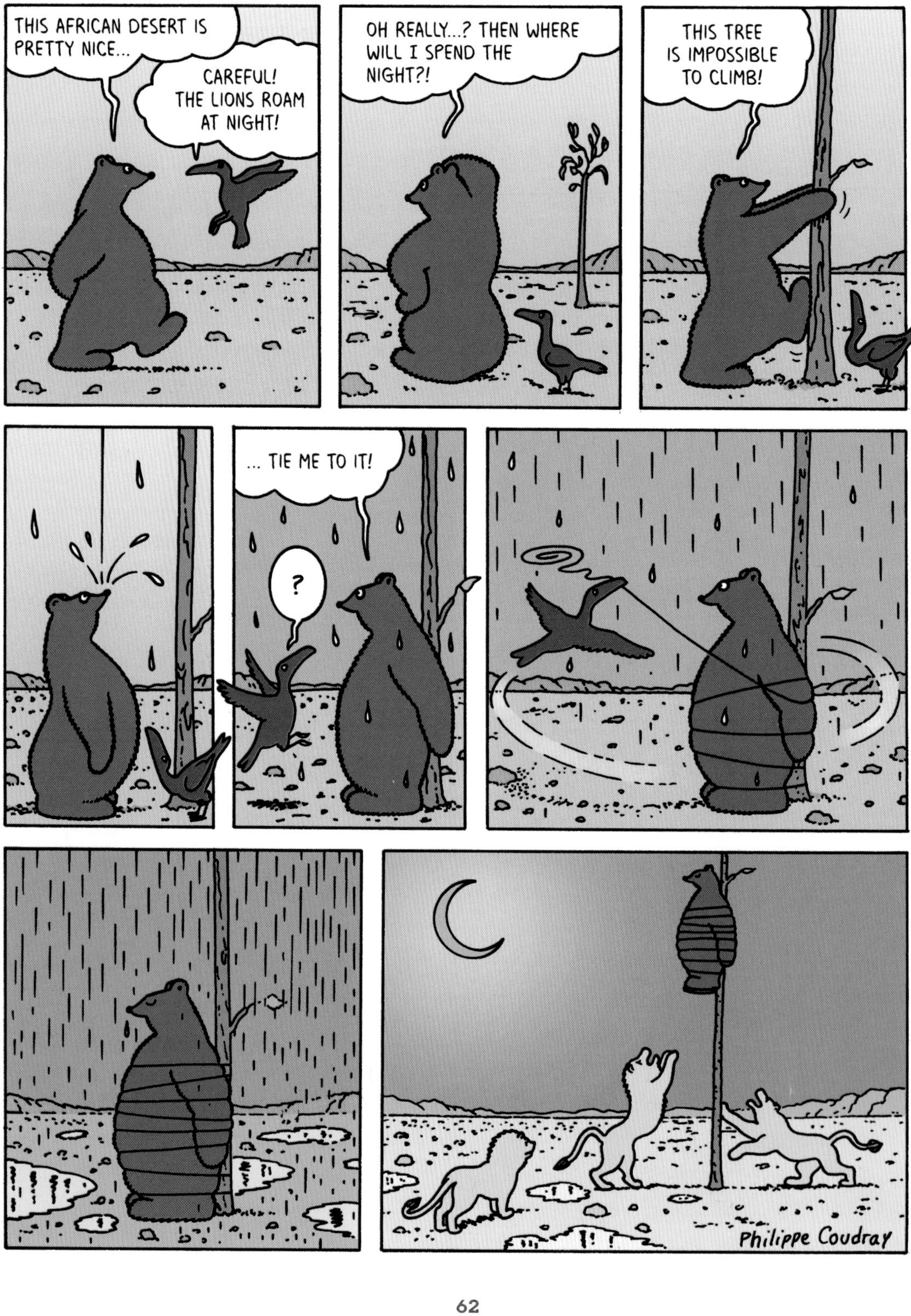
THIS AFRICAN DESERT IS PRETTY NICE...
CAREFUL! THE LIONS ROAM AT NIGHT!
OH REALLY...? THEN WHERE WILL I SPEND THE NIGHT?!
THIS TREE IS IMPOSSIBLE TO CLIMB!
... TIE ME TO IT!
?
Philippe Coudray

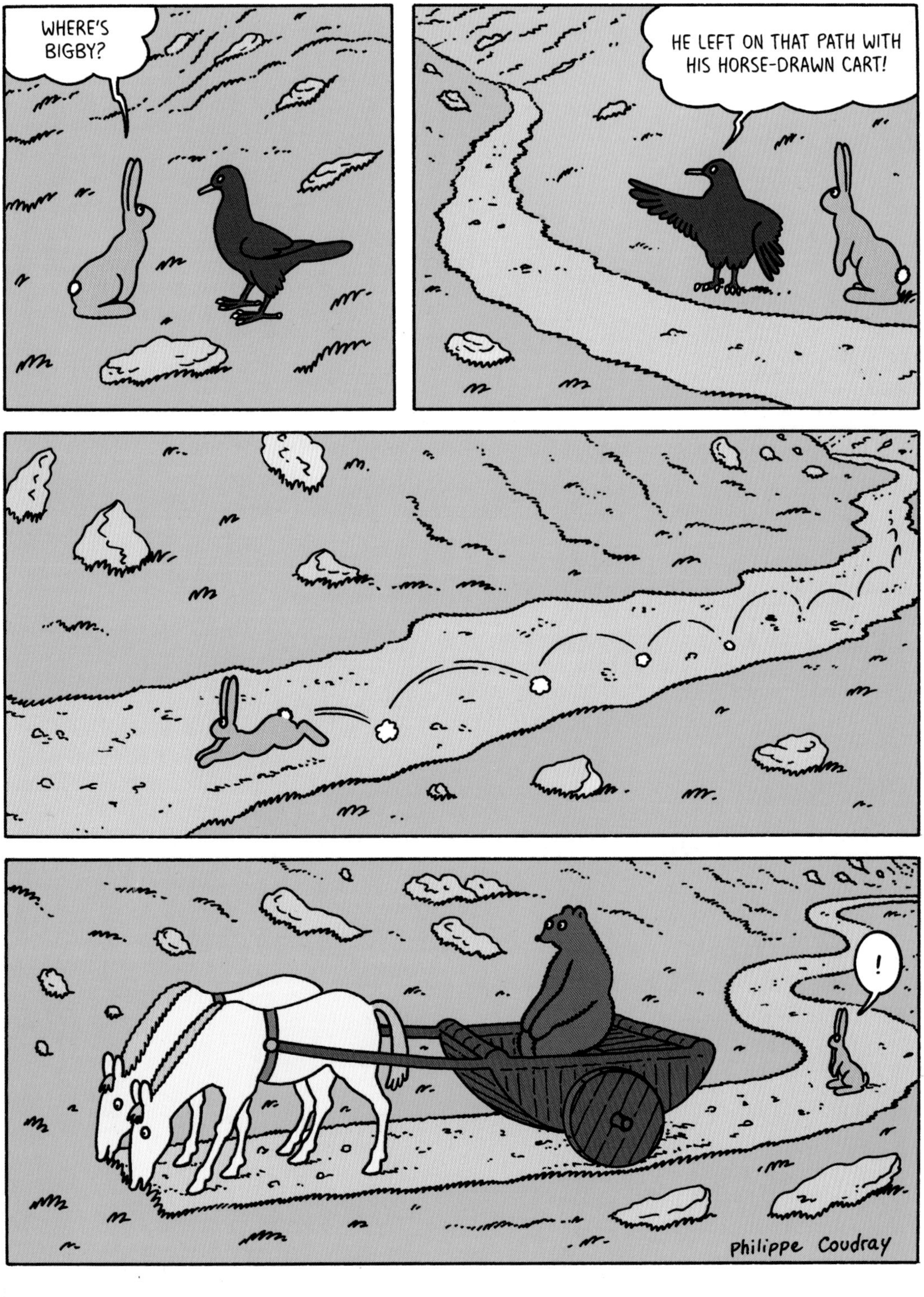
WHERE'S BIGBY?
HE LEFT ON THAT PATH WITH HIS HORSE-DRAWN CART!
!
Philippe Coudray

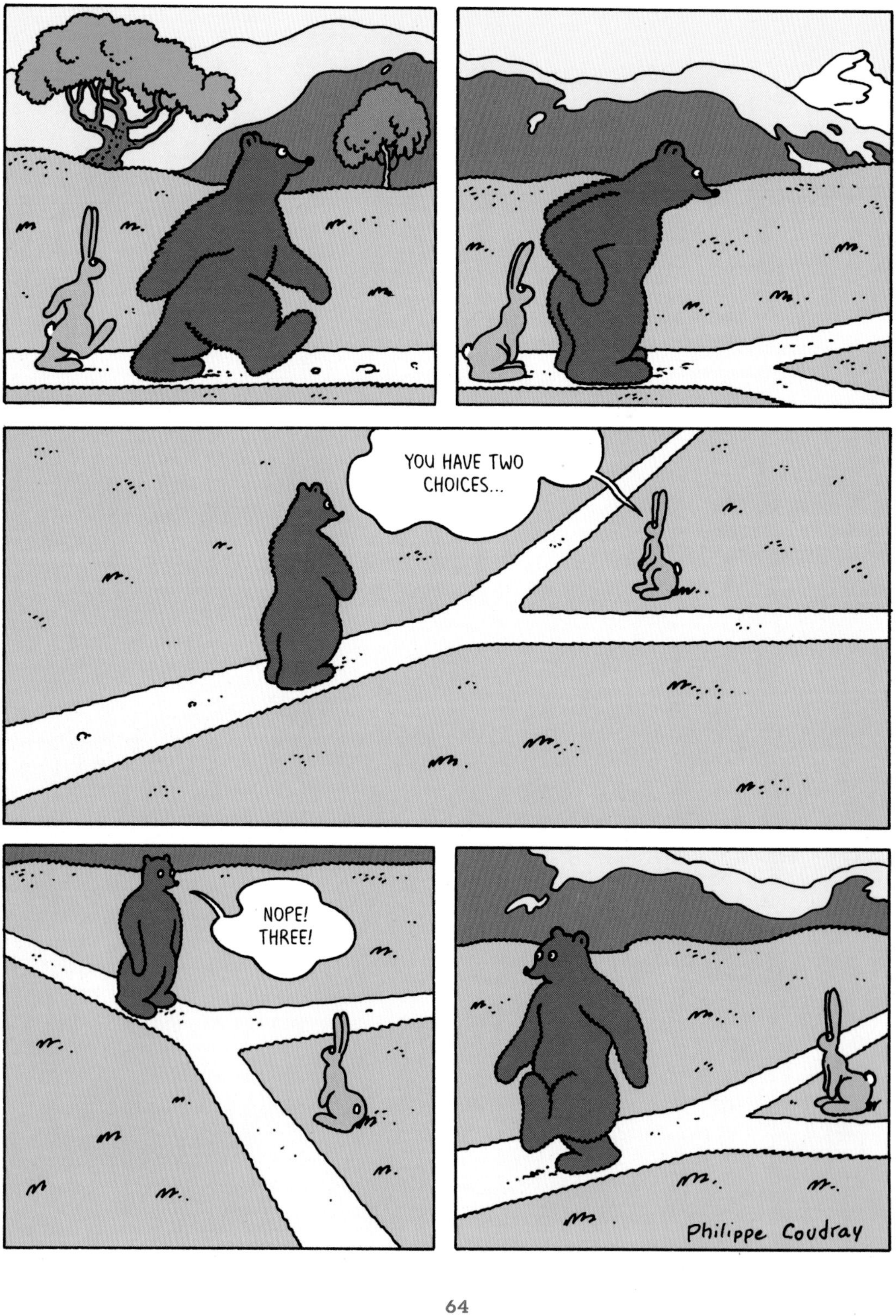
YOU HAVE TWO CHOICES...
NOPE! THREE!
Philippe Coudray

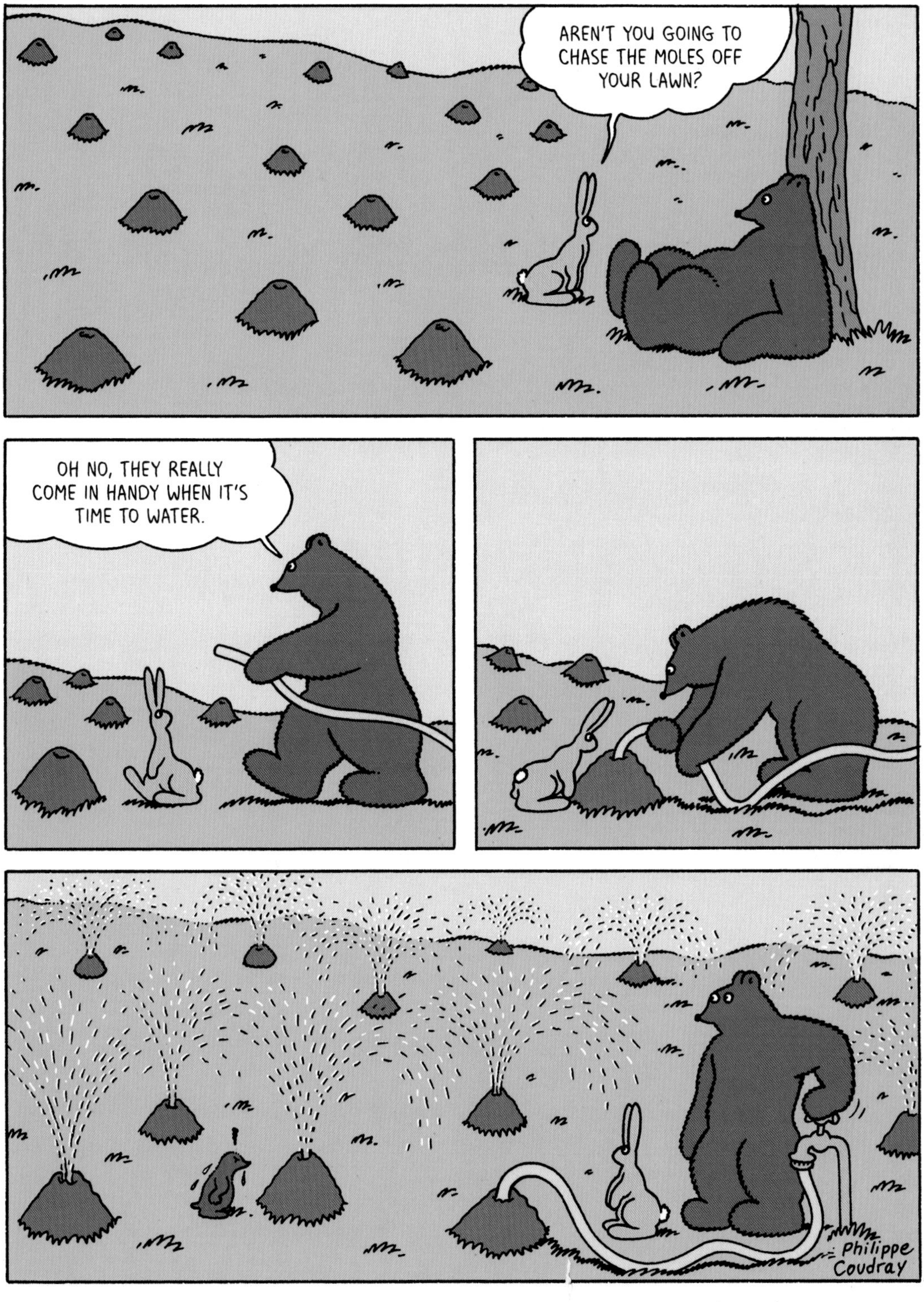
AREN'T YOU GOING TO CHASE THE MOLES OFF YOUR LAWN?
OH NO, THEY REALLY COME IN HANDY WHEN IT'S TIME TO WATER.
Philippe Coudray

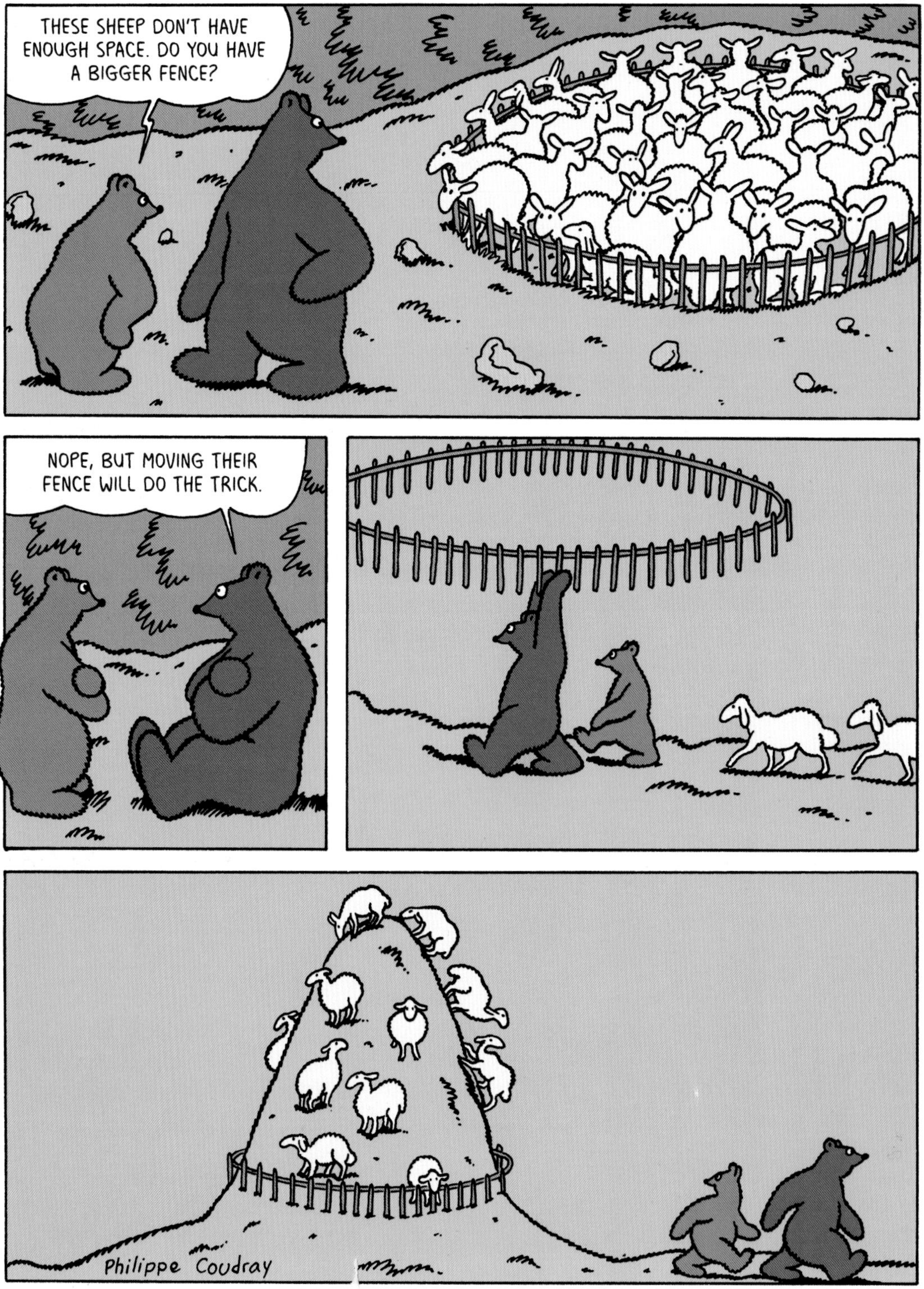
THESE SHEEP DON'T HAVE ENOUGH SPACE. DO YOU HAVE A BIGGER FENCE?
NOPE, BUT MOVING THEIR FENCE WILL DO THE TRICK.
Philippe Coudray

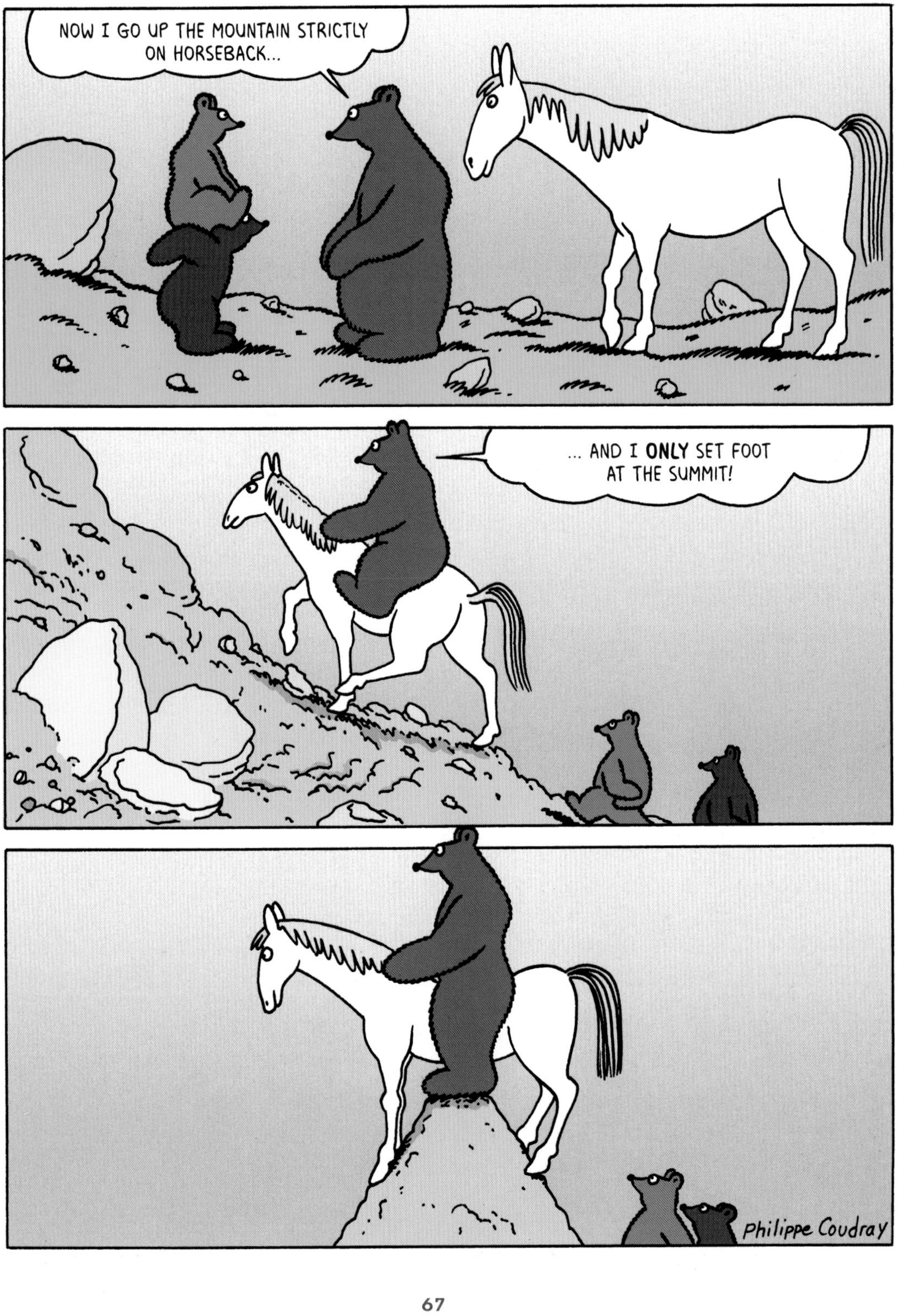
NOW I GO UP THE MOUNTAIN STRICTLY ON HORSEBACK...
... AND I ONLY SET FOOT AT THE SUMMIT!
Philippe Coudray

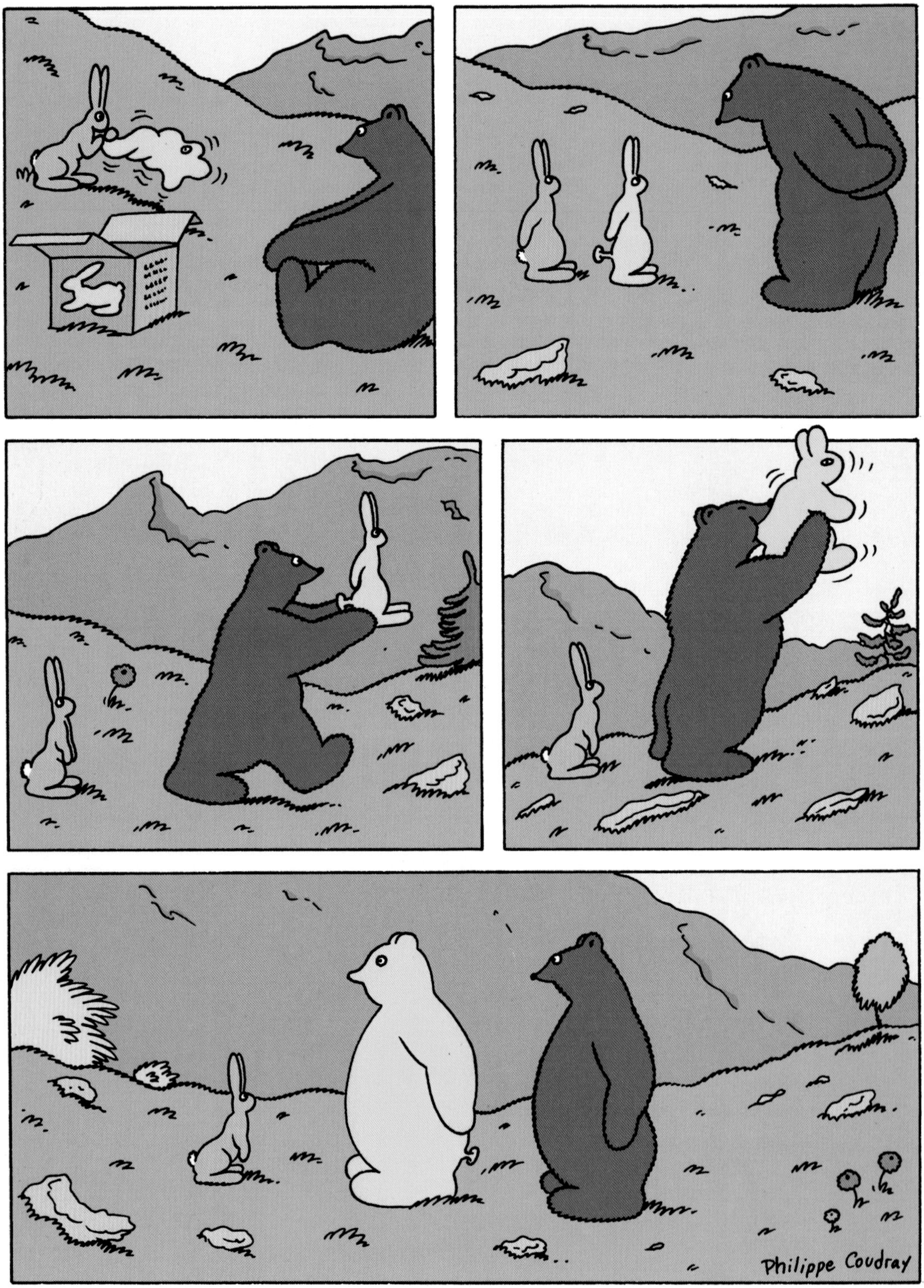
Philippe Coudray

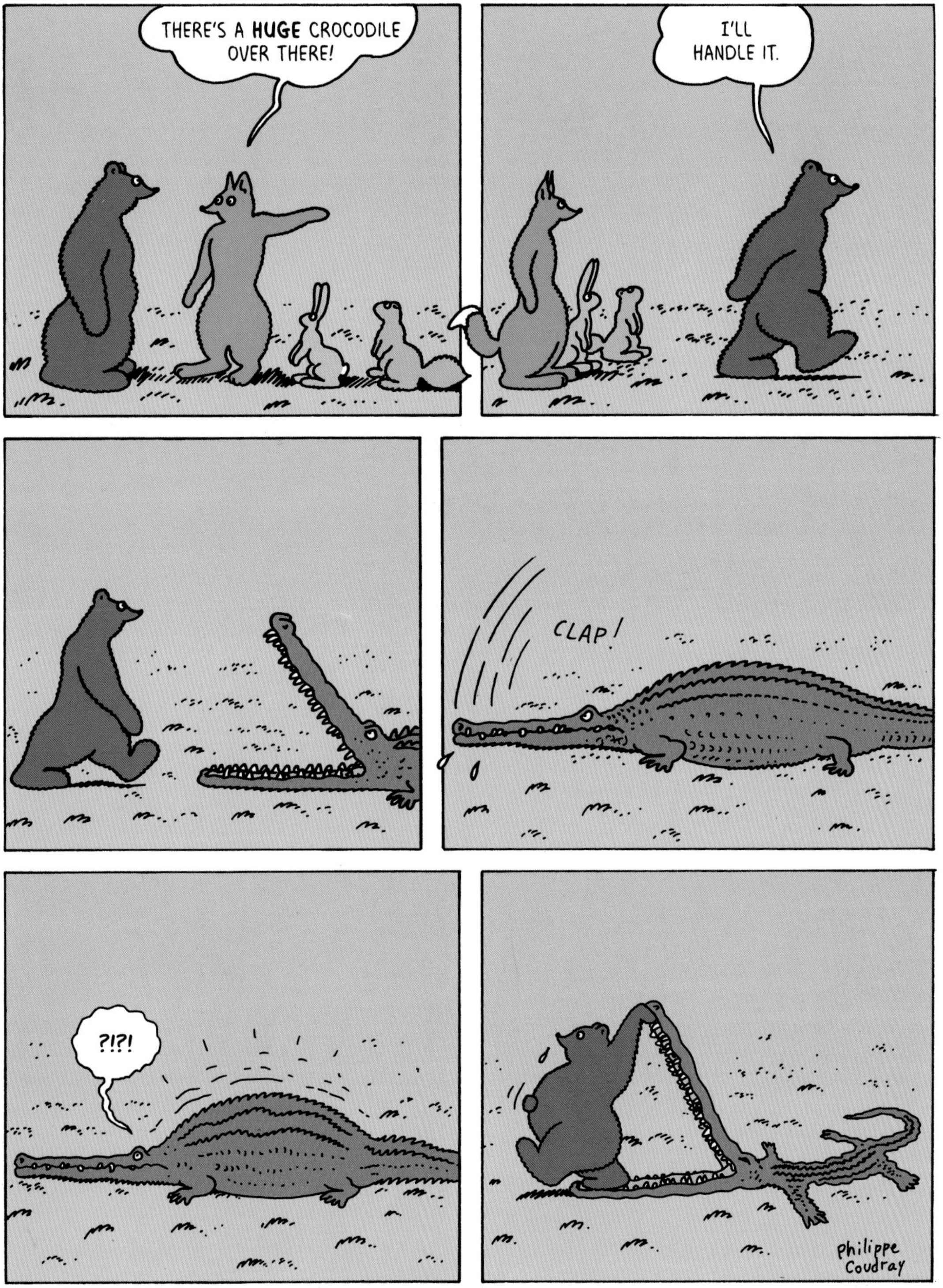
THERE'S A **HUGE** CROCODILE OVER THERE!
I'LL HANDLE IT.
CLAP!
?!?!
Philippe Coudray

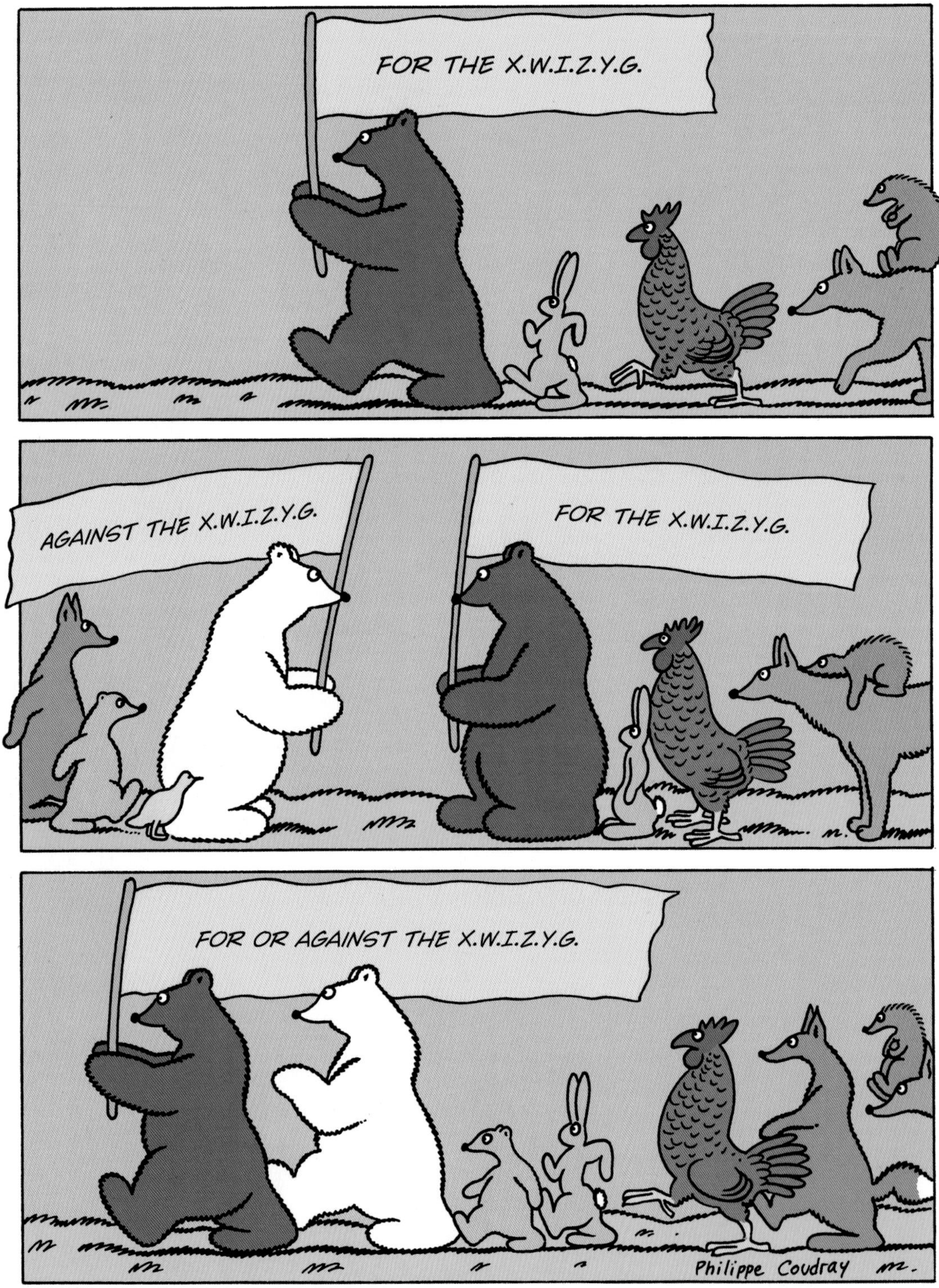
FOR THE X.W.I.Z.Y.G.
AGAINST THE X.W.I.Z.Y.G.
FOR THE X.W.I.Z.Y.G.
FOR OR AGAINST THE X.W.I.Z.Y.G.
Philippe Coudray

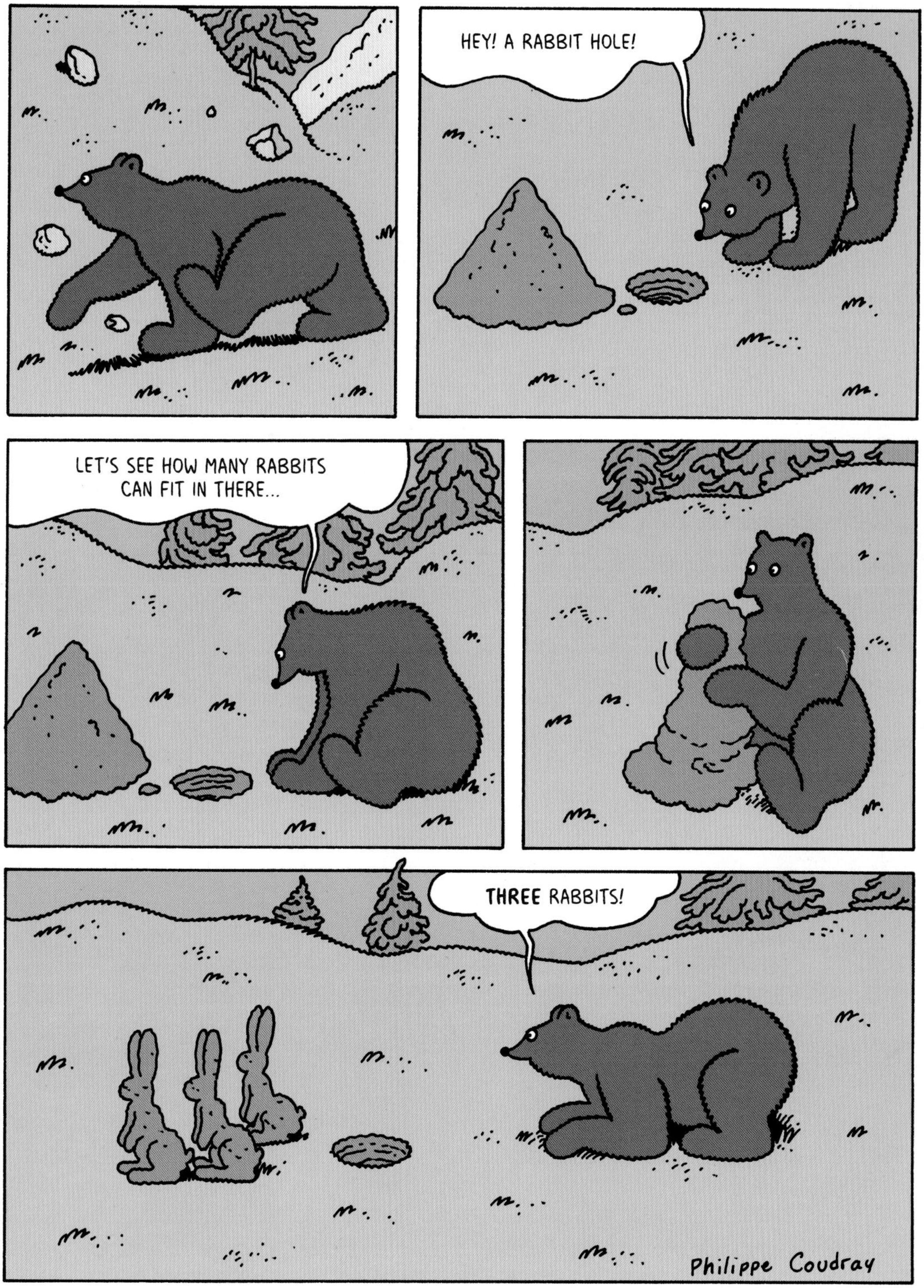
HEY! A RABBIT HOLE!
LET'S SEE HOW MANY RABBITS CAN FIT IN THERE...
THREE RABBITS!
Philippe Coudray

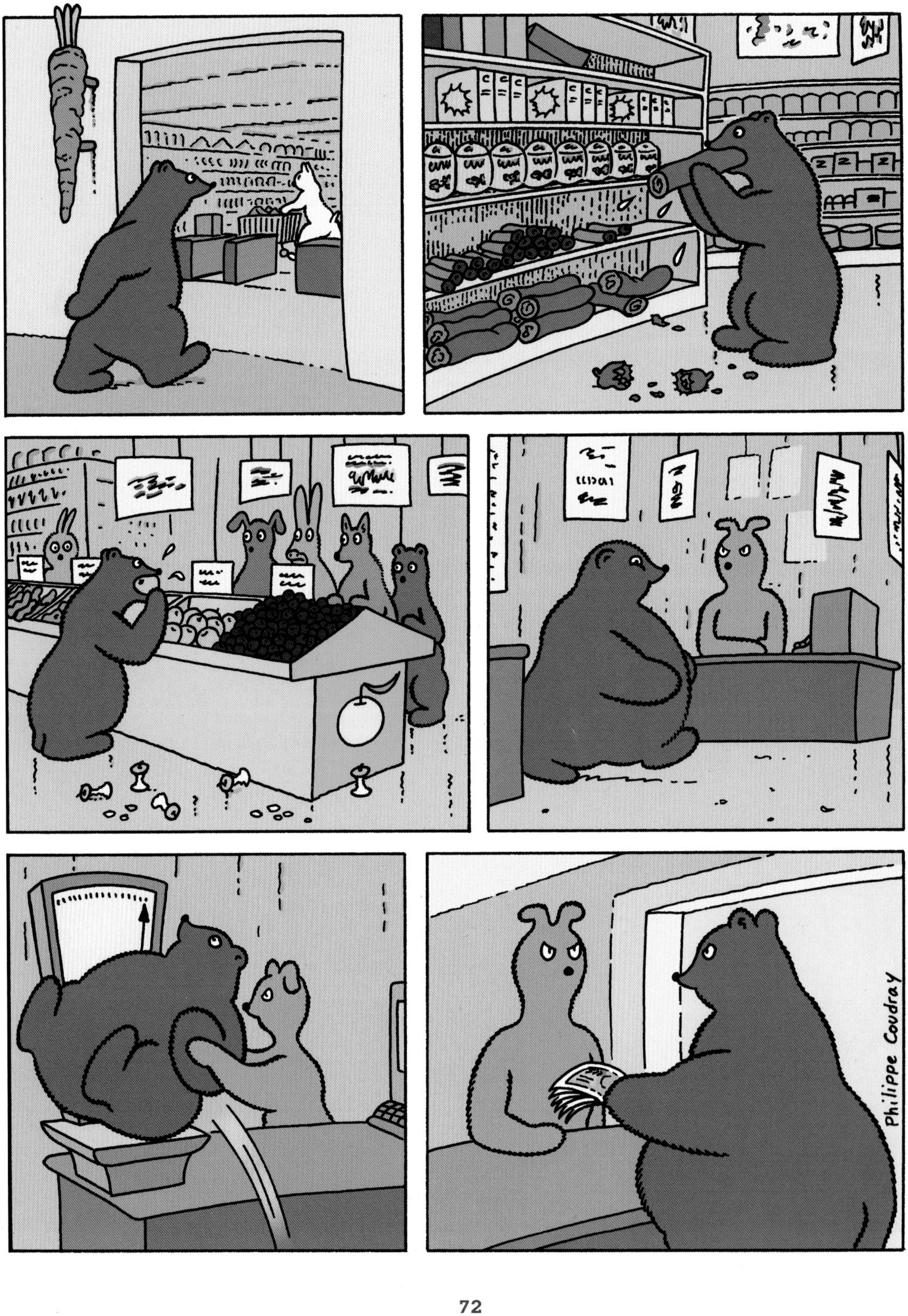
Philippe Coudray

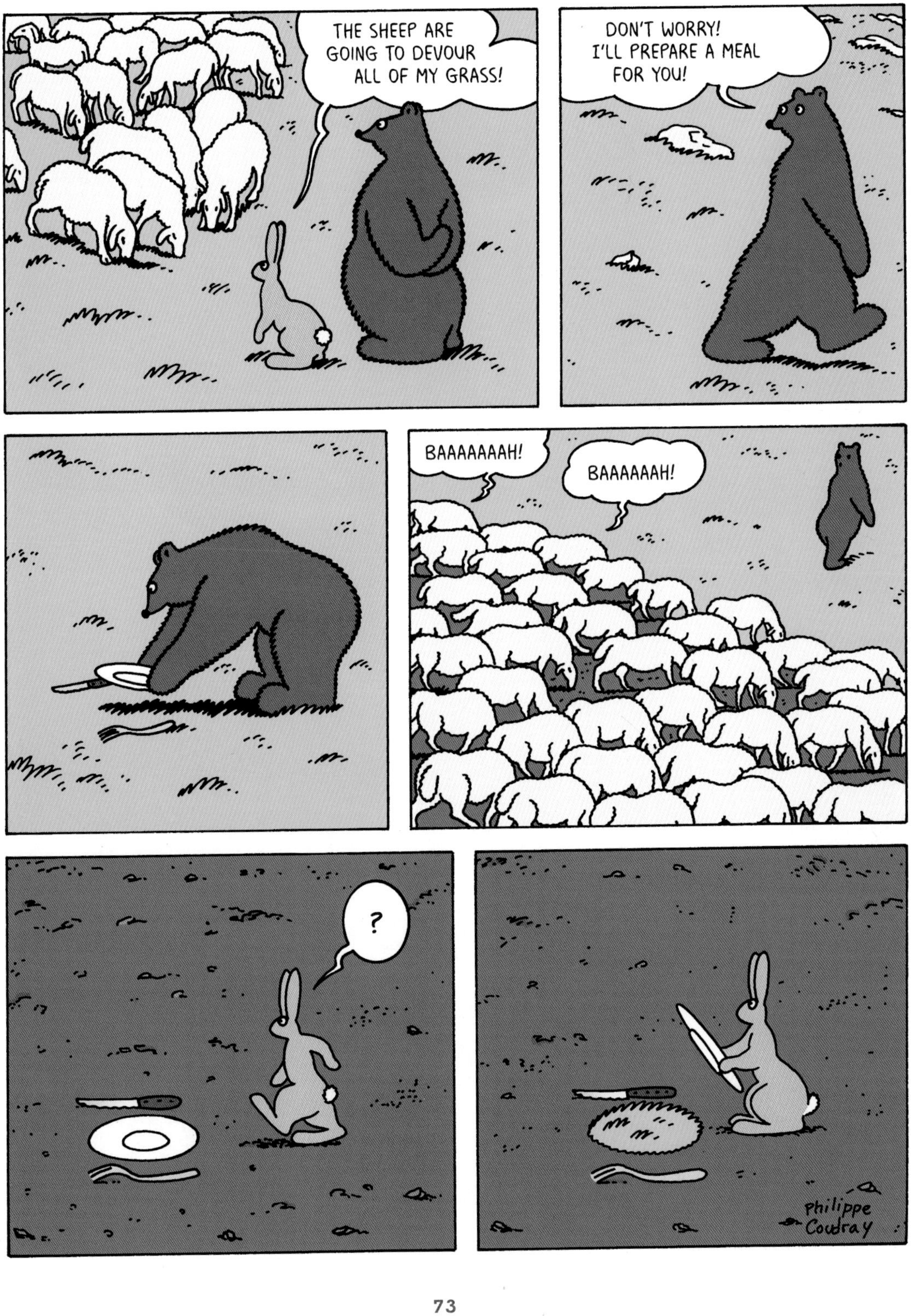
THE SHEEP ARE GOING TO DEVOUR ALL OF MY GRASS!
DON'T WORRY! I'LL PREPARE A MEAL FOR YOU!
BAAAAAAAH!
BAAAAAAH!
?
Philippe Coudray

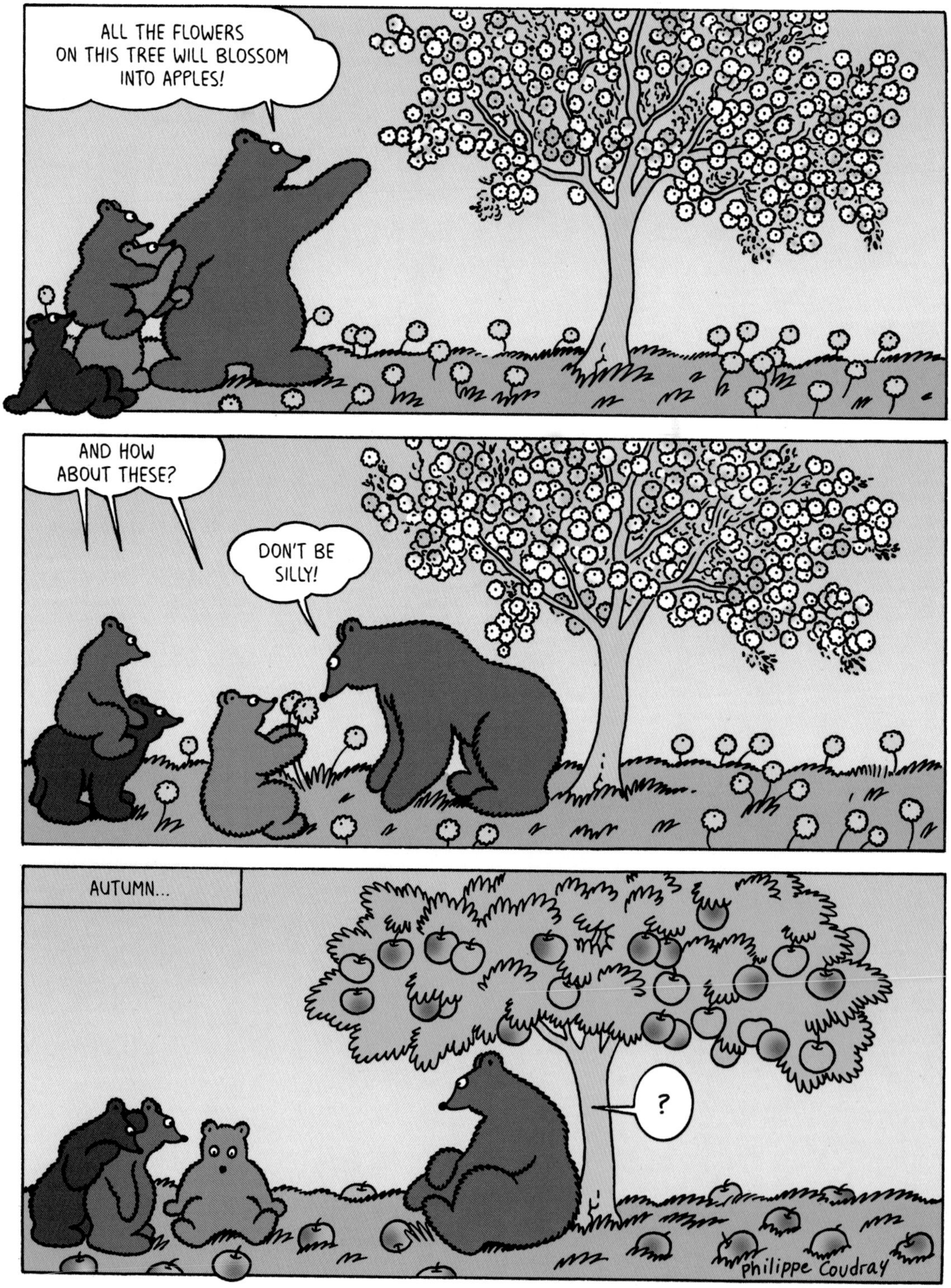
ALL THE FLOWERS ON THIS TREE WILL BLOSSOM INTO APPLES!
AND HOW ABOUT THESE?
DON'T BE SILLY!
AUTUMN...
?
Philippe Coudray

SUMMER

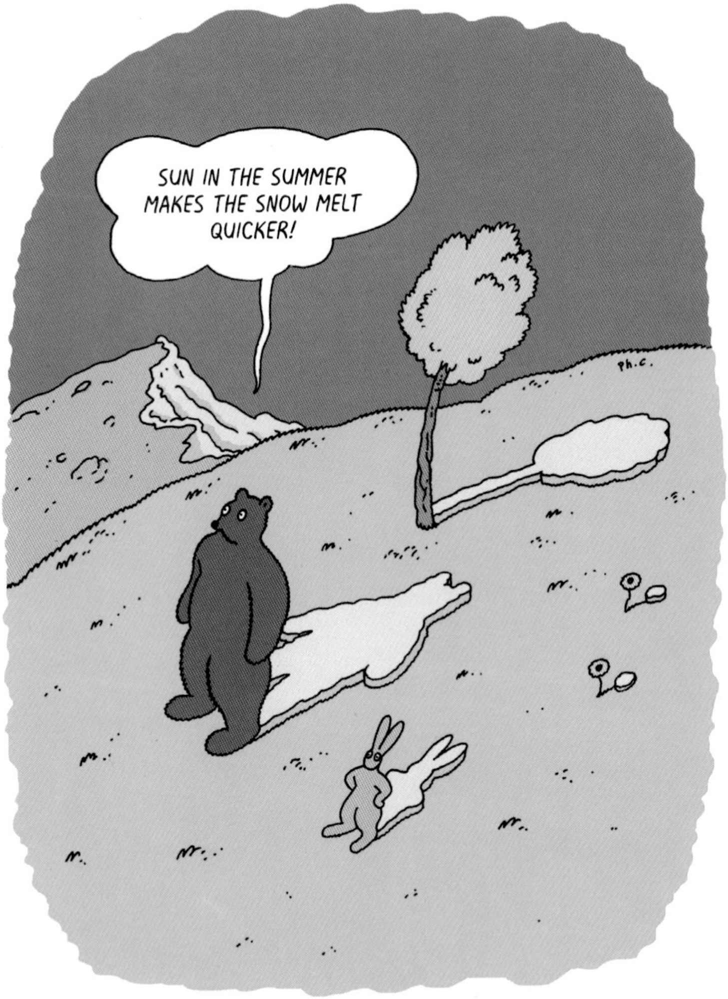
SUN IN THE SUMMER MAKES THE SNOW MELT QUICKER!
Ph.C.

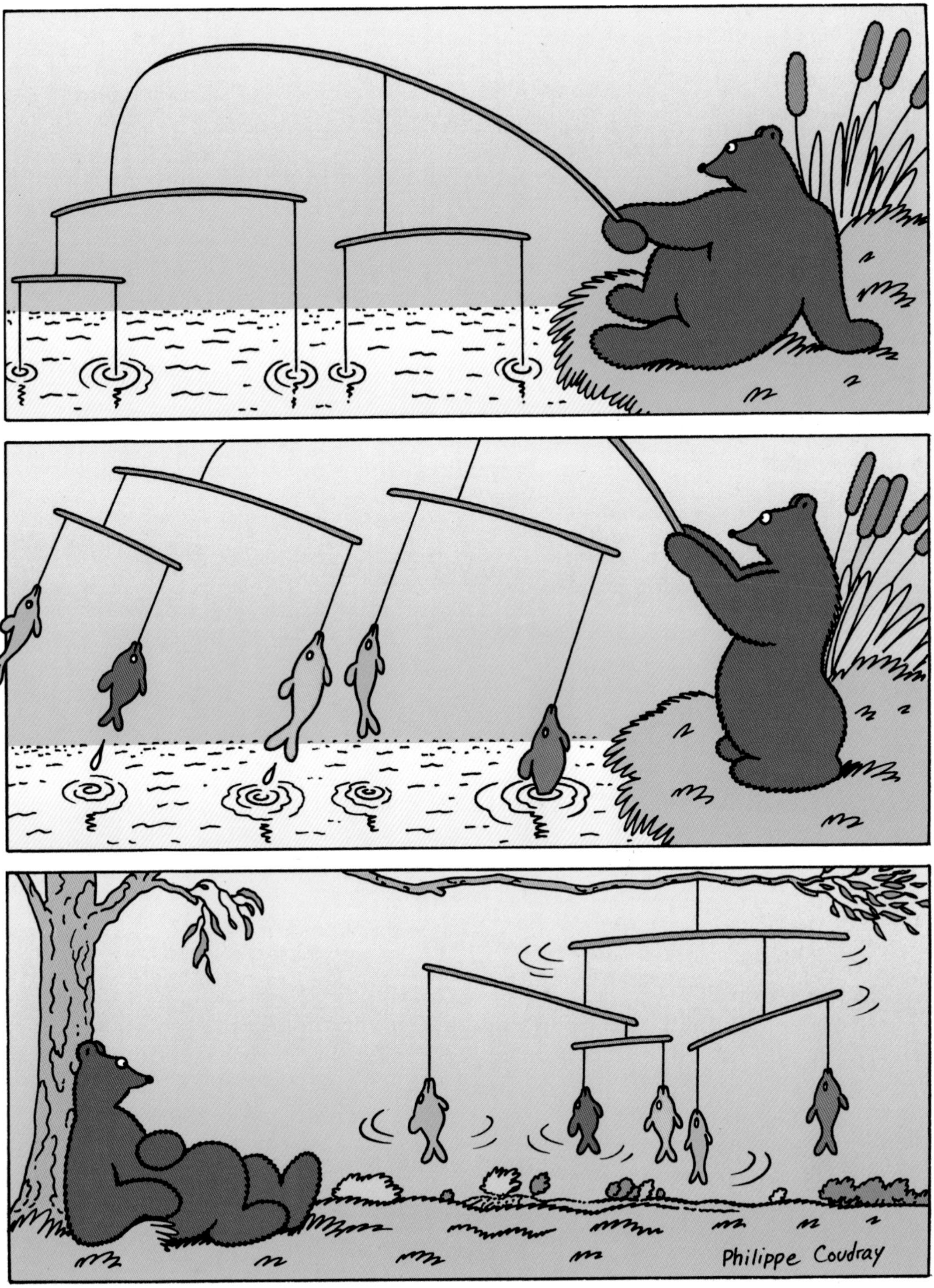
Philippe Coudray

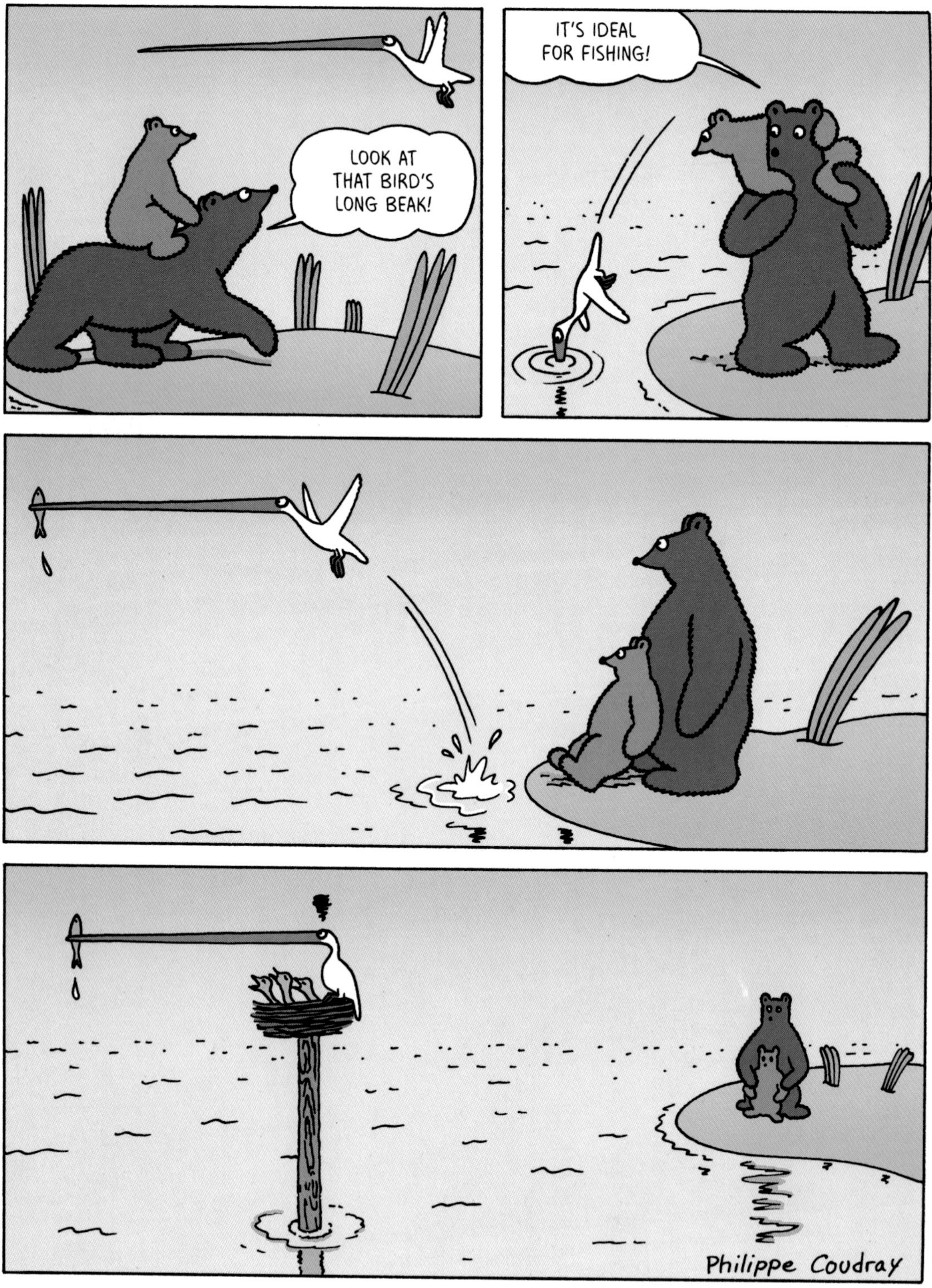
LOOK AT THAT BIRD'S LONG BEAK!
IT'S IDEAL FOR FISHING!
Philippe Coudray

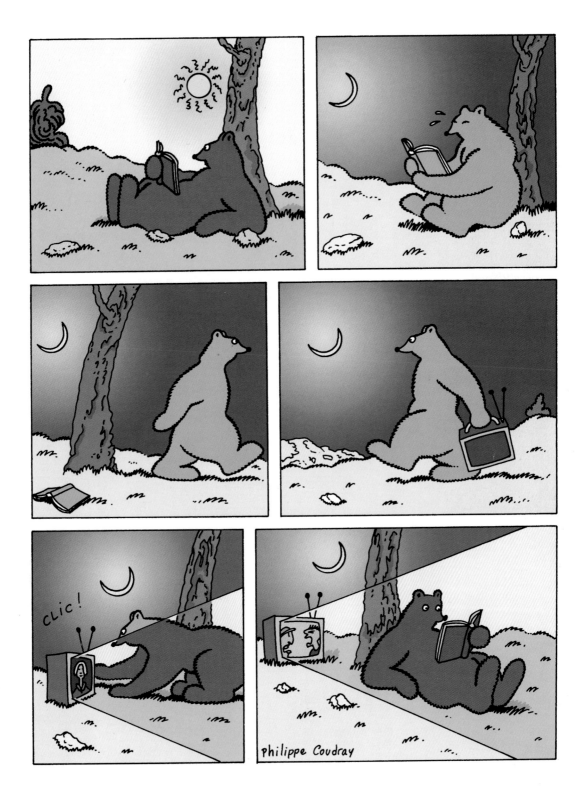

CLIC !

Philippe Coudray

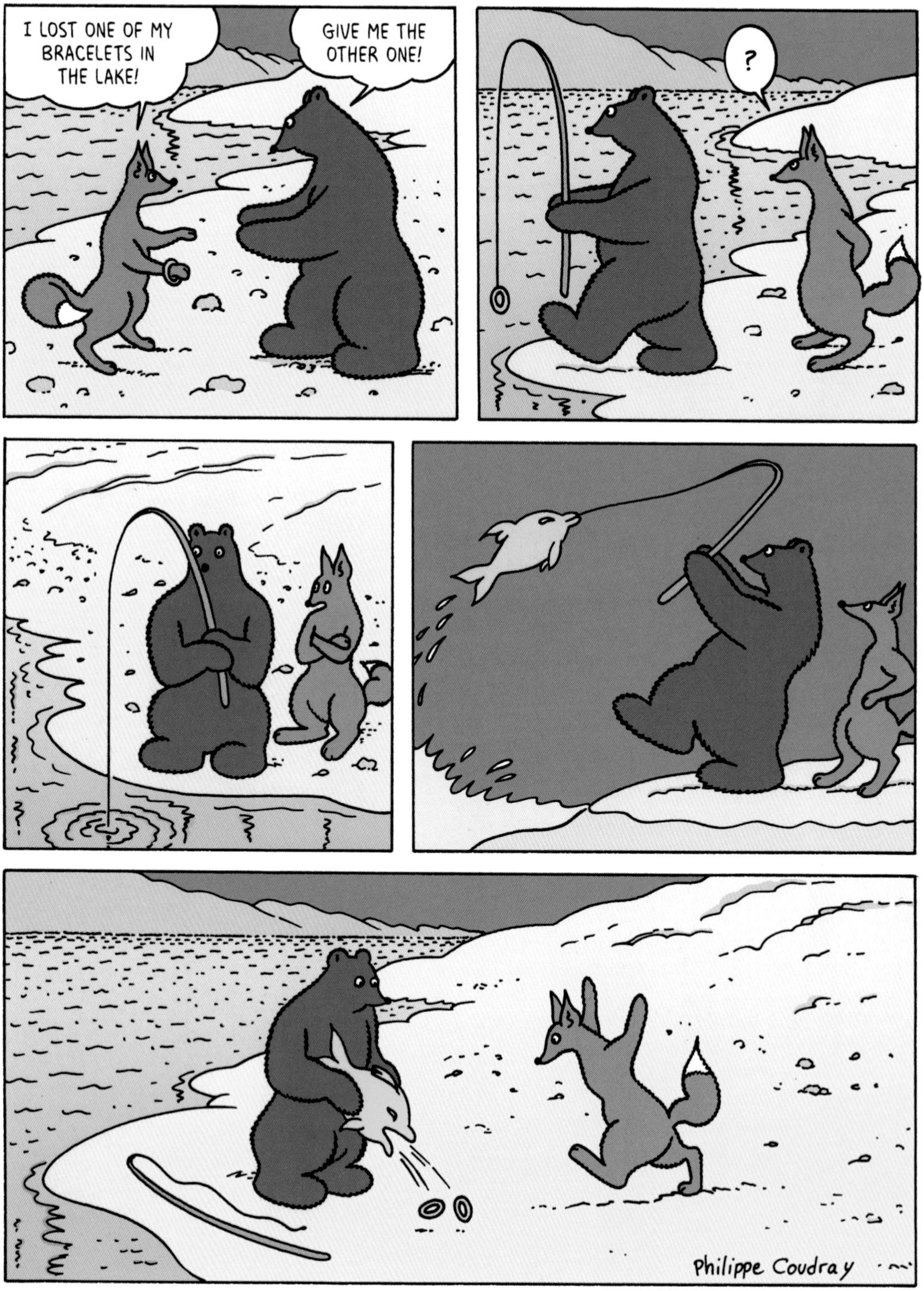
I LOST ONE OF MY BRACELETS IN THE LAKE!
GIVE ME THE OTHER ONE!
?
Philippe Coudray

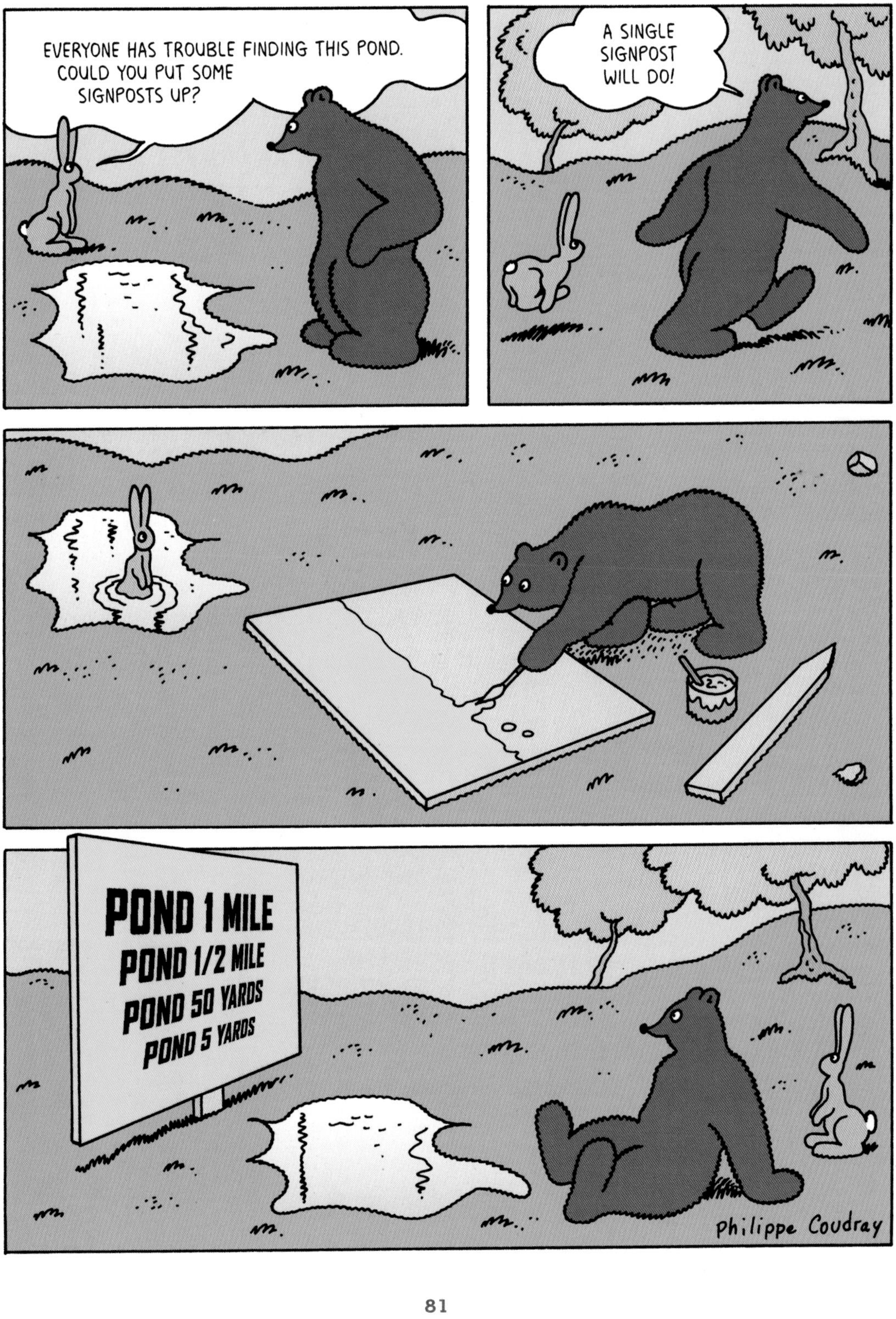
EVERYONE HAS TROUBLE FINDING THIS POND. COULD YOU PUT SOME SIGNPOSTS UP?
A SINGLE SIGNPOST WILL DO!
POND 1 MILE
POND 1/2 MILE
POND 50 YARDS
POND 5 YARDS
Philippe Coudray

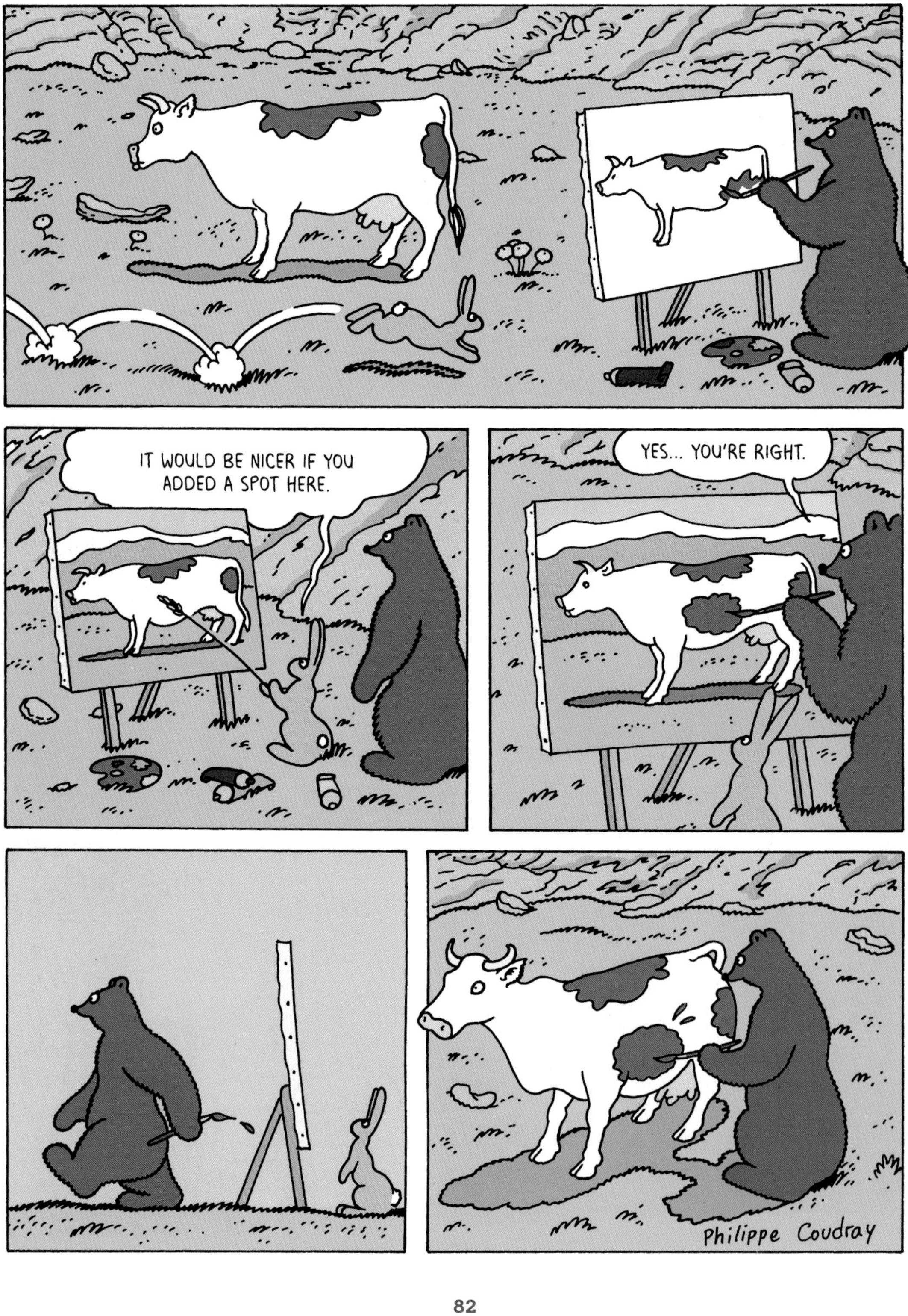
IT WOULD BE NICER IF YOU ADDED A SPOT HERE.
YES... YOU'RE RIGHT.
Philippe Coudray

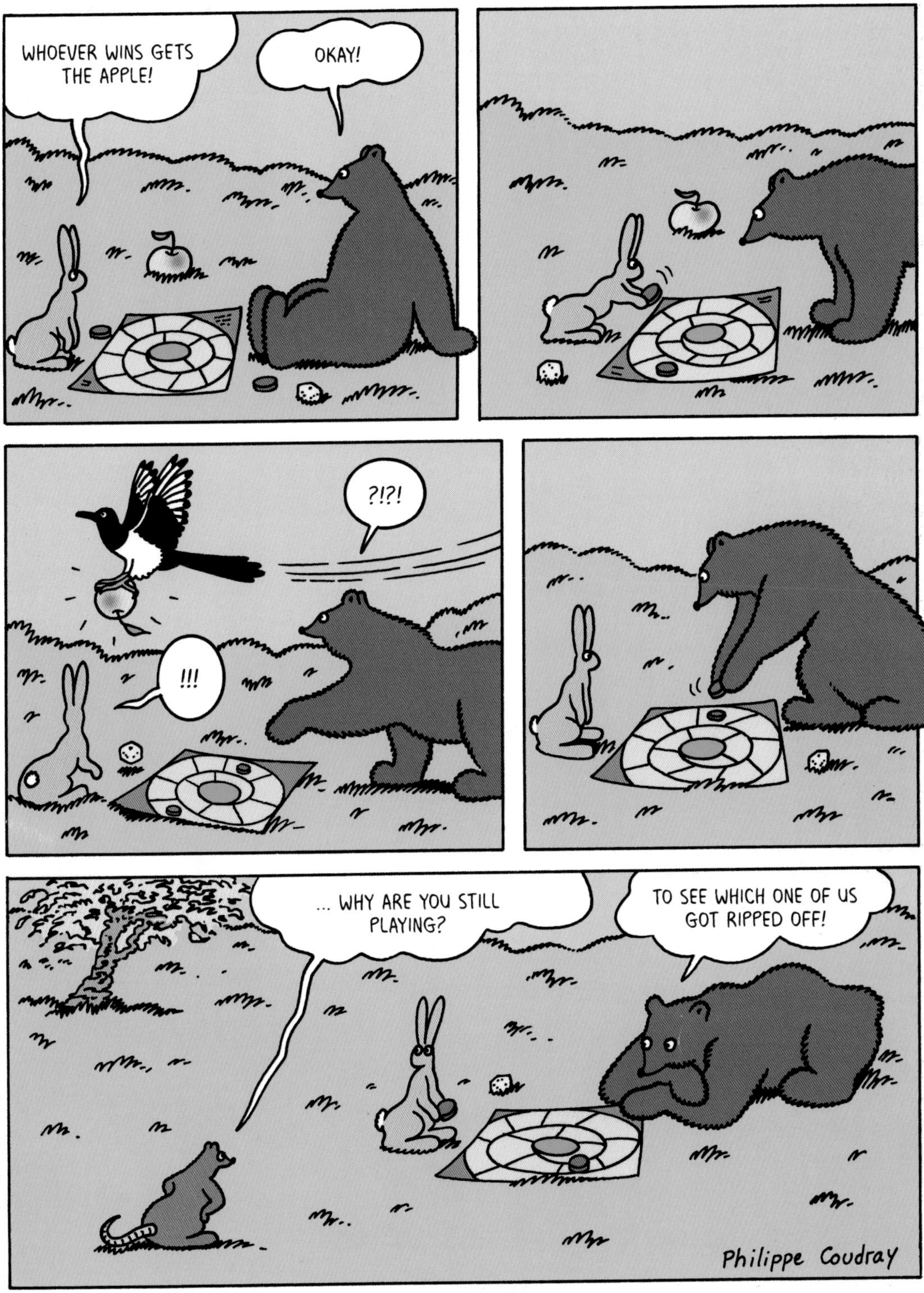
WHOEVER WINS GETS THE APPLE!
OKAY!
?!?!
!!!
... WHY ARE YOU STILL PLAYING?
TO SEE WHICH ONE OF US GOT RIPPED OFF!
Philippe Coudray

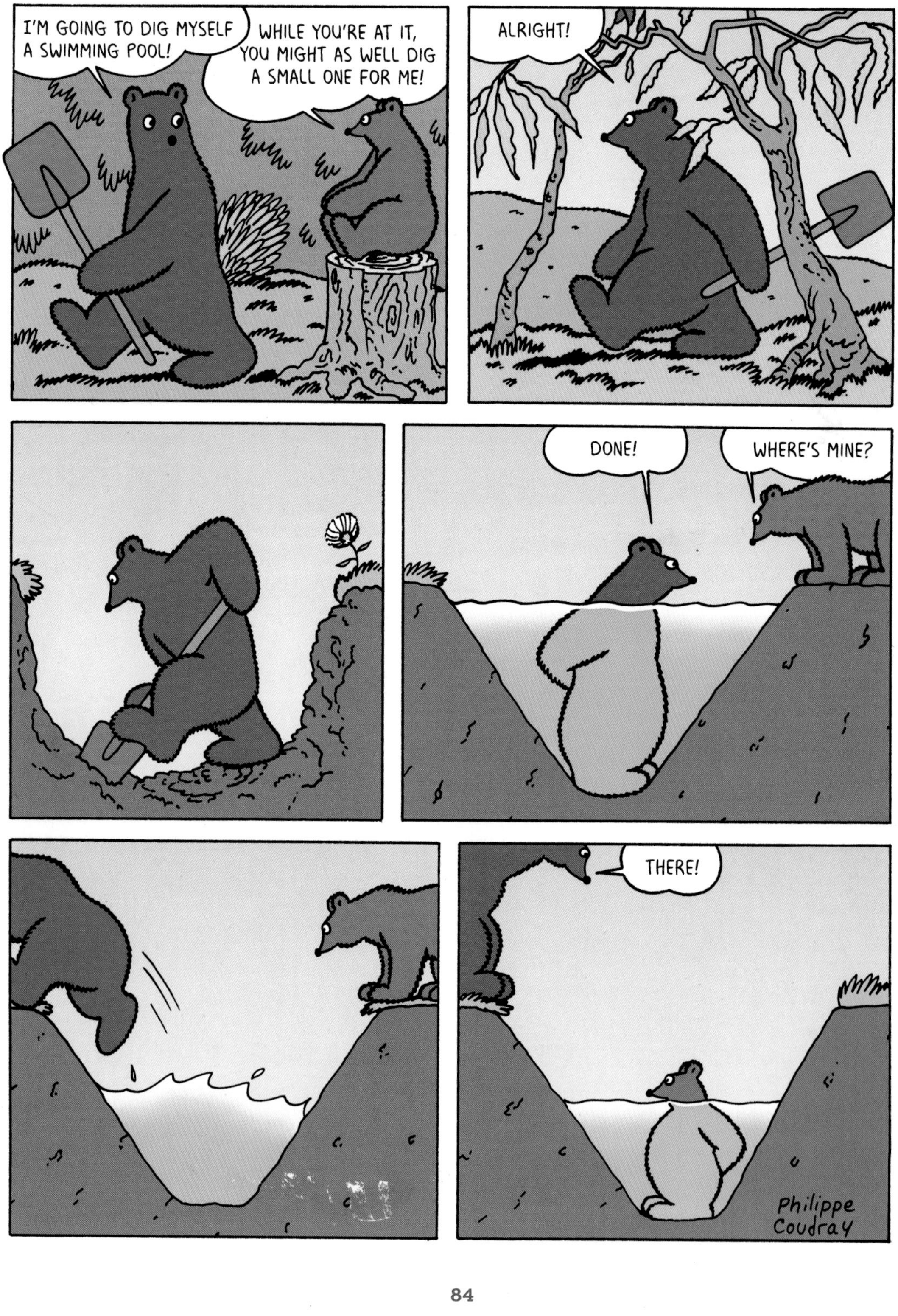
I'M GOING TO DIG MYSELF A SWIMMING POOL!
WHILE YOU'RE AT IT, YOU MIGHT AS WELL DIG A SMALL ONE FOR ME!
ALRIGHT!
DONE!
WHERE'S MINE?
THERE!
Philippe Coudray

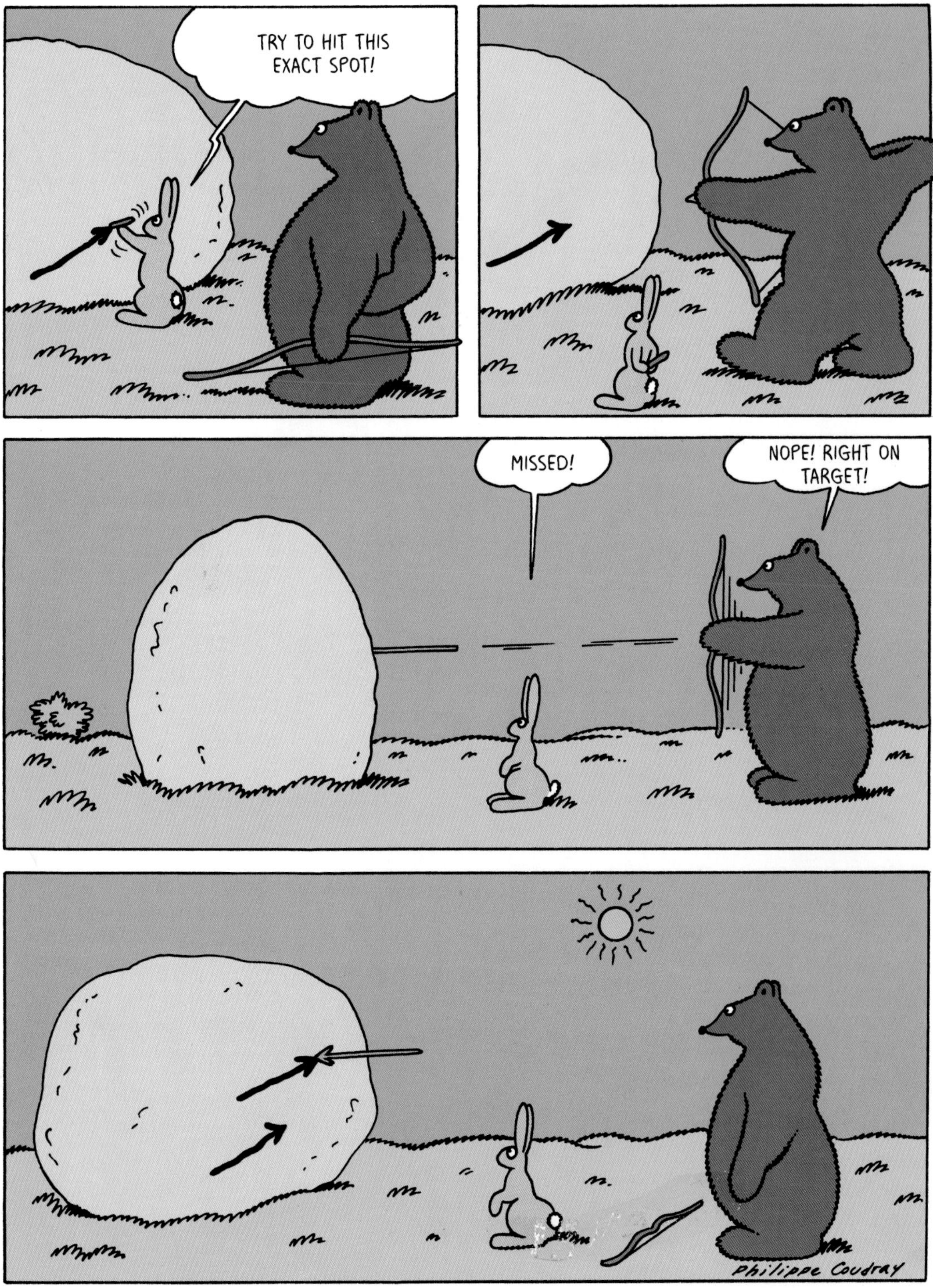
TRY TO HIT THIS EXACT SPOT!
MISSED!
NOPE! RIGHT ON TARGET!
Philippe Coudray

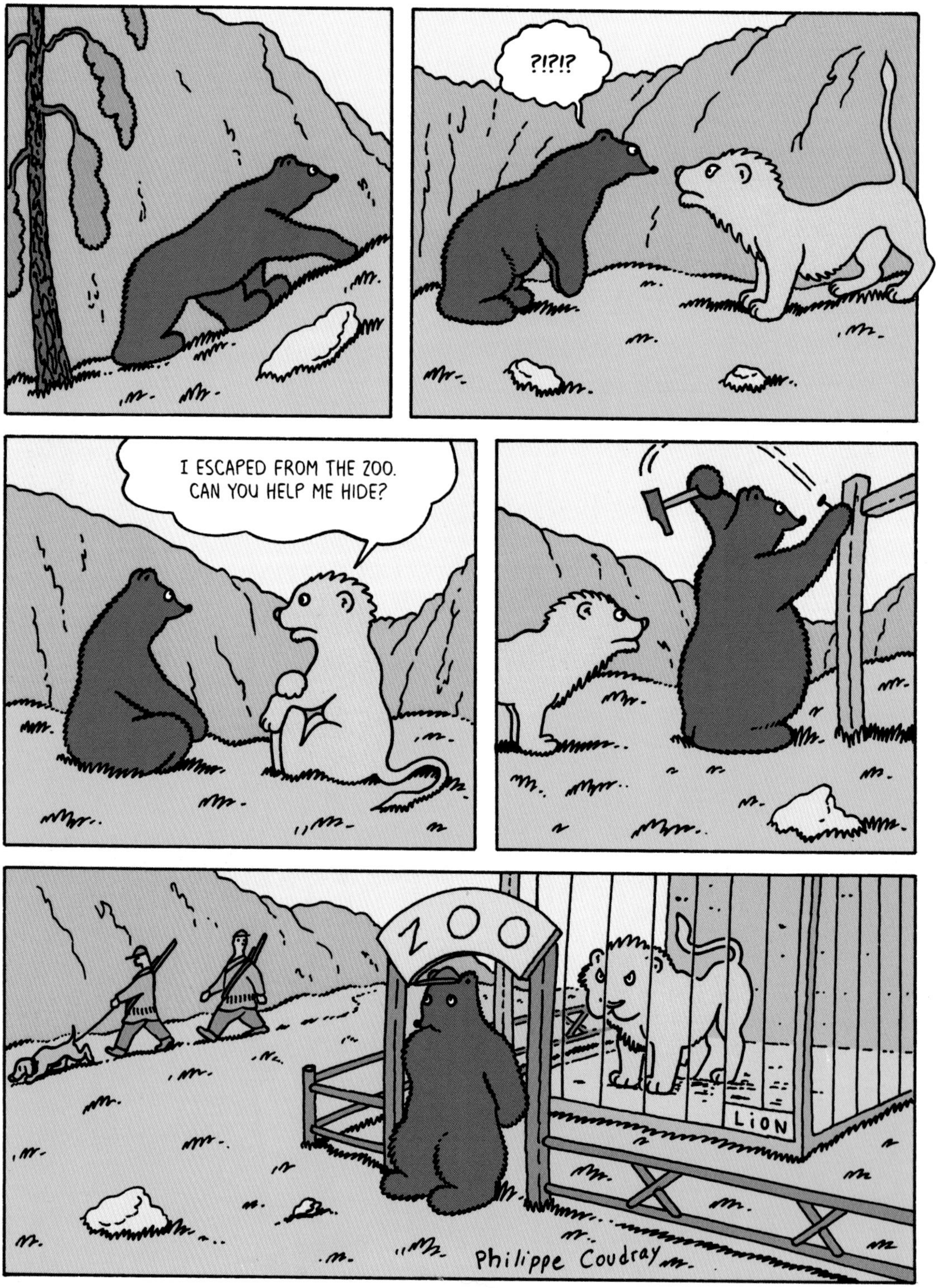
?!?!?
I ESCAPED FROM THE ZOO. CAN YOU HELP ME HIDE?
ZOO
LION
Philippe Coudray

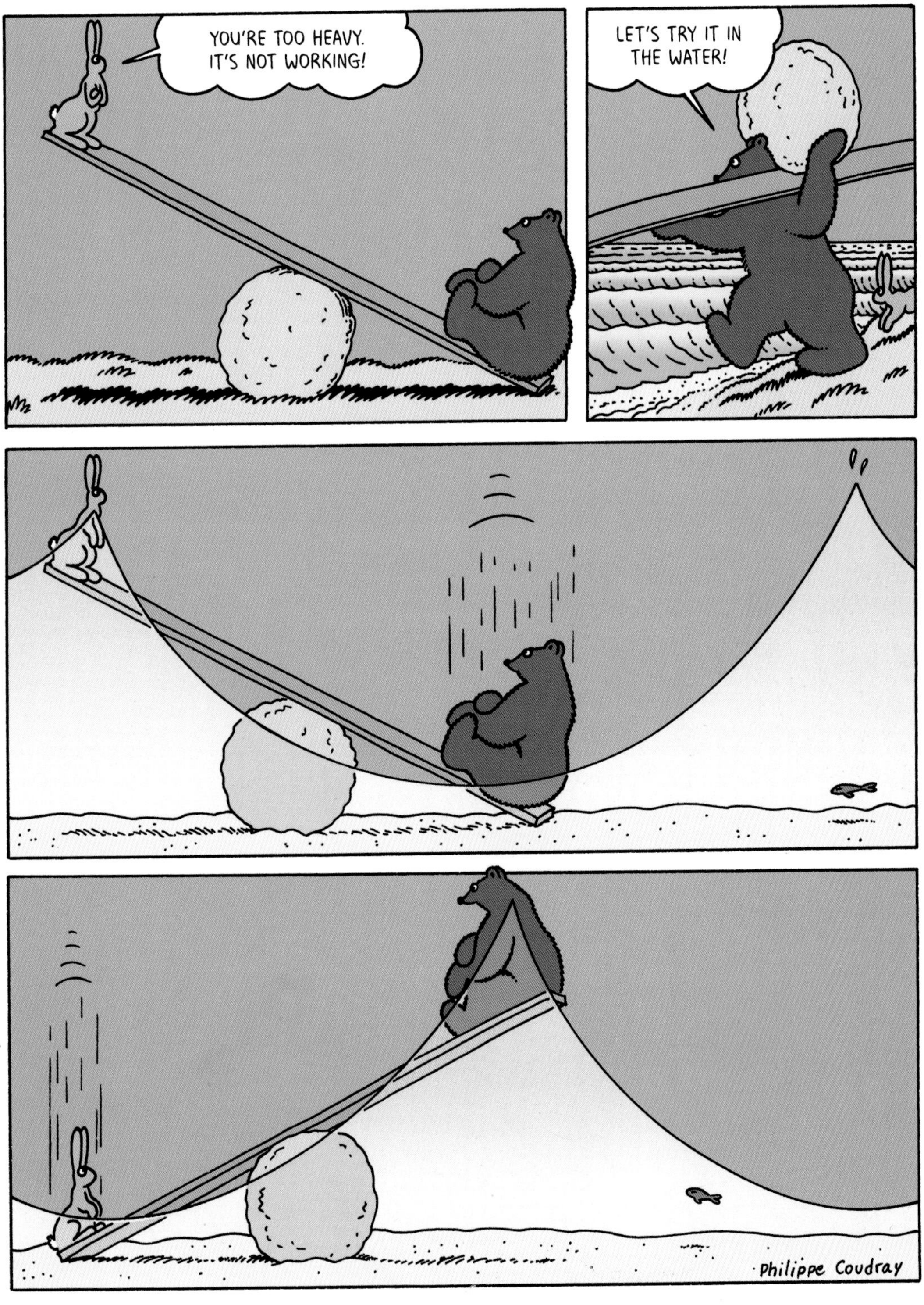
YOU'RE TOO HEAVY. IT'S NOT WORKING!
LET'S TRY IT IN THE WATER!
Philippe Coudray

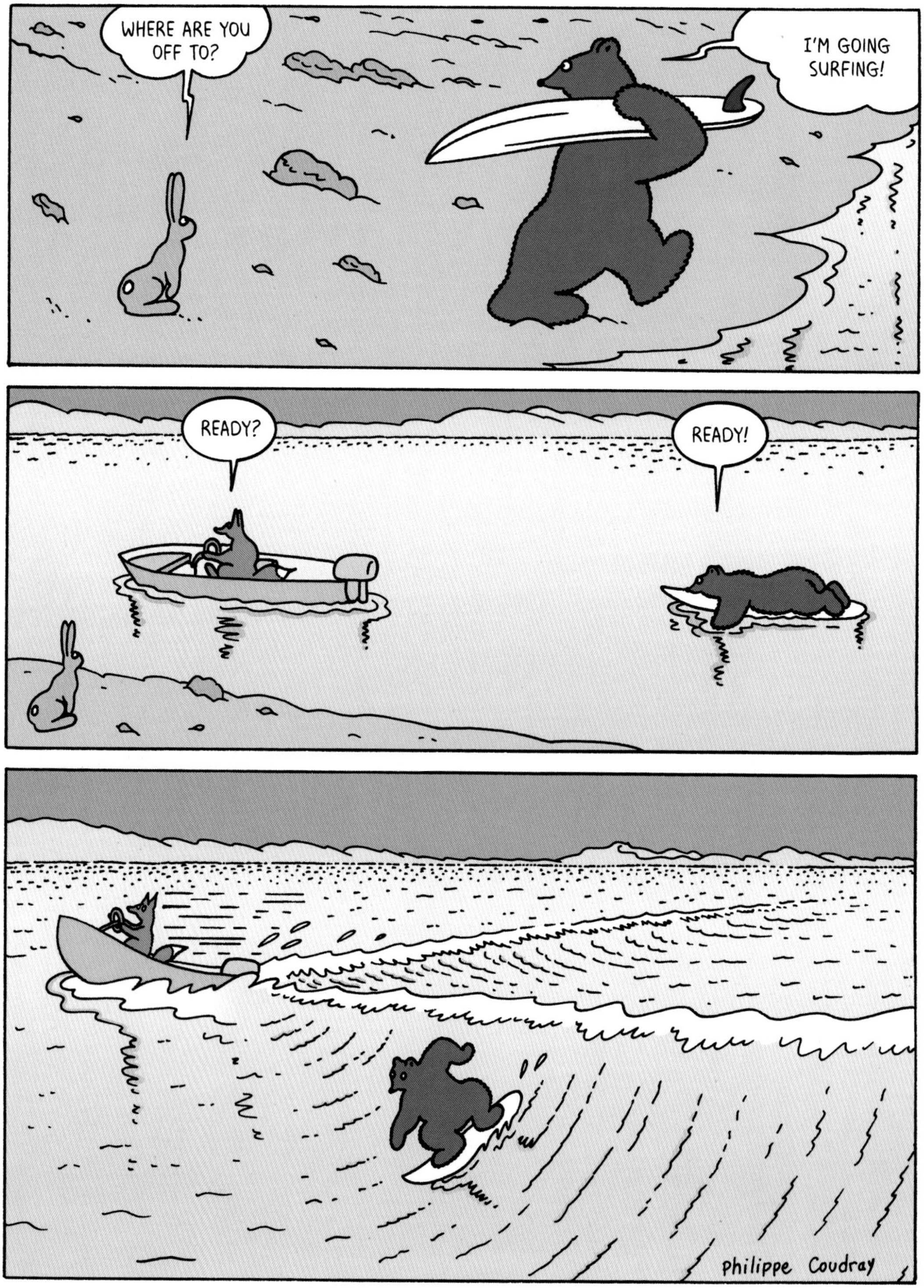
WHERE ARE YOU OFF TO?
I'M GOING SURFING!
READY?
READY!
Philippe Coudray

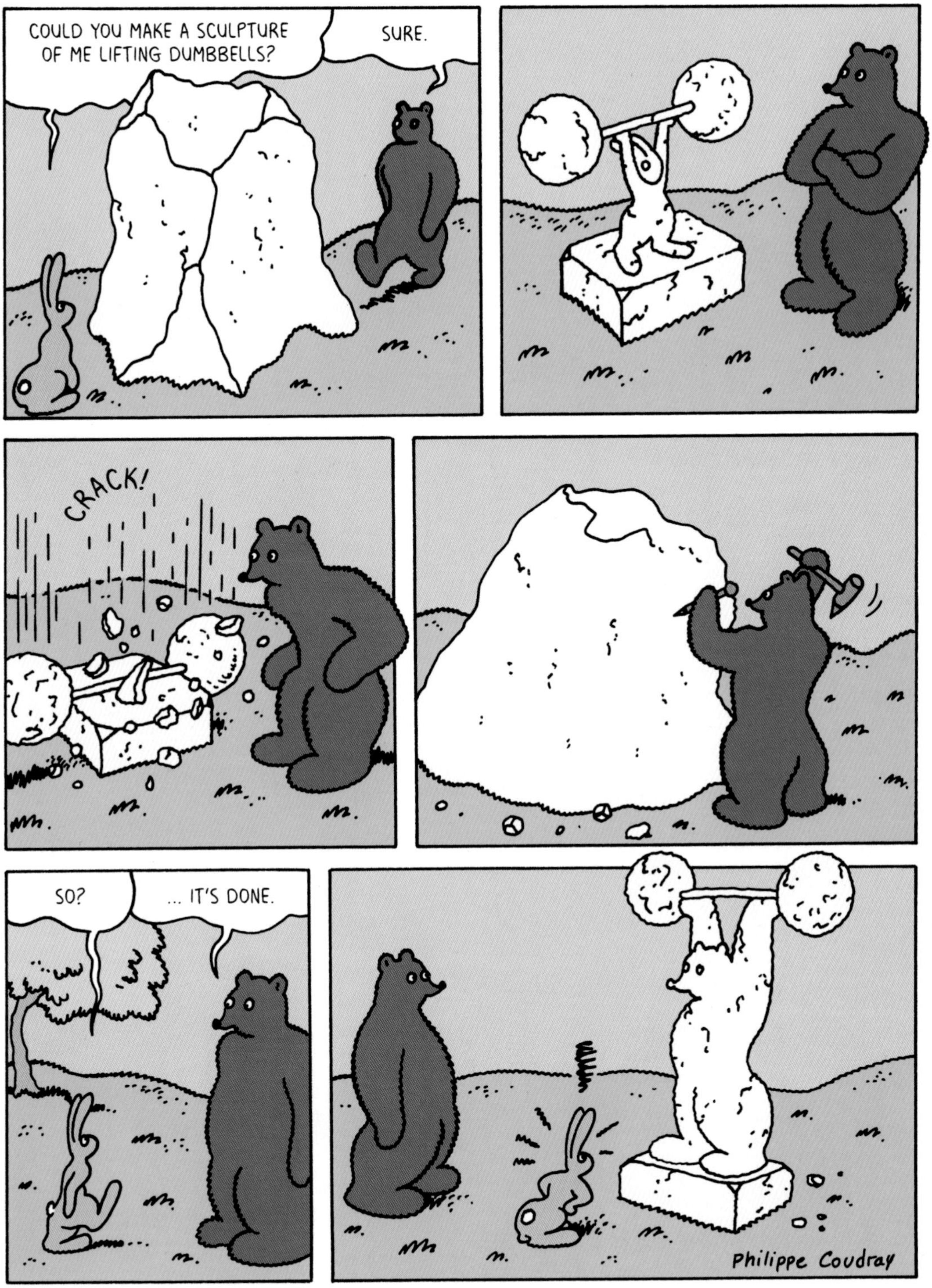
COULD YOU MAKE A SCULPTURE OF ME LIFTING DUMBBELLS?
SURE.
CRACK!
SO?
... IT'S DONE.
Philippe Coudray

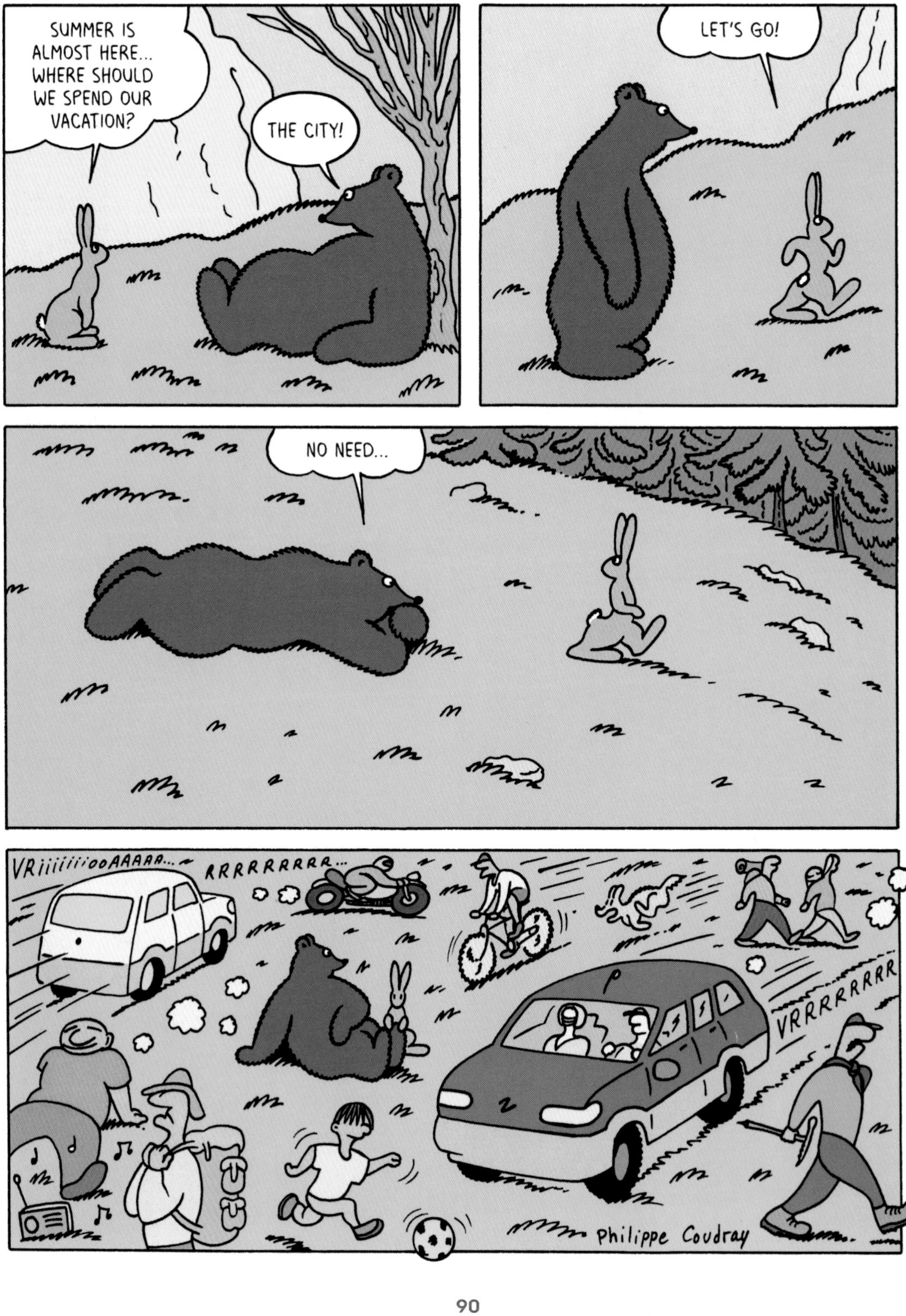
SUMMER IS ALMOST HERE... WHERE SHOULD WE SPEND OUR VACATION?
THE CITY!
LET'S GO!
NO NEED...
VRiiiiiiiooAAAAA...
RRRRRRRRR...
VRRRRRRRRR
Philippe Coudray

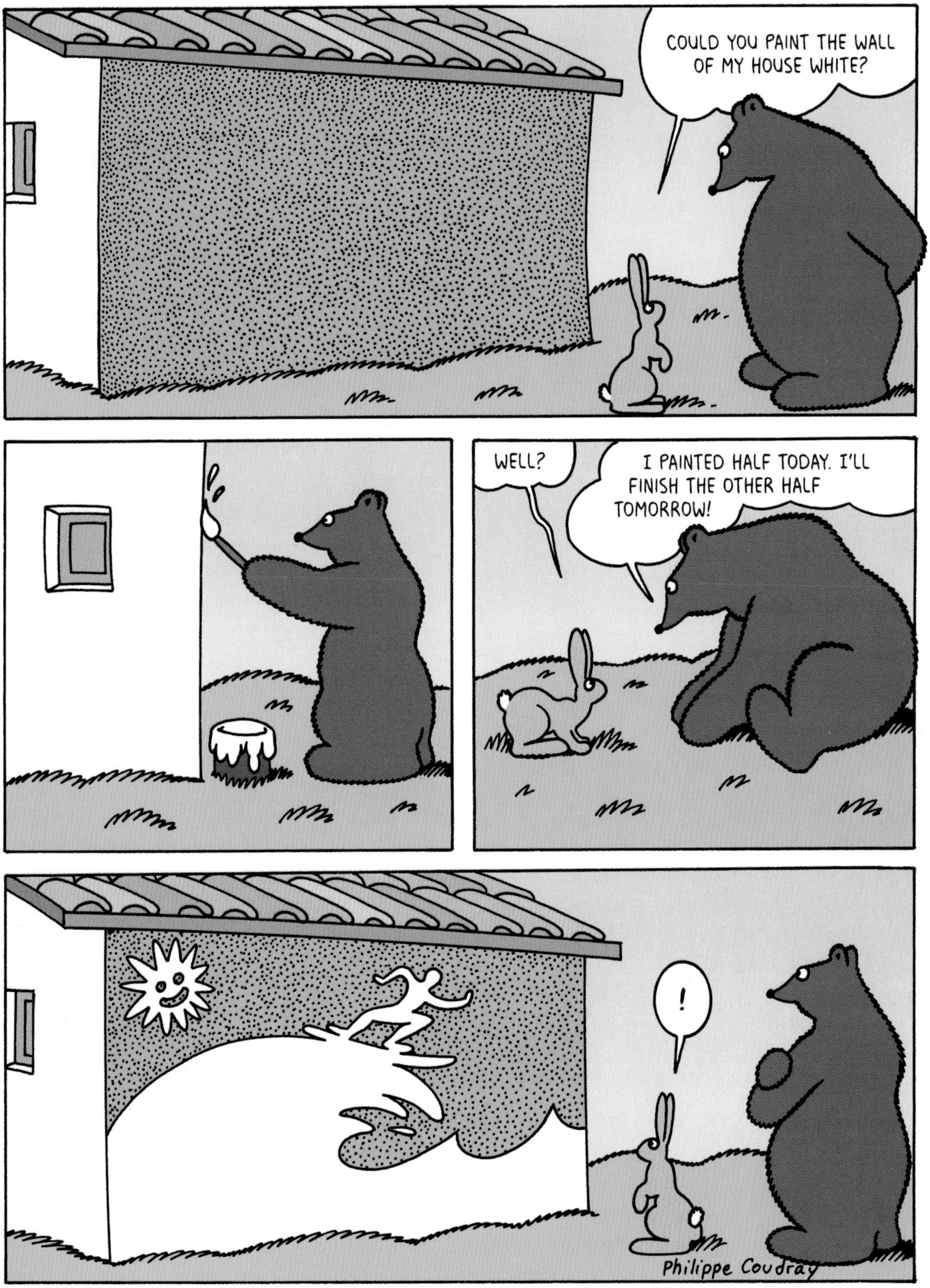

COULD YOU PAINT THE WALL OF MY HOUSE WHITE?
WELL?
I PAINTED HALF TODAY. I'LL FINISH THE OTHER HALF TOMORROW!
!
Philippe Coudray

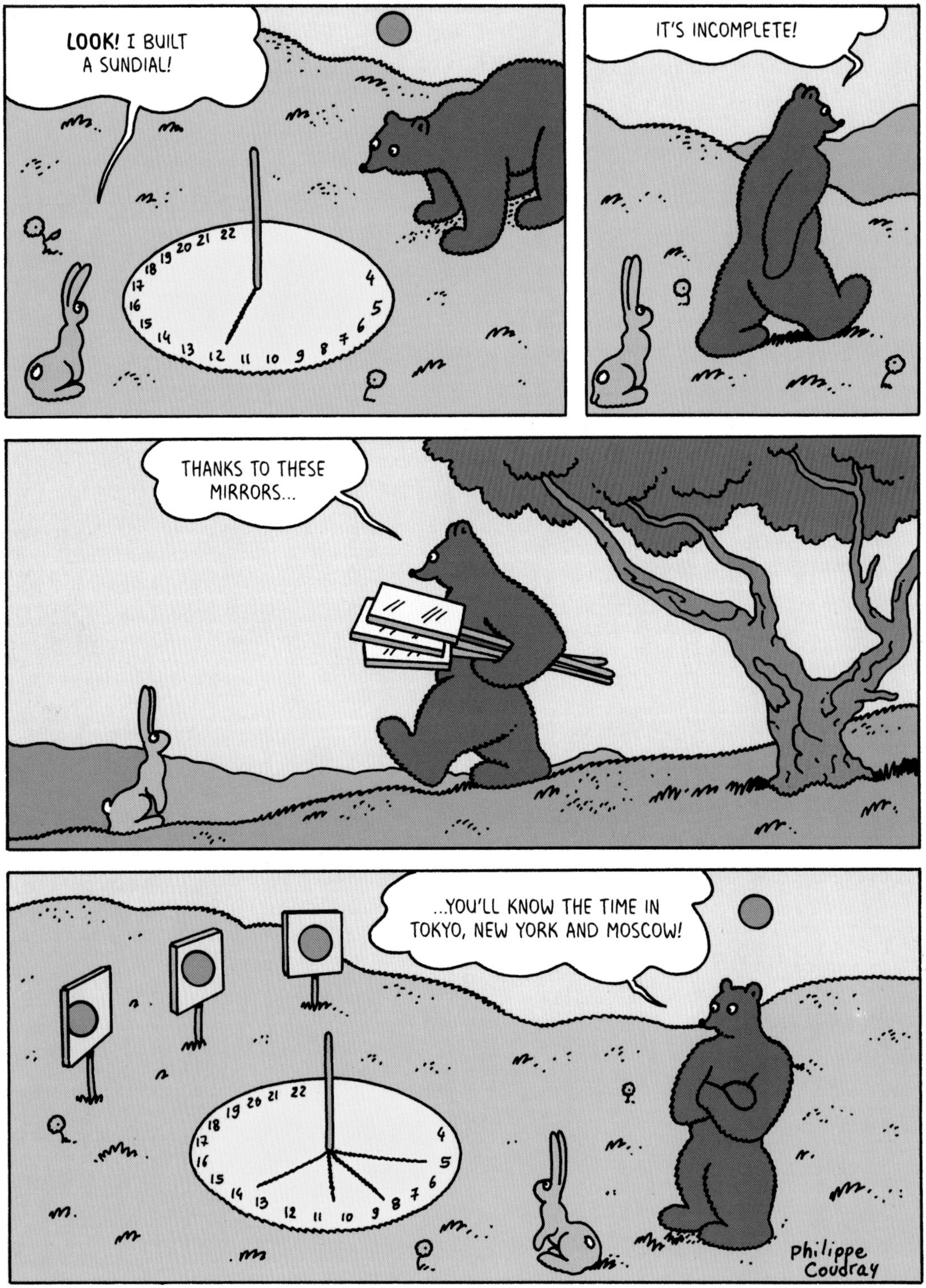
LOOK! I BUILT A SUNDIAL!
IT'S INCOMPLETE!
THANKS TO THESE MIRRORS...
...YOU'LL KNOW THE TIME IN TOKYO, NEW YORK AND MOSCOW!
Philippe Coudray

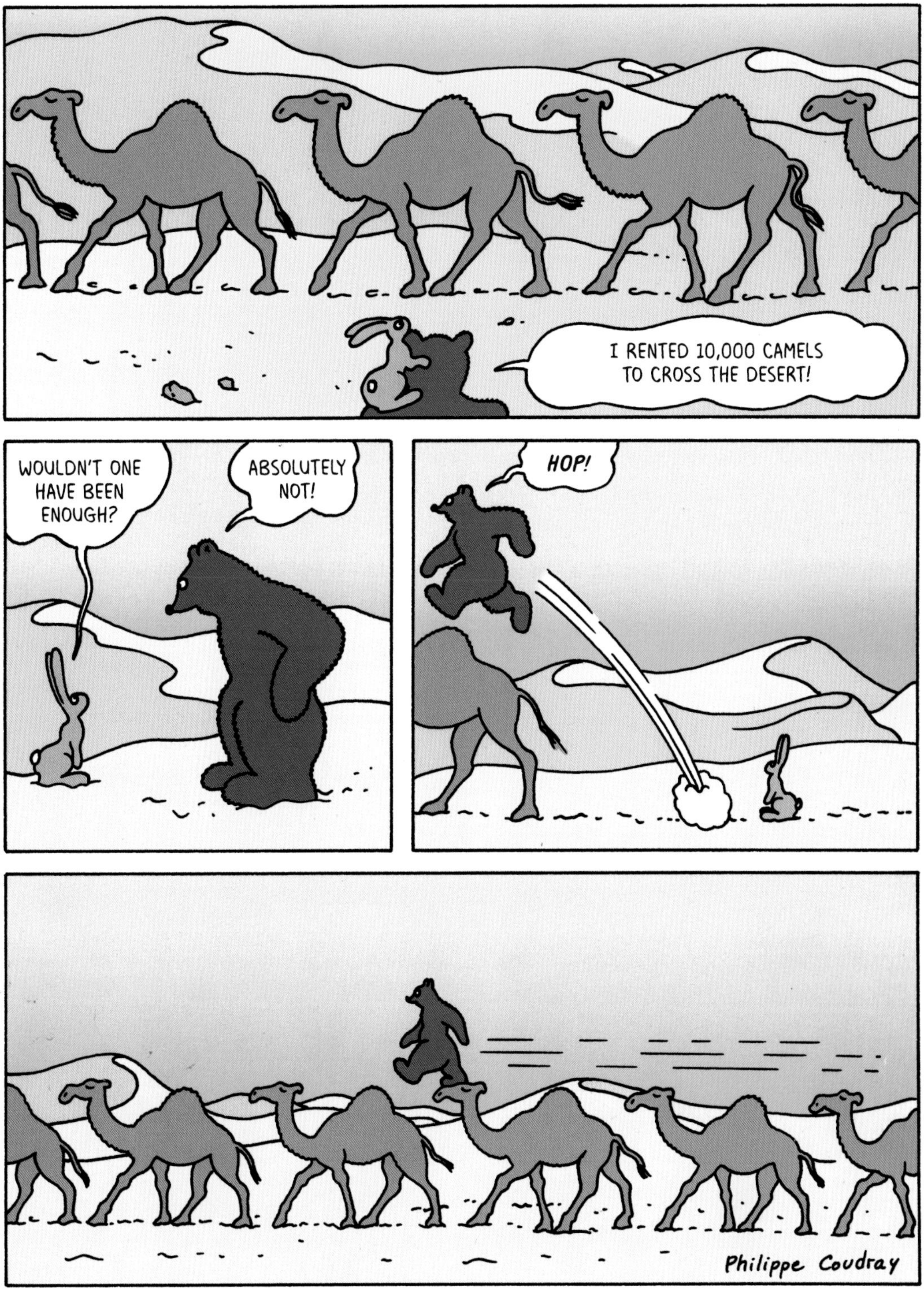
I RENTED 10,000 CAMELS
TO CROSS THE DESERT!
WOULDN'T ONE
HAVE BEEN
ENOUGH?
ABSOLUTELY
NOT!
HOP!
Philippe Coudray

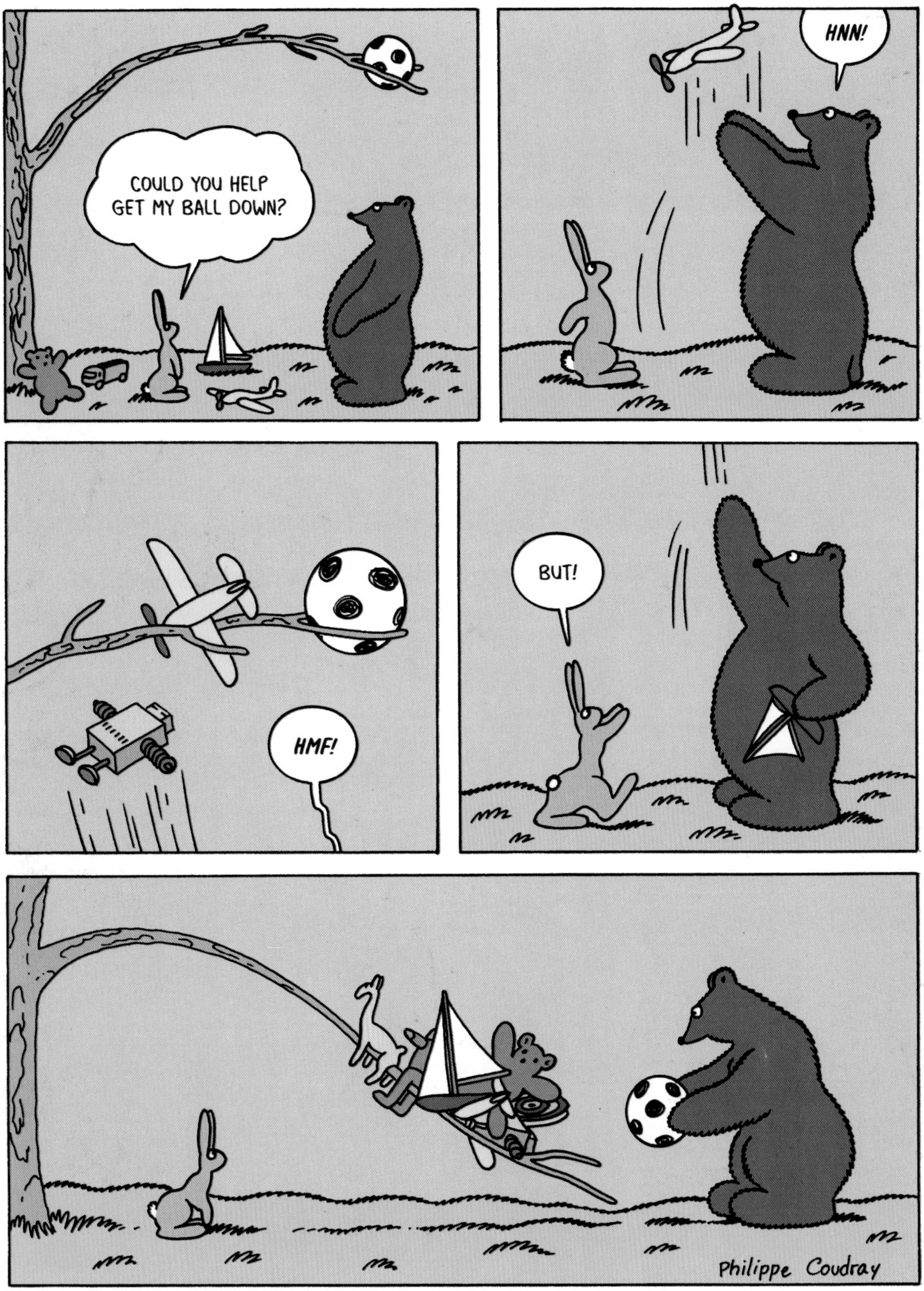
COULD YOU HELP GET MY BALL DOWN?
HNN!
HMF!
BUT!
Philippe Coudray

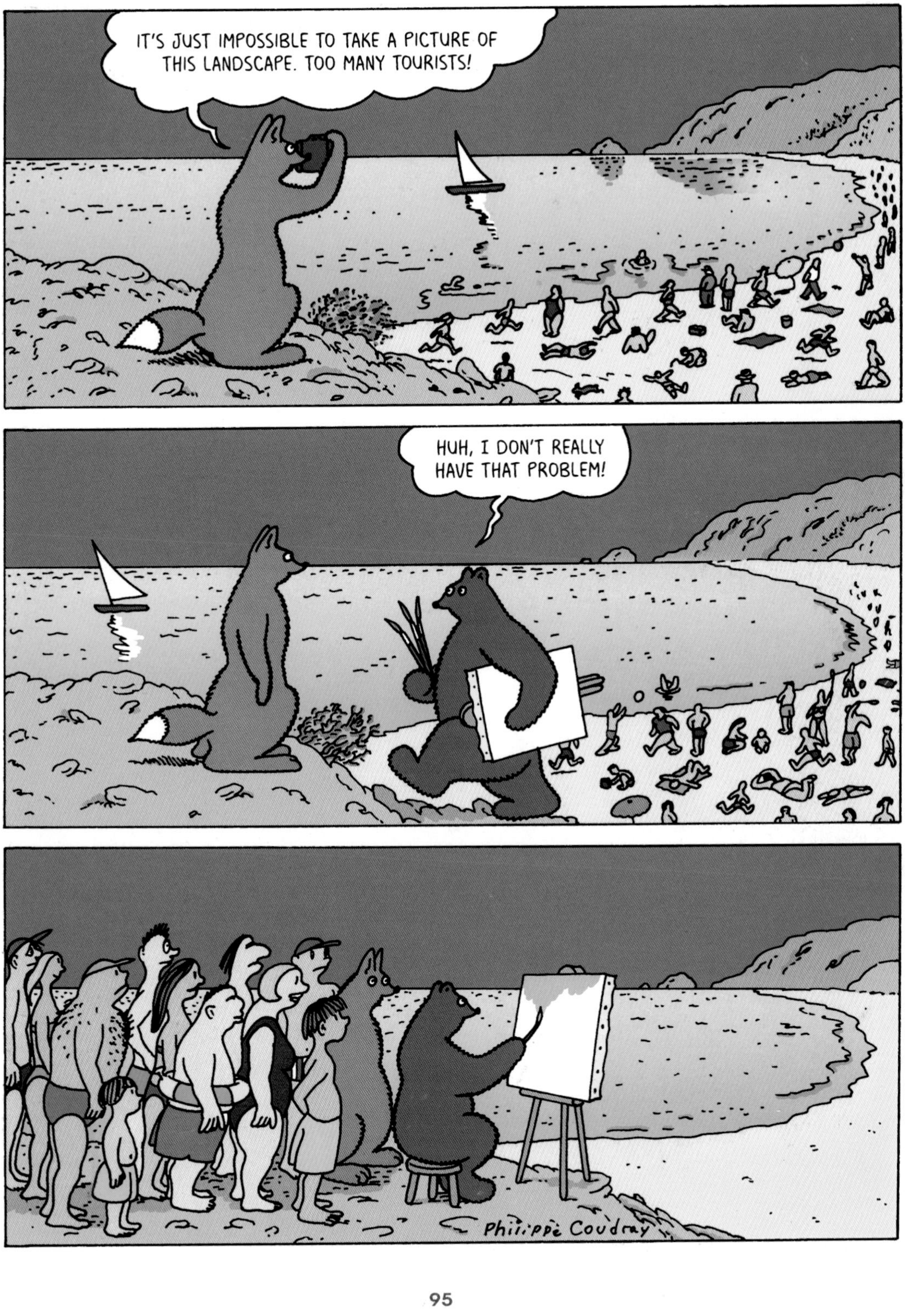
IT'S JUST IMPOSSIBLE TO TAKE A PICTURE OF THIS LANDSCAPE. TOO MANY TOURISTS!
HUH, I DON'T REALLY HAVE THAT PROBLEM!
Philippe Coudray

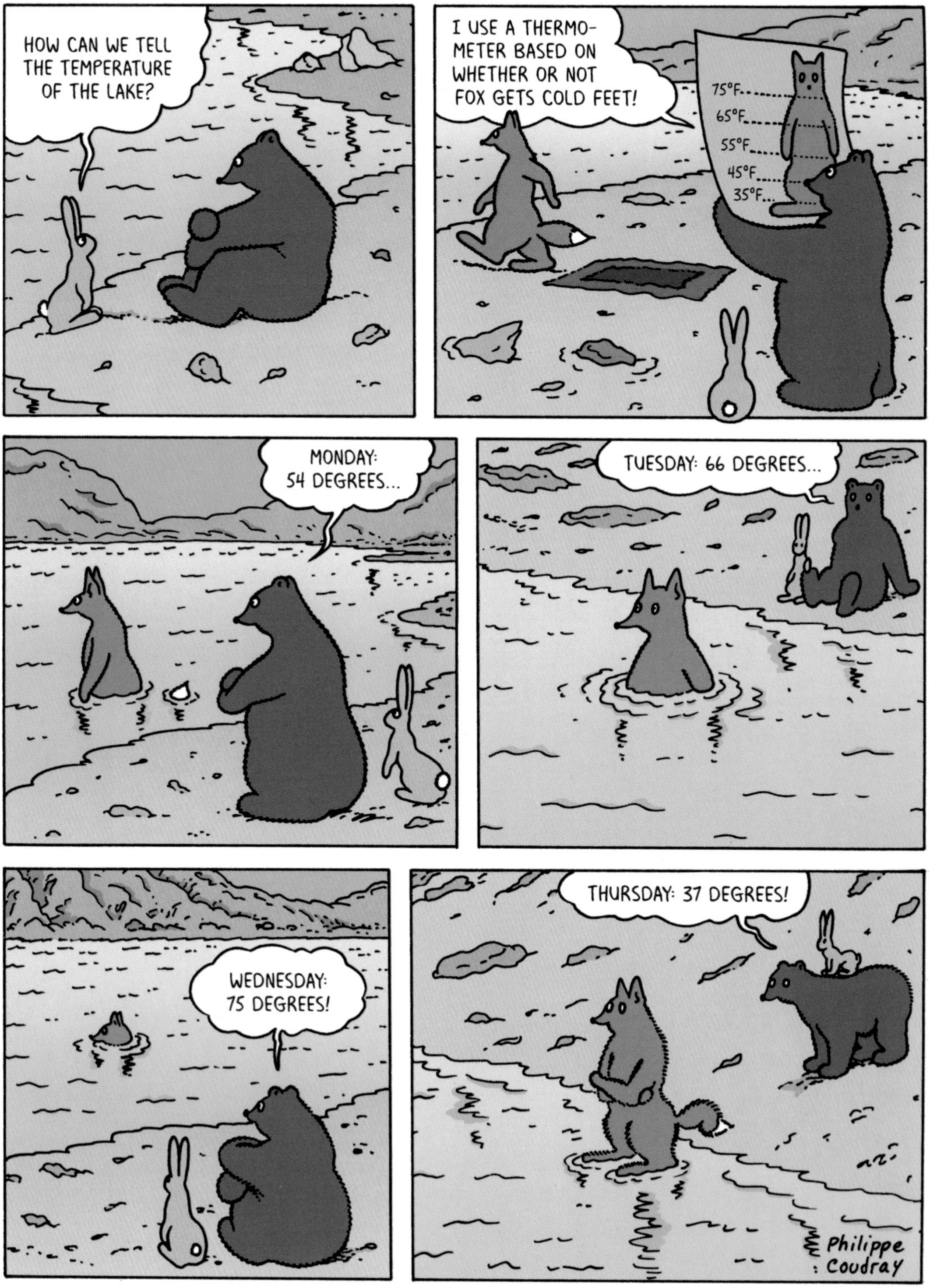
HOW CAN WE TELL THE TEMPERATURE OF THE LAKE?
I USE A THERMOMETER BASED ON WHETHER OR NOT FOX GETS COLD FEET!
75°F
65°F
55°F
45°F
35°F
MONDAY: 54 DEGREES...
TUESDAY: 66 DEGREES...
WEDNESDAY: 75 DEGREES!
THURSDAY: 37 DEGREES!
Philippe Coudray

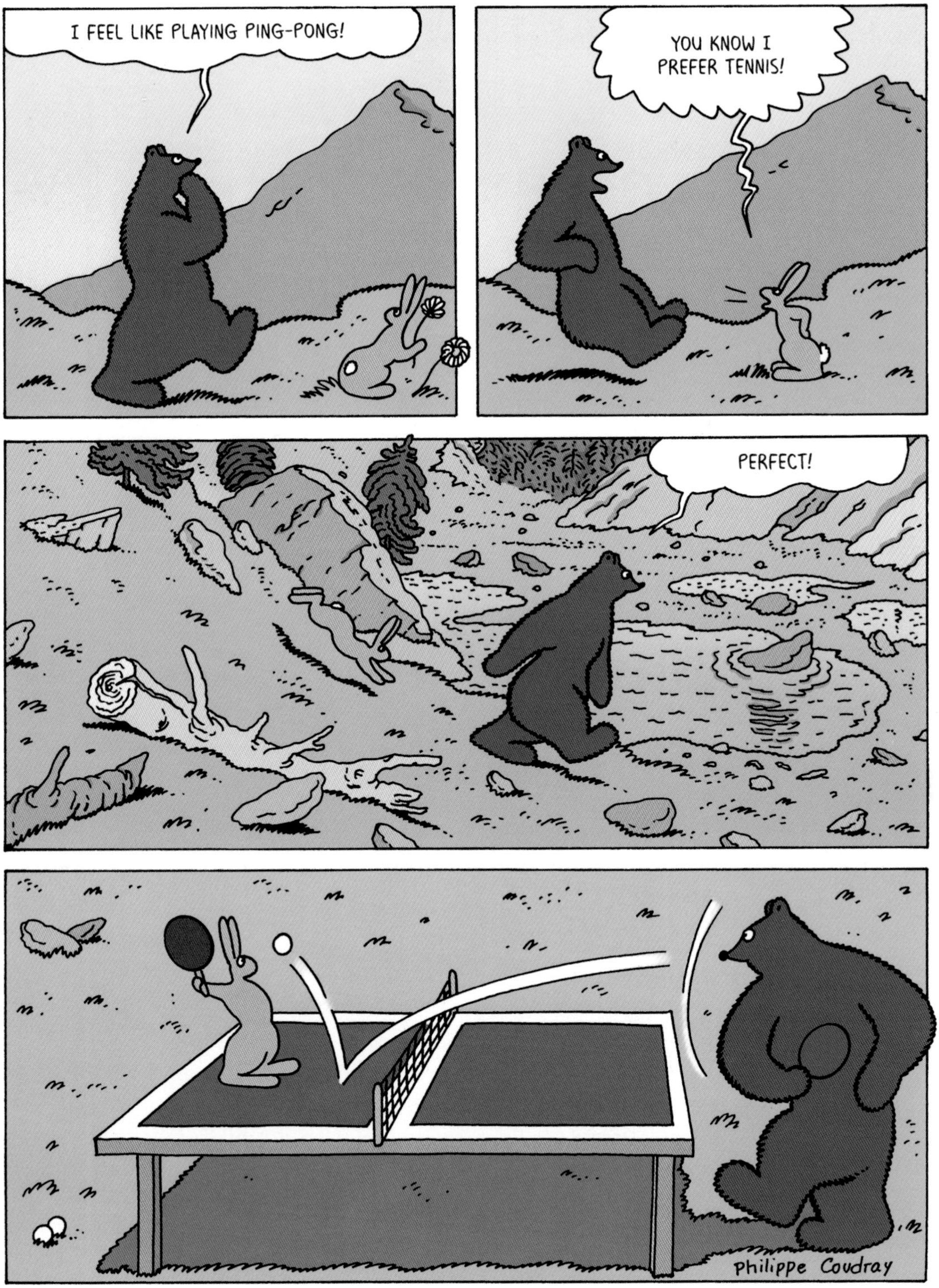
I FEEL LIKE PLAYING PING-PONG!
YOU KNOW I PREFER TENNIS!
PERFECT!
Philippe Coudray

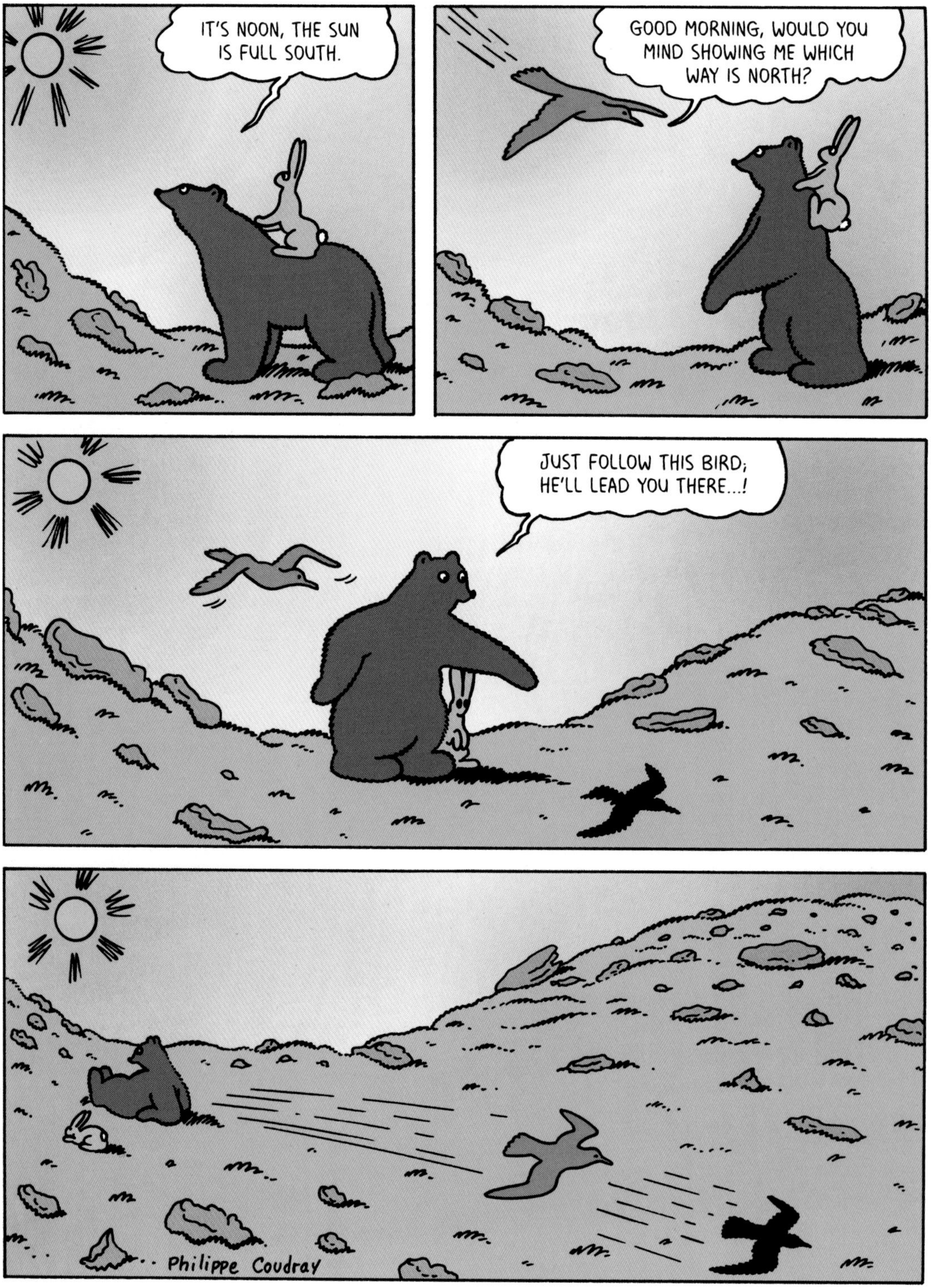
IT'S NOON, THE SUN IS FULL SOUTH.
GOOD MORNING, WOULD YOU MIND SHOWING ME WHICH WAY IS NORTH?
JUST FOLLOW THIS BIRD; HE'LL LEAD YOU THERE...!
Philippe Coudray

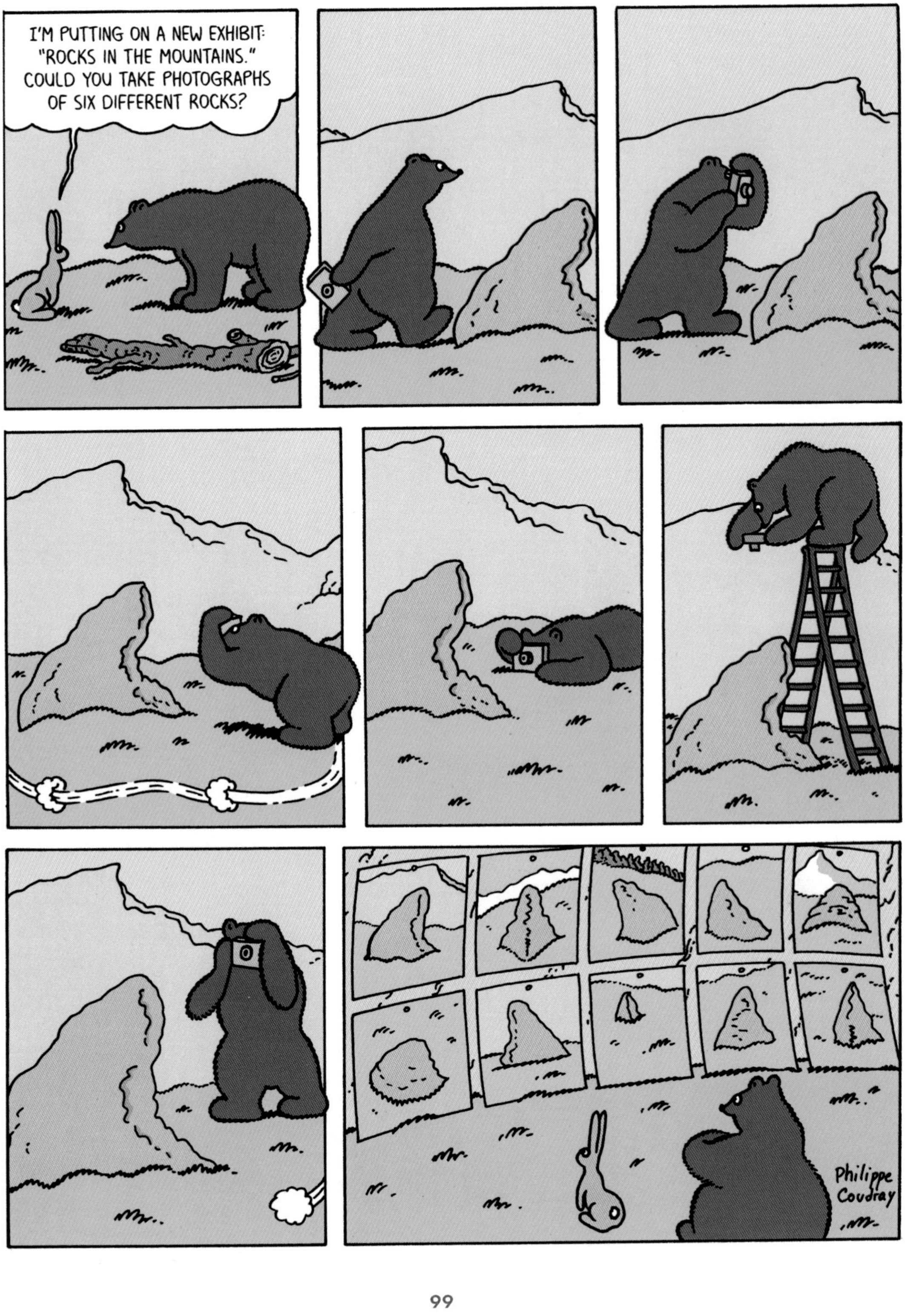
I'M PUTTING ON A NEW EXHIBIT: "ROCKS IN THE MOUNTAINS." COULD YOU TAKE PHOTOGRAPHS OF SIX DIFFERENT ROCKS?
Philippe Coudray

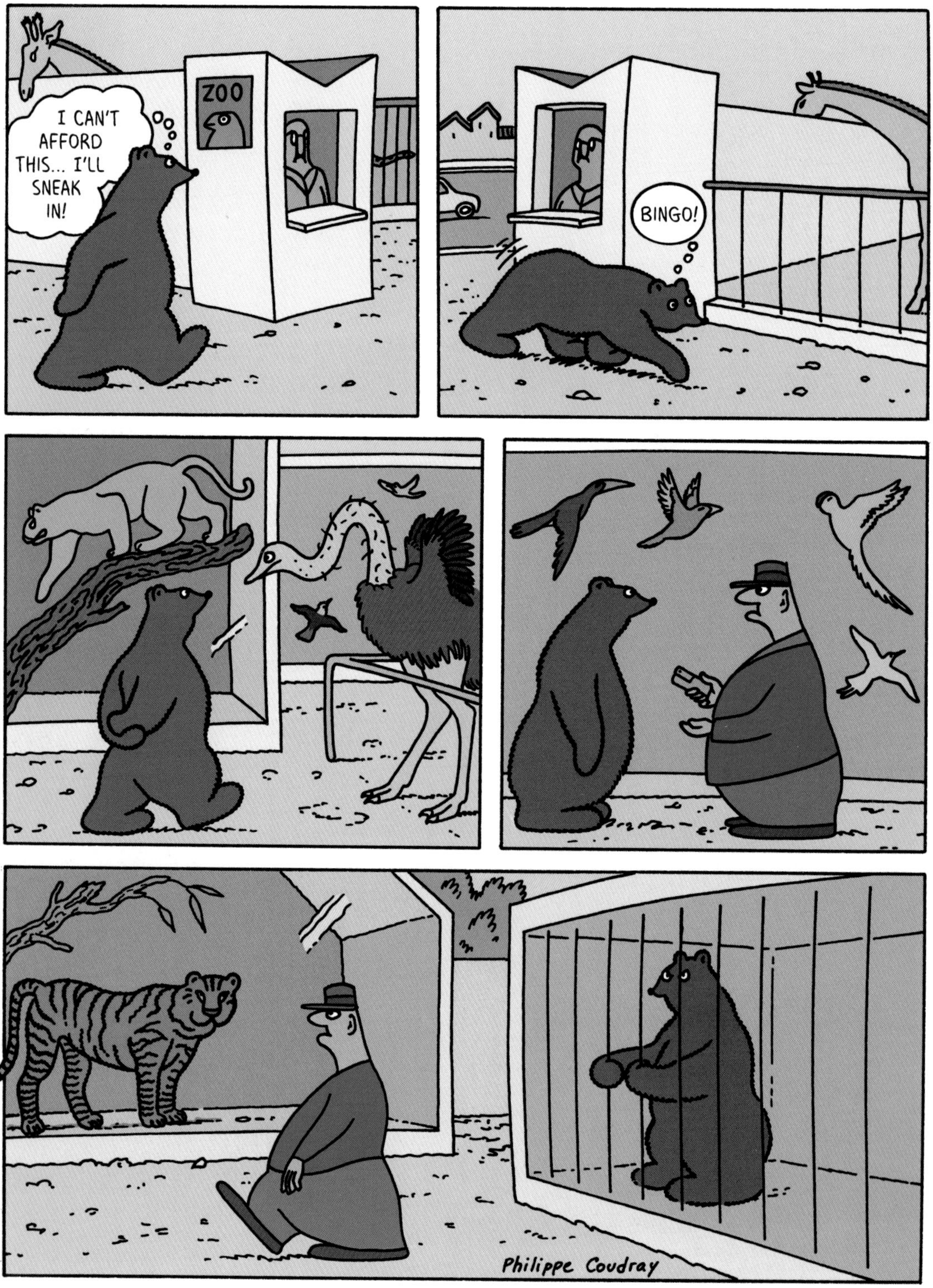
I CAN'T AFFORD THIS... I'LL SNEAK IN!
ZOO
BINGO!
Philippe Coudray

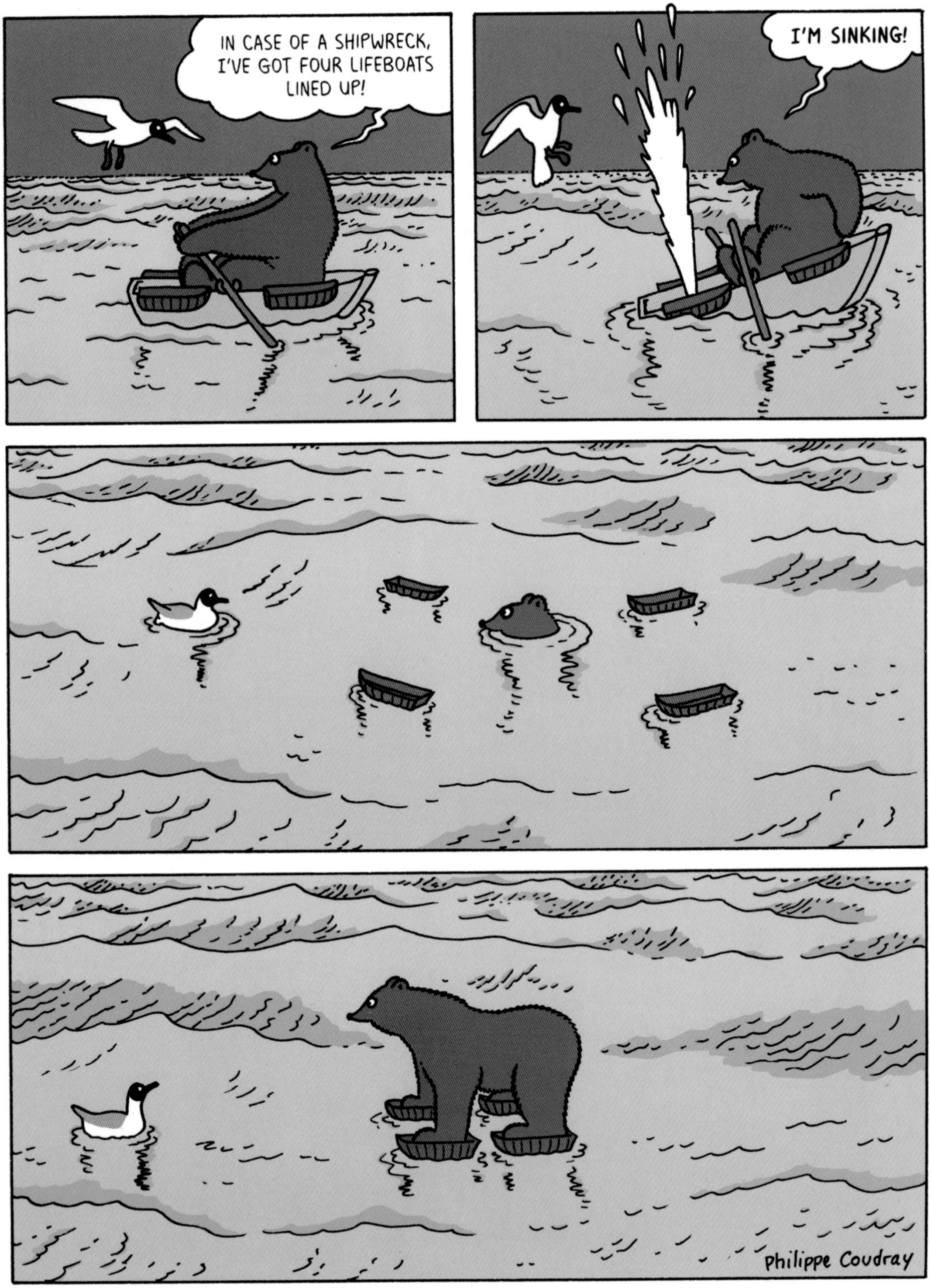
IN CASE OF A SHIPWRECK, I'VE GOT FOUR LIFEBOATS LINED UP!
I'M SINKING!
Philippe Coudray

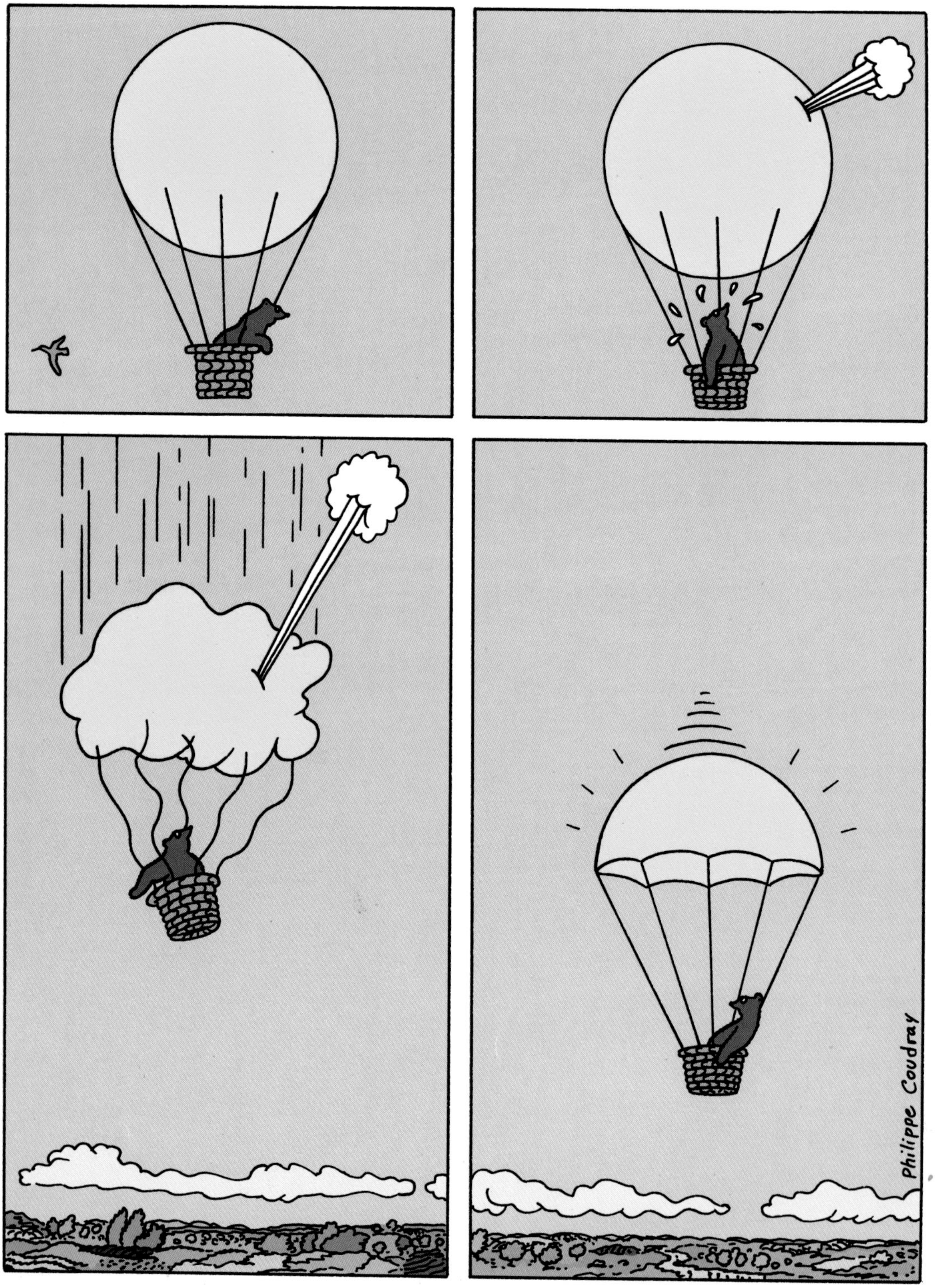
Philippe Coudray

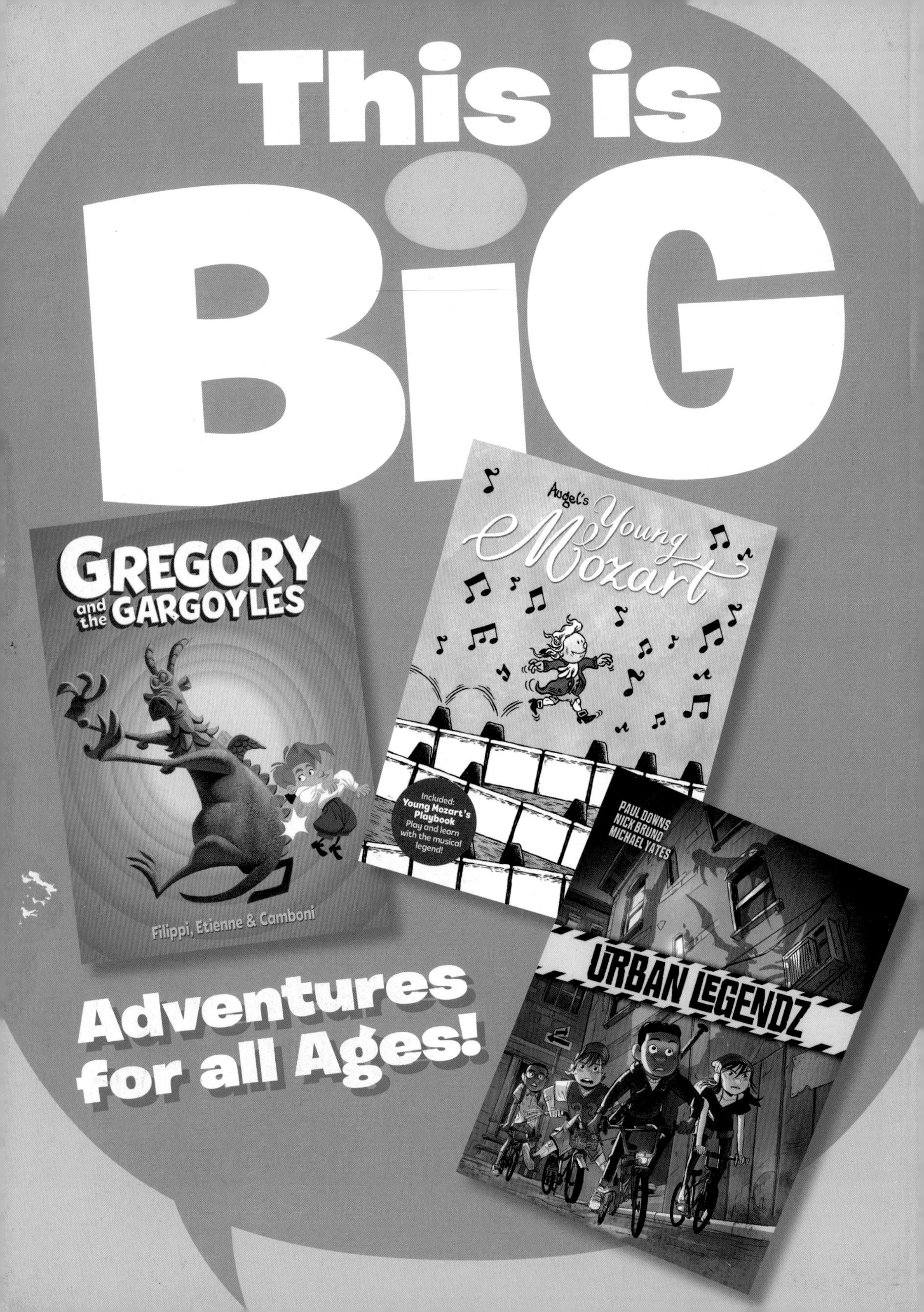
This is BiG
GREGORY and the GARGOYLES
Filippi, Etienne & Camboni
Augel's Young Mozart
Included: Young Mozart's Playbook Play and learn with the musical legend!
PAUL DOWNS
NICK BRUNO
MICHAEL YATES
URBAN LEGENDZ
Adventures for all Ages!